Hermit

Also by Chris McQueer:

Hings
HWFG

Hermit

Chris McQueer

WILDFIRE

First published in 2025 by
WILDFIRE
an imprint of HEADLINE PUBLISHING GROUP

1

Cataloguing in Publication Data is available from the British Library

ISBN 978 1 0354 0981 5

Typeset in Dante MT by CC Book Production
Printed and bound in Great Britain by Clays Ltd, Elcograf S.p.A.

MIX
Paper | Supporting
responsible forestry
FSC® C104740

Headline's policy is to use papers that are natural, renewable and
recyclable products and made from wood grown in well-managed forests
and other controlled sources. The logging and manufacturing processes are
expected to conform to the environmental regulations of the country of origin.

HEADLINE PUBLISHING GROUP
An Hachette UK Company
Carmelite House
50 Victoria Embankment
London EC4Y 0DZ

The authorised representative in the EEA is Hachette Ireland, 8 Castlecourt
Centre, Dublin 15, D15 XTP3, Ireland (email: info@hbgi.ie)

www.headline.co.uk
www.hachette.co.uk

Hermit

1

JAMIE

'She disnae love me,' I said, not even looking up from my Game Boy. I was maybe six years old, I think, sitting in my granny's living room. My maw and my granny immediately stopped the conversation they were having, and I could tell they were staring at me.

'Wit!?' snapped my granny.

I glanced up. 'Her.' I nodded at my maw. 'She disnae love me.'

My maw was laughing. Nervously, maybe, looking back on it. 'Aye, I dae,' she said, looking to me and then my granny, who was all worked up.

'Wit's he sayin that fur!?' my granny shouted.

'I don't know,' said my maw. 'I've nae idea.'

My granny told me to 'C'mere', and I went and stood in front of them both. 'Ye don't think yer maw loves ye?' my granny asked.

She loomed over me at that age, a massive personality. I was riddled with more anxiety in her presence than that of any teacher I had through school. I didn't ever really talk to her, but for some reason, I had just blurted that out. People on the telly were always saying 'I love you'. They would say it to their weans, to their partners, to anybody they were close to, and it always seemed so easy for them. A few days before, I'd heard somebody's maw say it to them when they were getting dropped off at school. All my maw ever said to me when she dropped me off was, 'Right, see ye later.'

I shook my head.

'How no?'

'She never tells me she loves me. She never cuddles me or anyhin.'

My maw laughed again here. '*You* never tell *me* that ye love me,' she said. 'But I still know ye dae.'

I shrugged my wee shoulders. I didn't know how to, like, articulate it back then, but I just felt as if she *should* be telling me that she loved me.

'We're gonnae need tae take ye tae the hospital then. C'moan,' my granny said, getting up off the couch.

'Wit? Why?' I asked. I felt a big lump rise in my throat, as if it had came all the way from my toes.

'Cause there must be something wrang wi yer brain if ye don't think yer maw loves ye, Jamie.'

'Aye, ye'll need an operation, I think,' chimed in my maw. 'Maybe a brain transplant.'

I started greeting then, I remember. My granny said 'C'mere' again, but no in the angry way she'd said it before; it was all drawn out and nice. I moved closer to her and she grabbed me. As my granny held me tight into her, I looked at my maw.

2

All I wanted her to do was say, 'I love you,' or join in and we'd have a big cuddle together like I'd seen American families do in films. All she offered me was a wee smile. She sat back and started reading her magazine.

'I love ye,' my granny said into my ear. 'An so does yer maw. Yer granda anaw. Everybody. It's awrite . . . it's awrite. They might no say it, but they dae. Noo go an play yer wee game.'

I pulled away from her embrace. I'd left a big wet mark down her top. 'Sorry,' I said, and went back to playing *Pokémon*.

My maw winked at me.

She never ever said 'I love you', even after that day. My da would say it, though. He never needed prompting. Especially if he'd had a few pints. That's why I always liked when he had a drink at the weekend.

My maw always seemed more uptight on a Friday. More snappy and naggy than normal. She'd say things like, 'This needs tae be done before yer da gets hame,' while she scrubbed the toilet or washed the windows or whatever. Doing pure trivial, non-essential cleaning stuff that could wait. Who actually cares if your windows are clean or not? But she'd be stressed out her box, running daft about the house. Cloths and bottles of cleaning stuff everywhere. The house reeking of air freshener and bleach, and every surface sanitised and gleaming. No even a single pube on the toilet floor.

I loved when my da came home from the pub. That smell of fags and lager on his breath felt so soothing. Like the way that aromatherapy stuff works for women, smelly candles and that, to make them all relaxed and chilled out, the smell of my da after the pub did the same for me. He was always more

3

of a laugh after he'd been to the pub. He'd say something cheeky to my maw, then turn to me and make a face, and it'd always make me laugh. If he had cans in the house, though, he'd get moody, and I'd get sent up the stair by maw. I never understood why until I was older.

I had this book I used to read when I was around that age. *The Encyclopaedia of the Unexplained*, it was called. A big heavy hardback. So heavy I could hardly lift it when I was a wee guy. It scared me to death, this book. The front cover was an aerial photograph of a supposed sea monster. It was a tiny fishing boat on a blue sea, but underneath it was this big black mass, bigger than any whale or squid or anything like that. Just some mad huge creature from the bottom of the ocean. Inside the book, in the sea monster section, it suggested the mass was either something like the Loch Ness monster or a giant, as-yet-undiscovered black jellyfish. Either way, it was terrifying.

The whole book was terrifying, to be fair, but the scariest bit was the ghost section. That's the one that gave me actual chills and made me shake with fear whenever I read it. The sea monster stuff was scary, aye, but sea creatures are easily avoided; just don't go into the sea, and you'll be fine. But ghosts? They can get you anywhere. The book had these horrible wee drawings of supposed ghost sightings, from the olden days through to actual black-and-white pictures, and then more recent ones as well. The drawings were scary cause everybody in them had their faces all contorted, mouths hanging open, eyes pure wide, clearly screaming. There was these pictures of folk with 'ectoplasm' coming out of their mouths and draping all over them. This sticky white fluid floating through the air and covering people. Apparently, it came from ghosts, but it just looked like jizz. It's funny now, looking back, I suppose, but back then I'd be sitting in my room at night, hands absolutely trembling while I tried to hold the book and look at it closer. Desperate to pull my eyes away, knowing fine well that I'd be unable to sleep for bad dreams and the thought that there was obviously ghosts in my house who were going to shower me with their ecto-jizz.

There was one section in this book that I only went near if I was feeling properly brave; it was normally only during the day I was able to read it. Because obviously, as everyone knows, ghosts can't hurt you – or even appear – during the day. It was this two-page spread, right in the middle of the ghost section, all about poltergeists. It started off by saying that poltergeist means 'noisy ghost' in German. I'd heard there was a film about them in the video shop near our house, but the book scared me enough; watching the video would probably have killed me, gave me a heart attack or something.

This section went on and on about how these ghosts could hurt you, and how it would feel like biting and pinching and kicking. It said, as well, that they were capable of moving objects and furniture around, and that if you had a poltergeist in your house, you'd definitely know about it.

I was sure we had one.

Occasionally during the week, but always on a Friday night, I'd hear banging and I'd hear my maw greeting. Surely, I thought, the telltale signs of having a poltergeist. I'd hear a plate smashing against a wall or something heavy being flung. Doors banging. My maw sobbing her heart out. My da shouting. I didn't know why they didn't just come up the stair away from the thing. I went down once during the night to suggest that they should do that, after the banging and greeting had been going on for hours and I couldn't sleep. I opened the living room door just a wee bit and I heard, 'Go back up the stair, Jamie,' from my maw. The big light was on, which was weird, as my maw never put it on. The living room looked different under its horrible yellow glow; it made everything look dead, like sickly and cheap and no nice. It all went quiet in the living room until I went back up to my room. Was only a few years ago I realised that the Friday night 'poltergeist' I'd been so scared of was actually my own da.

2

FIONA

Jamie was a quiet wee boy, always was. I could count on one hand the amount of times I heard him greet up until he was two. A lot of people would love that. A wean that doesn't greet? Being able to sleep through the night, not getting stressed out when it has a tantrum in Tesco, taking it out to restaurants and being able to enjoy your dinner and not get a riddy because it won't behave? Some women go mental, don't they? Hearing their wean screaming all the time, it makes something in their brain sort of malfunction, frazzles the circuit boards, like a sensory overload, and it makes them snap.

Truth be told, I'd have loved it if he'd cried more. There was honestly times where I'd forget he was even there or that I was supposed to be watching him, feeding him and just generally keeping him alive. I'd actually get a fright when he let out his quiet wee greet. Even when he was teething, it was never anything more than a soft moan. I used to zone out and forget he was in the room with me if he was sitting in his pram in front of the telly while I tidied up or something. I'd hear him make

7

a wee gurgling noise or, on very rare occasions, he'd laugh, and I'd shit myself. Sometimes I'd leave him in his room – hours on end, sometimes – and I'd go in to see him and he'd just be in his cot, staring into space; not sleeping, just awake and staring at nothing. Like he was on standby.

You know the way a wean's personality starts to come through as they grow and get older? Well, even from when he was only a few months old, I could tell he was going to be the same as me: a weirdo. It was just all these weird wee quirks he had. Lining up all his toys in straight lines, organised by height, colour, frequency of use, order of preference, and sometimes even based on how much they cost. Rows upon rows of toy cars, army men, animal figures, planes – anything he could collect, really. And he was shy, too. No just in a cute way; he was *really* shy. He still is. He can hardly look me in the eye, and I'm his own maw.

There's one incident from when he was a boy that really sticks out for me and shows how weird he was. Well, how weird he still is, I suppose. We'd always go to my ma's on a Saturday to see her and my da, and then later on just my ma. We'd watch the telly together, read magazines, drink tea, swap books, and just really have a blether and a catch-up. I'd tell her all about my week, work, what I'd been reading and what the wean had been up to. My ma loved hearing stories about him, and what daft wee things he'd said since she last seen him. The wean would play about with his wee toys or sit and watch whatever cowboy film was on the telly with my da.

One Saturday, right out the blue, he just says, 'She disnae

love me.' And pointed at me. Mid-conversation with my ma, and he just hits out with that. My ma was always giving me a hard time about how I was bringing the wean up, telling me where I was going wrong every chance she could. And now the wean had said this.

My ma turned and looked at me as soon as he said it. Honestly, the way he stood there, lingering, after he said it – it was like something out of *The Omen*. Didn't realise I'd birthed the next anti-Christ. Shoulders slumped, head bowed, looking up at us with his wee brow all furrowed.

'Why's he saying that?!' My ma shouted. How was I meant to know?!

'She never says she loves me,' he said. His head and shoulders were still slumped, like he was trying to make himself even smaller. I swear when I caught his eye, though, he smirked. A horrible little smirk. Blink-and-you'll-miss-it type of thing. Sometimes, I think he knew exactly what he was doing that day. Sometimes, I think it was the beginning of a lifelong campaign to drive me mental.

What I should have said was, 'Of course I love ye,' but I never said anything. I'm not the type to say things like that. It's just dead cheesy and a bit of a riddy. It's something only posh people say, or people who are on the telly. My ma and da never said it to me, I don't think, but I know they love me. People like us don't say it. We don't need to. Maybe folk that do say soppy stuff like that are just doing it for show. I think they are, anyway. Maybe if he was more normal, I'd have been able to say it. Maybe if *I* was more normal.

My ma gave him a big cuddle, told him he was being daft.

I gave him a forced smile and watched him go back to playing his game. He looked upset as he turned the thing back on. Then he wiped his nose with the sleeve of his jumper, took a deep breath, and the emotions that he'd briefly allowed to come up to the surface seemed to go away again.

My ma looked at me, and it was as if she was absolutely disgusted with me. As if she hated me. She left the room and I turned to my da, who smiled and winked. I felt a wee bit better. My da never seemed – and never claimed, either – to be the cleverest person in the world. He was forever saying the wrong thing and making arguments with my ma worse, and he was always making an arse of simple tasks. But sometimes, with just one look, and probably without him even realising, he could make you feel like maybe everything was going to be fine. Maybe that's a bit cheesy, but his obliviousness to any situation, no matter how serious, was always such a comfort.

In the weeks and months after Jamie said that, I thought about saying 'I love you' to him, but any time I went to do it, it was as if it would get stuck in my throat. I felt self-conscious, as if the words just wouldn't let themselves be said. Even after all this time, I still can't bring myself to say it to him.

3

JAMIE

I hear my maw's room door shutting. When she shuts her door, she does it so gently, like the door frame's lined with landmines or something that'll explode if she doesn't do it as softly as she can. Can only tell the door's been shut over cause of the wee click it makes as she pulls the handle back up.

She normally comes up the stair about half ten, and that's when I get up. I can't mind when my routine got as bad as it is now. I hate it, but once you get into a routine, it's hard to get out of it. You just get, like, trapped. I mean, I've never been a morning person, but I never used to be fucking nocturnal like I am now. Think I just started getting up later and later. Maybe it'll keep happening, and then eventually, for a wee while, I'll get up at a normal time, like a normal person.

I suppose it started when I was in, like, fourth year at school. If I didn't have to get up for school, then I just didn't get up, and if I didn't have to go to bed early so I could get up early, then I just didn't go to bed.

I didn't have any pals or even acquaintances. People who you

11

maybe wouldn't hang about with at lunchtime, but if you seen them in the corridor, you would give them a wee nod of the head or maybe a wee 'Awrite?' I wished I could be like the people I'd see at school who seemed to be pals with everybody – well, everybody apart from me. The lassies would just sort of sneer at me if I ever accidentally made eye contact with them. And fair enough, I've never been the best-looking or the coolest or the most popular or whatever. The guys, if they were alone, would pretend I wasn't there. If it was a group of them, my stomach would twist into knots as they moved towards me. They'd either kick me or push me or steal my bag or pull my jacket up over my heid. I started always wearing earphones so I wouldn't hear what they were saying about me, at least. Nine times out of ten, they'd be slagging the way I looked; I got that a lot. I've got horrible teeth, man. And a big nose. The odd time, they'd maybe slag me for being humming of B.O. Even the teachers seemed to have it in for me. I remember once in Geography, the teacher was doing the register. He shouted out my name, and before I could say 'Here', he went, 'I know you're here, I can smell ye.' The whole class burst out laughing, while I just had to sit there and take it.

School was a good laugh.

As soon as I found out I could leave at the end of fourth year after my exams and that, I just thought to myself, 'What's the point in even coming in?' So I just started going less and less. My maw didn't care. When I told her I was leaving, she didn't even try and stop me or say it might be a bad idea. Like, clearly, if I didn't go, I'd fail my exams, and then getting a job would be a lot harder. Which is exactly what happened.

'I'm no gawn back efter Christmas,' I said to her. I had been going maybe twice a week, on a good week, for a month, and nobody had said anything. Not my maw, not any of the people in my classes, not even the teachers. Clearly, I thought, nobody cared about me. Nobody noticed whether I was there or not.

'That's when I left school,' she said, 'and I've turned oot awrite.'

Aye, you've turned out great, hen; single maw, divorced, shitey wee house, nae pals and a son who's no good at anything.

'Wit you gonnae dae?' she asked.

'Dunno,' I grunted. I'd been expecting an argument, so I didn't know what to say back to her. 'I'll just get a joab.'

That was three year ago. Can't even mind the last conversation I had with my maw about getting a job or going to college or anything. The only time we actually talk in real life now is when she asks me, from the other side of my door, if I'm eating alright, or tells me to go for a shower.

A text comes through from her; she likes to check in before she goes to bed.

I've been to the shop. X

Did ye get chocolate spread?

I forgot. I'll leave money out and you can get it tomorrow. Sorry. X

Fuck sake. I get up and grab my onesie from off the floor. My maw's always on my case about it and says it's stinking.

13

She used to come into my room and take my clothes down the stair to wash them, but she's no done that in ages, and I don't know how to work the washing machine – so what am I supposed to do? Even if it does smell, and even if *I* smell, it's not as if we've ever got visitors. And I don't go out, unless it's out to the ice-cream van or the shop round the corner – and even then, it's only if I'm desperate. So who cares? I give the onesie a sniff. To be fair, it is a bit . . . ripe.

I tiptoe down the stair; I always tiptoe. I know I laugh at my maw for shutting her door pure quietly, but I always try and do everything as quiet as I can as well. No sure why we're like that. See those animal documentaries where it's like a wee mouse or a shrew or something and their weans, and they're always pure timid and scared of everything. Never leaving their nest in case something bad happens. That's basically me and my maw.

When I get down the stair, I check the cupboards, fridge and freezer to see what she's bought. I do a wee inventory in my head and try to work out how long it'll last me for. She goes for food twice a week, on a Tuesday and a Friday, so that means today's either Tuesday or Friday. Microwave burgers, chips, chicken nuggets, fish fingers, crisps, biscuits and fizzy juice. Class.

I would've liked to have some chocolate spread to have on a piece for my breakfast, but a burger will do, I suppose. I ping it in the microwave, grab a big glass of juice and head back up the stair, taking them two at a time to avoid the ones that creak.

Back in my room, I settle down into my chair and turn

on my PlayStation and laptop. The lamp in my room broke months ago, and the big light broke a few weeks ago, so I eat my breakfast by the light from my telly and my computer. I move my curtain slightly to see what the weather's like. It's pouring down with rain, one of those mad torrential summer downpours. I can see it coming down in big sheets, the different colours of the streetlights catching it and making it look all yellow and white and silvery.

I put on my headset and see who's online tonight. Lee's name comes up. Straight away, we're connected.

'Awrite, wee sacks,' he says into my ear.

'Awrite, prick,' I reply.

'You're up early.' He sounds distracted.

Sometimes we connect and just sit and watch YouTube videos. Sometimes the same ones at the same time, sometimes no. Sometimes we sit and talk aw night, and sometimes we hardly say two words to each other. It never feels awkward, but. Lee's the only person I talk to, but he has another pal called Seb. A mad American cunt. Sometimes, if he declines my request to connect and talk, he'll send me a message saying he's talking to Seb that night instead. I fucking hate Seb. I've never spoke to him, but I feel jealous of him. Him and Lee have been talking a bit more the last few weeks. I don't know what they get up to, but I've got a feeling it's maybe something dodgy. Lee doesn't really like it when I ask him about it.

Lee stays round the corner from me, but we've never actu-ally met or spoke in real life. He went to the same school as me, but we don't remember ever seeing each other there. I was a couple of years above him, but he says he saw me in the shop round the corner a couple of times, and he thought that I looked like a gamer. Then he recognised me in the 'people you may know' bit on Facebook and added me on there. He posted his gamertag once and I added him that night, and we've played together basically every day since. Sometimes I see him from the window when he walks to the shop, but I've never told him that. I don't want him to think I'm a stalker or anything.

'I know, man.'

We don't say anything for a few hours, but I like the sound of his breathing and his alternate grunts of frustration or excitement at whatever game he's playing. Makes me feel a bit less alone. It gets to about one in the morning, and I tell him I'm going to sleep. I can't be bothered. No with him, just being awake in general.

'Talk tae ye the morra, mate,' he says, and clicks off.

I turn everything off, climb under my covers and fall back asleep.

I wake up when I hear my maw's keys locking the front door from the outside as she heads to work. I check my phone. It's half eight, and there's light coming into my room from the gap in the curtains, since I never moved them back. I feel like I've had the best sleep ever, man. Suppose I should feel well-rested, since I've slept for a total of, like, twenty out of the last twenty-four hours. I sit up in bed. I think about maybe trying to go back to sleep, but since I'm up now, at a normal time for once, I'd be as well seeing what I can do with the day.

I've still got my onesie on. Maybe I'm just used to the smell of it now, but it's really not as bad as it was yesterday. It's weird being up and walking about the house at this time of day, in the daylight. I've never realised how clean the rest of the house is compared to my room. Suppose it's just my maw kicking about down here, and she's no very messy. Plus, she's no got anything else to do apart from clean.

You're meant to have a normal breakfast at this time of the day, I remember from my days of getting up at a normal time. I'm no really in the mood for another microwave burger, so I check the cupboard where the cereal and that is normally kept, but there's no much in it – just my maw's porridge. I read the back of the box and see what it's meant to be like. It doesn't look too appealing, but I suppose I could just fire loads of sugar in it and it'll be sound. There's instructions on the box for how to make it. Forty grams of the oats mixed with milk or water, and then pinged in the microwave for a few minutes. If you make porridge in the microwave and it's acceptable to have that for breakfast, then why not a microwave burger? Why's my body and brain saying that's no allowed? Weird, man. Maybe it's thinking what my granny would say about me eating burgers for my breakfast, since she doesn't approve of my diet at the best of times. She'd be buzzing if she saw me now, though, making porridge from scratch like a legend.

I take the bowl out the microwave, sit it down on the worktop and just look at it for a bit. It looks honking. Bit of sugar, though, and I bet it'll be class. I lean down and smell the bowl. It doesn't really smell like anything, but maybe my onesie is overpowering everything else.

I stir a big tablespoon of sugar into it and swirl it about; the stuff is so thick it's like mixing cement. I lift my spoon, and almost all of the porridge is clinging to it in one big dollop, wee drops of milk dripping back down into the bowl. Horrendous. I lick it like a big, bogging lollipop, like a lollipop you'd get in a fucking gulag or something. It tastes as bland and crap as it looks. I dump the whole mess into the sink.

I spy a couple of quid lying on the worktop and a note from my maw: 'Money for choc spread. X'. I could have a piece and chocolate spread, maybe even toast if I'm feeling fancy. Maybe I'll put on some denims. Maybe I'll even walk about a bit, see what's changed. Today will be a good day.

If I can just go to the shops.

It's easy for a normal person to go like that, 'Aw, I'll just jump out to the shop,' and not really think anything of it, but even the idea freaks me out. I'm craving chocolate spread, and if I want it, I'll have to go outside. Moments later, I'm up the stair and peeling off my onesie, searching in amongst the mess of my room for semi-decent clothes I can put on. A cloud of tiny wee flies rise up from the pile. They float in circles around my head. Must be at least two or three months since I last went outside. It should be warmer than the last time; people outside have been cutting about in T-shirts and shorts instead of big jackets. I find a pair of denims and a hoodie, put them on and head back down.

My keys are kept in a wee basket on top of a unit next to the front door. My hand hovers over them for a bit. I don't know what it is, but the thought of going outside now is making me feel pure sick and sweaty and nervous. I tell myself to get a grip and just grab them. But I can't. I shut my eyes and try

18

again. I feel them under my fingertips, all jaggy and cold. I pick them up. I try to make my hands place the key into the lock, but I'm shaking. Fuck knows what's the matter with me. I take a deep breath and try and steady myself, the key pure skittering around the hole. Eventually, it clicks in. I shut my eyes again, unlock the door and pull it open.

The fresh air slaps my face, and the bright sunlight is murdering my eyes. I stand for a minute, but I'm getting more and more nervous and I feel like I'm gonnae be sick. Nah, not today. I slam the door shut and lock it. I can't do this. Not today.

I'll just go back to sleep.

4

FIONA

'How's the wean?' my ma asks me while she stirs the tea. There's more than just a hint of scorn in her voice.

'Aye, he's fine,' I reply, buttering the bread, trying my best to come off as if everything really is fine. She drops the spoon into the sink with a clatter and it makes me flinch. I can feel her eyes boring into me.

'Wit's he been up tae?'

'Och, just the usual. I hardly see him.' There's no point in lying to her, really. She's like a human lie detector. I slap some ham down on to the bread.

'That's terrible, Fiona, hen,' my ma says, adding a wee tut at the end for emphasis. She lifts up the cups, mine and hers. Must be the millionth time I've heard her say this since Jamie left school. That must be nearly three year now, actually. Jesus Christ.

'A couple ae year oot ae school an no even a sniff ae a joab?' she goes on.

What does she want me to say? I absent-mindedly cut the pieces. 'I cannae *force* him tae get a joab, can I?'

'Aye!' she shouts. 'Wit did I dae when *you* left school?'

I don't have a smart-arse answer for her here. When I left school, just after I turned sixteen, same as Jamie, my ma took me into the city centre and got me a job in a newsagent's. She wouldn't take no for answer, just walked in and demanded that the guy employed me.

'Och,' I say. 'It wis different back then. There's nae joabs oot there noo.'

'So ye keep sayin. Wit's aw the other boays his age dain, eh? Aw they other weans like him, they're aw apprentices an workin in shoaps an at college. Wit's he dain? Nothing.'

I'm not looking at my ma, but I can feel her staring at me. When I eventually meet her gaze, feeling quite daft and guilty, she drags her eyes off me. I know she blames me for the way the wean is. I tried to raise him the way I wished she'd raised me, but it's become clear that her way must have been better. Even though I've turned out to be a loner, at least she made sure I was equipped to go out into the world and survive. I've not done any of that for Jamie. If I didn't want to do something, if I was too scared or nervous, she'd just force me to do it. I've let Jamie rot in his room, thinking I was doing a nice thing for him, letting him stay in his own wee safe space without a care in the world.

Nothing is said while we eat our pieces and drink the tea. I flick through a magazine but don't take it in. The primary colours of the pages, bright and intrusive, are just a horrible, lurid blur. Out the corner of my eye, my ma is sitting with her eyes on the telly, even though it's on mute. She's gripping her cup so hard I worry it might shatter. She catches me looking at her and I look away instantly. It's like a weird show of dominance. She's the matriarch of the pride, and I'm just a new mother who's let her down. A daft wee lassie. Maybe she'll take my cub from me and exile me out into the desert.

'I'll try and get him a joab, then,' I say, cutting into the silence. 'I'll find him something.'

She doesn't reply. Not that I wanted her to, anyway.

I finish my lunch and stand up, putting on my jacket.

'That you away, hen, aye?' she says.

'Aye, I better go and make sure the wean's awrite.'

'Bring him wi ye the next time. In fact, come up the morra. I want tae have a word wi him.'

Later that night, I chap Jamie's door. I can see the blue light leaking out from the gap between the bottom and the floor. 'Jamie,' I say.

Inside, I can hear him making weird noises, wee exhalations of breath and grunts and groans as he plays his game.

I try a bit louder and give the door another chap. 'Jamie.'

'Fuck SAKE!' I hear him moan. 'Naw, no you. It's ma maw. Hing oan.' I hear the sound of rustling plastic; I've never seen or heard him empty the bin in his room. I imagine it's probably piled waist-high with rubbish. Crisp packets, biscuit wrappers, and god knows what else. 'Wit is it?' he says.

'Can ye come oot fur a minute, please?'

More rustling. The door opens just a fraction and he pokes out his head. 'Wit is it?' he asks again, only he sounds more annoyed this time. He's a lot spottier than the last time I seen him. His hair badly needs a cut and is all greasy, clumps of dandruff and other matter clinging to it. A foosty smell eman-ates from inside. A heavy smell that feels like it's settling into my jammies, grabbing on to the fibres with tiny, stinky wee hands that won't ever let go.

'I was up at Granny's the day,' I say. 'She was asking fur ye.'

He rolls his eyes. In the blue light, he looks the palest I've ever seen him. He's like a wee ghost. Practically transparent. A normal reaction from a normal person here would be some-thing like, 'Aw, wis she, aye? How's she getting on?' But Jamie just sighs.

'I thought we could maybe apply fur joabs the night.' I'm trying to sound cheerful, as if I'm suggesting we go to the pictures or something. He does a big dramatic groan and slams the door shut.

'Jamie, c'moan,' I plead. But it's no good. I hear him go back to waffling away to his pals online. I imagine maybe there's some other wee guy, just like him, in another scheme or on the other side of the world having the same argument with his poor maw at the same time.

In bed, I try to text him. See if that'll get him to talk a bit more. He seems to find communicating with me a lot easier when it isn't face to face.

Do you want to try and look for
jobs tomorrow then? X

I stare at the screen for a bit, willing him to reply with something that shows even a crumb of positivity.

Aye if ye want

It's been a wee while since we done
up your CV. We'll get it sorted and
see what jobs we can find. X

Okay.

Okay. See you tomorrow. X

And that's it, end of conversation. Sometimes, through the wall, I can make out what he's saying when he's blethering away through his headset. 'Naw, it's ma maw,' I think I hear him say now. 'She's dain ma heid in.'

I turn off my light and try and go to sleep. When I hear him talk about me like that, it makes me feel like the worst maw in the world. Suppose I probably am.

5

JAMIE

'She's oan ma case aboot gettin a joab, man,' I say to Lee. 'It's a nightmare. Just wish she'd leave me in peace.'

'My maw's the same wi me,' he replies. 'Tried tae get me tae go fur wan in McDonald's.'

'I think that'd be class.' How have I never thought of applying for there? Maybe I'll apply for that tomorrow.

'Wit? Working in McDonald's?' Lee doesn't seem to share my enthusiasm. He says that like he's laughing at me.

'Aye. Just flippin burgers and that. Like SpongeBob.'

'If it wis just like that it'd be good, but see if ye had tae be the cunt servin cunts, that'd be murder.'

'Like Squidward. That'll be why he's in a bad mood aw the time.'

The only thing that fills me with more dread than going out-side is having to interact with other people. Imagine me serving folk in McDonald's – my old teachers and other people's maws looking down their noses at me, and angry das getting raging cause the ice-cream machine is broke. Nah, Lee's right. I'm not applying for there.

'Have you ever had a joab?' I ask him.

'I've had two. Hated them both.' He sounds distracted. We're both watching a top-five video on YouTube at the same time. It's the five scariest videos of ghosts ever caught on camera, apparently. I've got the sound off, cause it'll scare me too much.

'That's defo fake,' Lee says. 'I could make a class fake ghost video.'

'Did I ever tell ye aboot how I thought ma hoose wis haunted?'

'Naw, don't hink so. But ye dae talk a lot ae shite, so it's hard tae keep track.'

'Aw, shut up, man. Ye want tae hear ma story or no?'

My laptop screen shows night-vision footage of a guy and a woman lying in bed at night. Something grabs the bottom of their covers and pulls the duvet right off them, dead slow. The woman wakes up, pure screaming and throwing herself about the bed. Fuck that.

'That's a real poltergeist, defo,' says Lee.

'That's wit I thought we had in ma hoose.'

'Aye?' He sounds genuinely interested now.

'Aye, man. Used to hear loads ae banging comin fae doon the stair at night. Ma maw pure greetin an aw that. Used tae hear ma da shoutin, couldnae make oot wit he wis sayin cause he'd be steamin. This happened fur years, man. Then wan mornin ma maw had a black eye and ma da wis naewhere tae be seen.'

'Woaft, did the ghost kill yer da?'

'Naw, ya fuckin idiot. Ma da *wis* the ghost.'

'Yer da's a ghost?'

'Naw, read between the lines, man. Fuckin hell. It wisnae a poltergeist I could hear – it wis ma da, getting drunk and throwin stuff aboot. Shoutin at ma maw.'

'Awwwww right. Fuck sake, that's mental.'

'I know, man.'

That's the first time I've ever told anybody about that, I think.

'Did he hit her a lot?' Lee says after a wee moment of silence.

'Dunno. That wis the only time I ever seen her wi a black eye, though. Maybe he did, or maybe it wis just a wan-aff. My maw's never mentioned it since.'

'D'ye still see him?'

'Noo an again, aye. But I've no seen him in a while.'

'Dunno if I could even *look* at ma da if he hit ma maw,' Lee says.

I start to feel quite guilty. 'I know. He's still ma da, but, int he?'

'Aye, I suppose.'

The top-five video has concluded with a ghostly figure in a black cloak, walking through an abandoned factory. The subtitles say it's the soul of a guy who used to work there. The figure runs his hands over the machinery, and they look pure chalk-white. He turns back to look at whoever's holding the camera, and then runs towards a red fire-exit door.

'That wis shite,' says Lee.

I agree, but even with the volume off, I'm still creeped out by it, and I hope Lee stays up with me so I'm not alone. I stare at my own reflection in my laptop screen as it goes into standby mode. Sometimes my face kind of creeps me out a wee bit. I don't what it is, but I just don't look *right*.

'D'you know anybody that's died?' Lee asks, yawning, after a few minutes of silence. His voice is low and quiet.

'Just my granda,' I reply. 'A few year ago. Hink I was thirteen or fourteen.'

'Wit wis he like?'

'He wis funny. My granny wis always annoyed at him, but he'd always make her laugh, and then everythin wid be awrite. I don't remember much aboot him other than that.'

'How'd he die?'

'Think he had a heart attack. My maw woke me up wan morning and said he'd died during the night.'

'That's shite, man. Least you goat some time wi him, but. Mine died before I was born. My granny anaw.'

I don't know what to say, so I just say, 'I'm sorry.'

'Don't be sorry,' he replies. 'Cannae miss wit ye've never had.'

That feels like quite a profound thing for him to say, and it takes me by surprise. I turn my laptop back on, and Lee yawns loudly in my ears, making them ring a wee bit.

'I'm gonnae get tae bed,' he says. 'Am fucked.'

'Sound, mate,' I reply. My headset goes silent, so I crawl into bed. When I shut my eyes, I start trying to picture my granda, but I can't get his face right; it's all wrong. I wish the ghost videos creeped me out more so I didn't think about him. I try to picture ghosts floating around in the air, then they morph into jellyfish, then all of a sudden I'm remembering being at Ayr Beach with my maw and my granny and my granda. My maw and my granny are sitting on a wall overlooking the sand, watching me and my granda walk right down by the shore. I can't remember why my da wasn't there that day, but I can mind him saying goodbye to me that morning.

As we're walking, my granda puts a hand on my shoulder. 'Look at that,' he says, pointing at a jellyfish in the sand.

'Cool,' I say, walking towards it. 'Is it deid?' I kneel down next to it.

'It's alive!' my granda says. He pushes me forward, giving me a fright, but then gently pulls me back away from it. I turn to look at him as he laughs, and his face is perfect this time. His tache is thick like a nail brush and he's got a belter of a tan. He's smiling, and I can see the gaps where some of his teeth are missing.

'Tam!' my granny shouts, coming towards us. 'Don't let the wean near that hing, ya fucking idiot.'

'Och, don't worry, Isabel,' he says, ruffling my hair. 'He's fine. He's no scared ae anyhin.'

The sound of my maw's footsteps coming up the stairs jolts me awake. I grab my phone and check the time. Half ten. I think I went to sleep about half six this morning. If my maw's home at this time of the day, it means today's either Saturday or Sunday. Time and dates and months and all that mean nothing to me, man. I feel like I'm pure apart from the rest of the world, cut off like a prisoner, or like I'm in *Big Brother*. Maybe I'm in some kind of computer simulation to study the effects of what a wee guy gets up to when he's left to rot.

'Jamie,' my maw says from just outside my room door. Her

voice is a bit, I don't know, *angrier*-sounding than it usually is. It gives me a mad sick feeling in my belly. 'I'm gawn up tae see Granny.'

'Awrite, sound,' I reply, pulling the covers up over my face.

'C'moan,' she shouts and rattles my door. The thing sounds like it's going to come off its hinges. 'She wants tae see ye.'

'Wit?' I realise I couldn't tell you the last time I seen my granny.

'Move. The sooner we go, the sooner we can get back.'

This means I'm going to have to go outside. Fuck. And interact with another actual person. Two actual people. All this visit is going to be is me getting grief off the two of them. Just off my maw is bad enough, but my granny is on another level.

'I cannae,' I shout. 'I'm . . . no well.'

'I don't care, just hurry up. Ye need tae shower as well.'

I get up and open the door a wee bit. She's standing biting her nails. 'Dae I *need* tae go?' I ask.

'Aye. Move.'

'Fuck SAKE!' I shout, and slam the door in her face. I don't mean to be horrible to my maw – I don't want to be – but it's the only way for me to avoid situations like this. Normally, she'd just admit defeat here, but today she's no having it.

'You're coming wi me tae Granny's. That's it. Or I can go and get her and bring her doon here. Ye don't want that, dae ye?'

I do not want that. If she sees the state of my room, she'll kill me. 'Fine.' I sigh. Maybe if I have a shower, I'll feel better about going outside. Maybe it'll be good; maybe my granny will slip me a tenner. I grab my denims, pants, socks, T-shirt and a hoodie up off the floor, open the door and creep out just wearing my boxers.

My maw is still standing there, on her phone. She looks me up and down. 'You're so skinny,' she says, almost sounding surprised.

'I've always been skinny,' I reply, and slink by her, heading down to the shower.

'Make sure you scrub that hair.'

The water pelts out the showerhead, battering down into the bath. I don't remember the shower being as loud as this the last time I went for one. Maybe it's a new shower or something. I step into the stream and let it hammer into my back and ribs. I put my head under and watch as loads of black fluff and hairs and crumbs are washed off me. After thirty seconds or so of standing there, not moving, I press the button to turn off the shower. That'll do.

When I open the toilet door, my maw's in the hall, putting her shoes on. 'You done awready?' she asks.

'Aye.'

'Did ye wash yer hair?'

'Aye.'

She eyes my damp scalp suspiciously. 'Let me smell it.'

I'm just a wee bit taller than her – I get my height from my da – so I bend down for her, and she does a big comical sniff that makes me smile. I feel like a wee boy again. Suppose I am just like a big wee boy, really.

'Naw ye didnae,' she says.

'I know.'

'It's awrite, just hurry up and get ready. Ye don't smell as bad as ye did, at least.'

I run up the stairs, two at a time. If I can just get ready and out the door fast, then I won't have time to think about it too much, and I won't get all freaked out like I did the other day.

When I emerge from my room, phone in hand so I can use it as a distraction from conversation at my granny's, my maw's at the bottom of the stairs, waiting. 'Ye look nice,' she says. 'Ye look weird when ye wear real claes.'

'I know, man.' I walk down the stairs slowly, adjusting myself and trying to get used to wearing something that isn't my onesie.

'Don't call me "man", am yer maw,' she says, kidding on she's acting the hard man. I try to hide my smile, but I can't. She is actually quite funny.

She opens the front door and I'm feeling alright, but then I stop four stairs from the bottom. 'Wit's the matter?' she asks.

My chest feels like it's tightening, like there's somecunt grabbing me from the back and squeezing me pure hard. I can't breathe.

'Jamie?' she says, but I can't answer her. She comes up towards me. 'Take a deep breath. You're awrite.'

'I cannae go ootside. I don't know wit's the matter wi me.' Each word is alternated with a rapid breath. I'm hyperventilating or something, whatever they call it. I have to sit down.

'It's awrite, it's awrite.'

'I feel like am gonnae die.'

'Yer no gonnae die, calm doon. C'moan, stawn up.' She

32

helps me to my feet. I feel mega dizzy, man, like I'm just off the waltzers.

Before I realise what's happened, she's guided me outside. It's no as sunny as it was last time I opened the door, but it's still hurting my eyes. I can't tell whether the air on my face is warm or cold. I've not known anything other than room temperature for months, so maybe I've lost the ability to tell. This must be how it feels when prisoners get out the jail, or when astronauts come back to Earth after being in space for ages. I'm all shaky. My maw has her hand on my back and pushes me gently towards the motor. It's weird feeling her touch me.

When she sits me down in the front seat and shuts the door over, I start to feel normal again. Maybe I'm allergic to outside; that'd be mental. Maybe I'm going to have to live in a big bubble or something.

'You awrite noo?'

'Aye,' I say. 'I think so.'

'Who's that?' my granny says when me and my maw walk into her living room. She puts her glasses on pure theatrically. 'Fiona, who's this wee boay?'

My maw laughs. 'Aw, it's just that weird wee guy that stays up the stair in ma hoose.'

I feel my face go hot and red.

'I've no seen you in YEARS!' my granny says. She stares at me like I'm a really hard crossword. My granny's house is roasting – think she must have the heating on, even though it's summer – so I take off my hoodie and sit down on the couch. My maw sits next to me while my granny sits in her chair across from us.

'Jesus Christ, hen,' my granny says to my maw. 'Look how skinny he is!'

I try and cover up my arms with my hands so she can't see how thin they are. They're like pencils. I can make a circle with my index finger and thumb right around my arms, from my wrist right to the shoulder.

'No a pick oan him,' my granny says. 'Is she no feeding you?'

'I make ma ain dinners,' I say, hoping that it'll impress her.

'How dis yer ma no make them?'

My maw shifts uncomfortably in her seat. 'We eat at different times,' she says. 'And we like different stuff.'

'That's a sin.' My granny sighs, looking as if she's feeling sorry for me. 'Poor boay.'

'It's awrite. I like makin ma ain stuff.'

'Ye should come an stay here fur a couple ae nights. I'll fatten ye up.'

The thought of staying here – no internet, no being able to talk to Lee, eating mashed totties and pies and corned beef or whatever it is old people eat – makes me feel sick.

My granny shakes her head at both me and my maw. I turn and look at my maw. She looks worried. I always wonder if they actually like each other. My maw's an only child, same as me. Only children are normally pure spoiled, but my maw wasn't. They didn't have a lot of money, and I think my granny was pure strict with her. I was spoiled, though – big time. First grandwean and all that. Was allowed to just do whatever I wanted. Maybe that explains a bit about the state I'm in now.

34

My granny and my maw disappear into the kitchen to make the lunch. Pieces and ham and cheese for them, probably, and maybe a piece and jam for me. Chocolate spread if I'm lucky. A cup of my granny's extra-sweet tea as well, hopefully. Think she puts about four sugars in mine; it's class.

'Right,' my granny says, putting down my lunch in front of me and sitting down with her own. 'Wit ye dain aboot getting a joab?'

I take a big bite of my piece straight away to give me time to think of an answer.

'He's been lookin,' my maw jumps in while I chew away at the thick bread and strawberry jam.

I haven't been looking, but I appreciate her sticking up for me. I nod in agreement.

'Where?' my granny replies, quick as a flash.

'McDonald's,' I say. I turn to my maw.

She looks surprised. 'That'd be good fur you,' she says.

'Ye should be aimin a bit higher than that, son,' my granny says. 'Wit aboot an apprenticeship? Be a joiner or a plumber or suhin. They're aw loaded.'

I was shite at techie in school, and I really don't fancy doing that as a job. All the boys I went to school with who got apprenticeships were all the boys who bullied me. No chance.

'Aye, maybe,' I say.

'I think ye should go tae college,' says my maw.

'Aye, maybe.'

It's hard to keep up the pretence that I'm interested. I don't want a job and never will. Who'd employ me, anyway, man? I can't do fuck all, and I'm heavy stupid.

'Look,' my granny says. She leans forward in her chair and sits her cup down. 'I don't care wit ye dae. McDonald's is fine. As long as yer bringin in money. Yer ma cannae afford tae keep ye aw her days.'

I nod. 'I know.'

'So ye need tae get doon that joab centre. Ye'll get money aff them, and they'll help ye. An apply fur college anaw. Anything. Awrite?'

'Awrite.' See, having my maw and my granny on at me like this all the time, it's actually driving me insane. Just leave me alone, honest to fuck. I don't let them see my frustration; I channel it into picking at the skin around my thumb, next to the nail. It's all hard and scarred and scabby now. I started doing it a while ago, think it was the last year of school, when I was getting a hard time off folk. A teacher had commented that no one would sit next to me because I was stinking. As you can imagine, the cunts in my class had a field day with that. But I can block out anything by picking at my skin. It makes everything go away. All I can focus on is the pain; sometimes it bleeds when I get really bad, but it feels good. Feels like a release or something. I told Lee about it one night, and he said it was self-harm, but he's even more daft than me and doesn't know what he's talking about.

I feel my maw's hand gently prise away my index finger from the bit I pick at. Twice today she's touched me. This is weird, man. I hope she doesn't fancy me or something.

'See, as long as yer tryin and getting interviews, or bringin in money somehow,' my granny says, 'we'll get aff yer back aboot it.'

Suppose I can just wing it. Apply for a job a day, then just not answer if they phone me. That'll be fine. I can do that. I'm honestly doing any future employers a favour; I'd be a nightmare working anywhere. I'm quiet, I'm shy, I'm weird, I'm honking. If, by some kind of miracle, I actually have an application accepted somewhere and do well in an interview, they'd sack me soon after, cause they'd see I'm hopeless. Be good if I could just win the lottery. Although I'd need money to buy a ticket, and to get money I'd need to get a job. Seems a big gamble to try and get a job in the hope I'd win the lottery.

'Just promise us ye'll at least try?' my maw says. Her and my granny are staring at me, pure leaning forward.

'Aye, awrite,' I say. 'I'll try.'

6

FIONA

I was dead like Jamie when I was a wee lassie. Looking at him now is like seeing how I'd have turned out if my ma hadn't been so hard on me. Sometimes I wish I could have his life, not have to go to work or ever interact with anyone, but it's just not healthy, is it?

The way he spoke to me about school when he was still going, how much he hated it, really reminded me of my own time there. It was hard not to feel sorry for him, so I'd just let him stay off whenever he wanted, really.

When I was younger, the school I went to was just round the corner from my ma and da's house, so I'd walk to school myself in the mornings. I'd got home one night, and told my ma I'd been getting bother off a couple of lassies in the year above me. The next morning, she said she was going to walk me round to see the lassies and have a word. I was worried having her there would only make things worse, making it look like I was her wee spoiled princess. But then I pictured her standing at the school gates, coiled and ready for action, hackles up like an angry dog, watching over me. If anything was to happen, she'd sort it out. Even the teachers were scared of her.

'Just go an play wi yer pals,' she said, 'an I'll be waitin here fur ye until the bell goes. I'll make sure naecunt touches ye.'

As I stepped between the gates, my ma patted my back, encouraging me to go and mingle. I had ten minutes to kill before the bell went.

There was a few steps down into the cauldron of hatred that was the playground. I walked down them with my head bowed, trying to avoid eye contact with the lassies that had decided to bully me. They huddled together, four of them, directly across from the stairs. I went and stood next to the tree I liked to wait at, using it as a sort of shield between me and them.

'Fiona,' my ma shouted after a few minutes.

I went over to see her.

'Wit ye dain?'

'Just waitin fur the bell.' I shrugged a wee bit.

'Why don't ye go an stawn wi yer pals?'

'I don't have any pals,' I said.

Looking back on this, I can see it's dead sad, but it was just normal to me. The look on my ma's face, though: pure pity. Like she was a hairdresser and I was a customer who'd just dropped into the conversation that they were riddled with bone cancer or something.

When I turned eighteen, I remember my ma and da – well, my da especially – being really excited for me to be able to go to the pub. I couldn't think of anything worse. Who would I go with? Myself? My ma and da? I don't know what would've been sadder.

Jamie turned eighteen a year ago, and my ma said the same thing to him. 'Eighteen noo, eh?' she said. 'Be able tae go fur a pint wi yer pals, get yerself up the dancing anaw.'

Jamie looked less than enthused at the prospect of either of these activities. 'I've nae pals,' he replied bluntly.

My ma looked at me and rolled her eyes, 'Another recluse in the family.' She spat the sentence out at me.

I feel terrible getting on at him about washing, about going out, about getting a job. I know if my ma hadn't been so hard on me when I was his age, I'd have ended up in the same rut as him. He's just the same as me; it's like looking at a mirror that shows you the past. My ma pulled me out of my rut. I need to do the same for Jamie. I know it'll be hard for him, and hard for me to be strict with him, but one day, even if it's away in the future, he'll thank me for it.

7

JAMIE

'Awrite, Captain Gay,' says Lee into my ears. It's two in the morning, and that's me just up. If I'm getting a hard time about getting a job, or if I've had a row, or if I've just fucked up at something, I just sleep and sleep and sleep. That's been me since I got back from my granny's yesterday. A text from my maw says she'll help me apply for 'jobseeker's', whatever that is.

'How am I gay?' I sigh into my mic. It's too early in the morning for Lee's shite. 'An wit dis it matter if I am?'

'Yer a VL, int ye?'

'VL, fuck sake. No heard that patter since school.' It stands for 'Virgin Lips', which means you've never been kissed.

'I'll take that as an aye, then.'

'It's no a big deal,' I say. 'It's no as if I've ever even tried tae dae anything aboot it.'

'It's awrite if ye are,' he says.

'Disnae mean am gay.'

'Ye'll no find oot till ye break yer VL. Wi a guy, probably.' He laughs at his own joke.

'Aw, shut up, man.'

Lee sighs, and then tells me to press play on a video he's picked about aliens. It's only got a hundred views, and it seems to just be a slideshow of mutilated dead cows.

'Aliens come down, kill them, and steal their blood and eyes,' he says. 'Oh fuck, look at that wan. It looks like your maw.'

'Fuck up. It looks like *your* maw.'

'Oh, good comeback, mate. Just make the same joke I did.'

The video cuts to a wee guy sitting in his bedroom and talking to the camera about the cows being all fucked up by aliens. He's spotty and has glasses and curly black hair. If you were to divide wee guys up into different groups, then he'd definitely be in the same group as me – fucking weird.

'He looks like you,' Lee says. 'Bet he's a VL anaw.'

'Aye, he does a wee bit.' But at least this wee guy is confident enough to sit and talk to a camera about something he's interested in. Lee said once that me and him should start a podcast, but then we realised we didn't have anything we could talk about.

The video fades to black.

'Wit ye want tae watch noo?' Lee says.

'Dunno, man,' I say. I feel weird for some reason. Maybe it was just looking at the pictures of fucked-up cows. 'You pick.'

'Ye awrite?' he asks. 'Ye don't sound awrite.'

'I'm fine.'

'Wis it cause I asked ye aboot being a VL?'

'Talking aboot school an lassies an that just makes me feel a bit, I don't know, anxious.'

'Aw,' he says quietly in reply. 'Sorry.'

He doesn't say anything else, and neither do I. I sit back and listen to him breathing.

'Here, eh, by the way,' he says after a couple of minutes. 'I hink we're incels.'

'Wit?'

'Incels. Involuntary celibates.' He says 'involuntary celibates' like he's trying to sound dead clever. Like he's imparting some sacred knowledge to me. To be fair, I don't know what he's talking about.

'Yer gonnae have tae explain that tae me.'

'Right, well, listen.' His voice goes all low, like he's telling me a secret. 'I've been on these mad forums.'

When you hear the words 'mad forums' from someone who's as online as Lee is, alarm bells should start going off. The guy uses proxy servers and VPNs and all that kind of stuff to hide what he does on the internet. Fuck knows what he gets up to when he's no talking to me, or what he's trying to hide. I try not to think too much about it. I'm quite online, but no as online as he is. He's on a different plane of online existence, using mad websites I've never even heard of.

'. . . an it says an incel is defined as somecunt who cannae ever get their hole.'

'That could be anybody in the world, mate. My maw's no had a boyfriend since she split up wi my da. Is she an incel?'

'Naw, she's just ugly.'

'Am gonnae make something tae eat,' I say. 'Back in five minutes.'

'We are defo incels,' is the last thing I hear before I take off the headset.

Down the stair, I check in the freezer to see what there is. A couple of frozen pizzas are lying in the top drawer but I don't think I could eat a whole one, so I opt for a box of Micro Chips instead. I've never been a big eater but I feel like my appetite's just disappeared, like I'm only eating now because I feel like I have to. I type 'incel' into Google on my phone while I wait for the microwave to announce that my chips are ready.

Incels, a portmanteau of 'involuntary celibates', are members of an online subculture who define themselves as unable to find a romantic or sexual partner despite desiring one, a state they describe as inceldom.

I've never had a girlfriend, and I don't really want one, to be fair. Suppose it might be nice, right enough. I click on 'Images' to see some examples of incels. They all look like me. Skinny, spotty, shite haircuts, bad clothes. I click off the images because it's gave me a mad sick feeling in my belly. It makes me feel a bit dirty reading about these guys, man. I don't like it. I wish Lee hadn't told me about them.

I head back up the stair and sit and stare at the state of my room in the twilight for the first time in a bit. What Lee's saying is making me feel dirty and weird. I know I am dirty, but this is the first time I've actually *felt* like it. I don't plan on sorting it out anytime soon, but it is an absolute tip. I know how much of a mess it is. I'm always aware of it, but nearly all the time I can just block it out. I imagine this is what an incel's room would probably look like. Actual knee-deep in

44

rubbish and old food, man. Empty bottles of juice everywhere. Manky old socks and pants. Toys and that from when I was a wee boy that I've not got rid of. There's a wee old toy motor, Mr Bean's Mini, that sits among a load of other shite on my chest of drawers. I buried it out the back garden when I was maybe nine or something, just to see how the metal and paint and that would react to being underground for a few months. I fancied myself as maybe growing up to be a scientist, and was always doing wee 'experiments' as I called them. Turned out I wasn't clever enough to be one, but it's okay. I dug it up a few months later, and I've kept it in my room since. Wee bits of dirt are still stuck inside it, like round the seats and that. I imagine that's how the inside of my body looks. All the rust and eaten-away paintwork is my spotty face and greasy hair.

'You want tae watch something?' I say to Lee as I put my headset back on.

'Naw,' he replies. 'The night's aw aboot findin oot if we're incels or no.'

'We're no incels, Lee. C'moan tae fuck, mate. I've googled it. These cunts are no right. They aw look like school shooters.'

'I know it's a bit creepy, but it's interesting. Nice tae know that it's no just us that's like this. There's other cunts as well. We're shunned by society because women don't find us attractive. It's no oor fault we're like this.'

'We're no incels, Jesus Christ. The reason we're the way we are is cause we don't go oot. We don't dae anyhin apart fae . . . this.'

'Think aboot how much yer maw an yer granny annoy ye.

How the lassies treated ye at school. How they laughed at ye, mate,' Lee says. 'We've been doomed tae fail in life because ae how we look. Mind you were saying how your da hit yer maw? Bet there wis a good reason fur it, actually.'

'I dunno, man . . .' I reply. 'Gonnae no say stuff like that.'

'I'm tellin ye. See, since realising how fucked up the world is if you're like us, I fuckin hate lassies.'

'I don't hate lassies, though. I just want tae be left oan ma ain.'

'Fine, suit yerself,' Lee says and clicks off. That's the first time he's ever hung up on me.

'Fuck SAKE!' I shout. I didn't mean for it to be so loud; it just comes out.

My maw bangs on the wall straight away. 'Jamie, gonnae shut up,' I hear her say.

I tell her to shut up in retaliation, but I do it under my breath so she can't hear me. I'll talk to Lee tomorrow when he's calmed down a bit. Suppose when *I've* calmed down a bit too. He's annoyed me, actually, by calling me an incel. Imagine popping up to your pal and basically going, 'Here, mate. I've done some research, and you're actually a skinny, spotty, virgin creep.'

How long's he been sitting on this for as well? I get up off my computer chair and climb back into bed with my chips. I lie back and scroll through Facebook for the first time in a few days. Some boys from my year at school are all away on holiday together. There's a picture of the four of them, no tops on, in front of a bar. They're a lot more muscular than me, and they actually look a lot older than me. Wouldn't be hard, considering I've got all the muscle of a twelve-year-old.

A lassie I'm related to somehow – a cousin, maybe – is pregnant; my maw's liked the status. This lassie looks like she's got her life together. Must be a nice feeling. Lee's just shared some kind of football meme that I don't understand. Means he's still online, so I could message him if I really wanted to talk.

Before I realise it, I'm scrolling through Google, looking up incels again. I click on a link to an article that's just called 'The Black Pill':

'You take the blue pill,' Morpheus says to Neo in The Matrix, *'the story ends; you wake up in your bed and believe whatever you want to believe. You take the red pill, you stay in Wonderland, and I show you how deep the rabbit hole goes.'*

In the incel community, a blue pill is a person who hasn't yet woken up to the fact that society discriminates against males and not females. A red pill is, you guessed it, someone who has. They've realised that the odds are stacked against them so that they'll likely never find a partner unless they fight back and try to alter their appearance, the way they dress and even their entire personalities.

Then there's the black pill. While redpilled incels believe there are routes out of inceldom through going to the gym or other more dubious self-improvement strategies, blackpilled incels believe their situation is permanent and inescapable. To them, it's all down to genetics – men are either sexually attractive or they're not, and no amount of self-improvement can change this.

Now this is when incels become particularly dangerous. Some may simply LDAR (Lie Down and Rot), retreat to their bedrooms and lock themselves away, giving up on life completely. Or they might turn violent . . .

Fucking hell, is that what I've done? Just decided to lie down and rot?

Some incels may opt for the 'Rope' – incel speak for suicide.

Nah, man. Fuck this. I'm not an incel. I'm not going to lock myself away anymore; nor am I going to kill myself just because I can't get a girlfriend. There's guys on these forums saying they can't get their hole cause their wrists are too skinny or they've no got a big enough jaw. The only reason I don't have a girlfriend is cause I don't want one. Well, also the fact that the only women I ever come into contact with are my maw and my granny, and I wouldn't know how to talk to one. It's probably the same for these freaks, man. Lee needs to get a grip. I'm going to sort myself out, starting tomorrow.

8

FIONA

I pull up outside the house. Ours is the only house in the street in darkness. I'm sure everyone must talk about us, me especially. I wonder if they even know I've got a son, whether they remember the skinny, shy wee boy who used to play out in the street by himself.

I used to watch him from my bedroom window while he walked slowly up and down the street, kicking a discarded can or clanging a bit of wood off the metal fences. During the summer, he'd try and catch bumblebees in empty bottles of juice. Gingerly approaching them, hunched over, trying to sneak up on them, then hesitating as he tried to place the mouth of the bottle over them, afraid he might get stung. Then he'd pick flowers and drop them into the bottle. Some stones. A few blades of grass. A twig. A perfect wee home for a bee. I remember asking him once when he was doing this what he wanted to be when he grew up.

'A scientist,' he replied confidently.

Sometimes he'd just sit on the front step, lost in his Game

Boy, for hours and hours. He'd have a nice wee glow about him by the time he went back to school after the summer holidays. If he sat outside in the sun like that now I imagine he'd sizzle and smoke like a vampire. Sometimes, other maws at the school gates would ask where we'd been on holiday. 'Spain,' I'd lie, wanting to appear like a normal, well-put-together maw. Wanting them to think we had a normal life. Not wanting them to know that my son was basically a stranger to me. It was easier to just let him be, to let him live in his own wee world, rather than trying to force him to spend time with me.

I don't know; maybe it was just laziness on my own part. Maybe it's the fact that sometimes when I look at him, I see his da staring back at me.

I go inside and turn on all the lights, trying to make the house look as normal to outsiders as possible. I like to keep the house as spotless and minimal and tidy as I can. It's not hard; Jamie doesn't really come out his room. A wee spill on the kitchen floor or crumbs on the worktop is the only way I know he's came out his room that day.

I text him, trying to be funny.

You alive? X

Aye

Well, that's a relief. I wonder what time he got up at today. I wonder if he's eaten. I wonder if he's okay.

Can you come down the stair? X

I can hear his voice faintly through the ceiling. I don't think he's playing his game, because when he's playing that, he makes loads of wee noises. Like squeals and croaky screams. Sounds like maybe he's talking to himself. Or to some wee pal, maybe. Some weird guy on the internet, more likely. Then I hear his room door creak open.

'Wit is it?' he shouts.

'Can ye come doon? Just fur a minute.'

'Sake.'

If I hear him say that one more time, I'm going to rip my hair out from the root and stuff it in my mouth and scream.

He takes the stairs two at a time; he does that when he's in a mood. I try to make myself look busy in the kitchen. I don't know why. I grab a plate from the sink and hold it. I stare into the dirty water in the basin. He approaches, but I smell him before I see him. If he was in a cartoon, he'd have a greeny-brown fog hanging over him, following wherever he went. Maybe a houseplant would wilt and die as he passed. He had a shower yesterday, though; maybe it's being in his room that makes him so stinking. He stands in the doorway between the kitchen and living room, in that horrible onesie. Under the big bright light, he looks so impossibly pale. Like some kind of cave-dwelling creature that's never seen sunlight. That's what he is, I suppose.

'Wit is it?' he repeats.

'I said I was gonnae help ye apply fur joabs.'

'Aw, aye.' He doesn't look at me when he talks. He sounds and looks miserable.

'We'll make a CV. It'll be good fun.' I can't even bring myself to make 'good fun' sound like anything other than the grim-mest activity on earth.

He sighs.

I slip the plate back under water.

'Awrite,' he says.

I tell him to sit on the couch while I go and get my laptop from up the stair. When I come back, he's perched on the arm of the couch, looking around the room. Like a stranger in his own home.

'How've ye been?' I ask him.

'Wit?' He scrunches up his face.

'How've ye been? Wit've ye been up tae?'

He shrugs his bony, angular shoulders. 'Awrite. Just been dain the usual.'

'That's good.' I sit down next to him and open up the com-puter. 'Wance ye've goat a CV, it's easy tae get a joab.'

I look down at his hands, because I can hear him fidgeting. He's picking at the skin around his thumb. His fingernail digs under a wee flap.

'Stoap that,' I say.

'Stoap wit?'

'That.' I nod at his thumb as a little bead of ruby-red blood forms on it.

'Aw.' He tucks his hands under his thighs.

'Right. Ye don't have a lot tae put oan it, but we can pad it oot.'

He sighs.

I start typing his name into a Word document. Big bold letters at the top. *JAMIE SKELTON*.

He doesn't look impressed. In fact, he looks like he'd rather be doing literally anything else. He removes his hands from under his thighs and rubs his knees with them, then balls them into tight fists. His da used to do that before he'd lose the rag with me.

'We need a personal statement at the tap, like a wee bit aboot you and wit kind ae worker you'll be. Stuff you're interested in as well.'

He's not listening.

'Jamie?'

He lets out a big groan.

'Wit'll I write?' I ask.

'I dunno. Anyhin ye want.'

'Well, it's no wit *I* want. Wit dae *you* want it tae say?'

He groans again and runs his hands through his greasy hair.

'I'll just put that you're hard-workin, enthusiastic and that you're a good time-keeper,' I say.

He gets up and heads for the door in a huff.

'Jamie, come back.'

'Naw. I don't want tae dae this. Just you make me wan and send it tae places.'

'You need tae help. Am no dain everything fur ye.'

'Sake.' He sits back down.

I feel my own hands curling into fists as they rest on the laptop. It's getting harder and harder to get through to him, but also harder to keep my cool. He reminds me so much of his da. The sighs, the moaning, the storming about, the snapping at me when I'm doing nothing except trying to help him. It scares me sometimes.

I rattle out a personal statement while he stares at the screen, his face devoid of all emotion and feeling. I always wonder what's going on in his wee brain. What does he think about? What are his hopes for the future? What does he want from life?

'Does that sound awrite?' I ask, finishing off the paragraph with, '*I feel I will be an asset to your company.*'

'Aye, witever.'

I can see he's going to lose the rag. There's no point in keeping him here while I do this; I'm only making him stressed, and I don't want him to resent me.

'Right,' I say, holding my face in my hands, trying to calm down. 'I'll finish this fur ye, if you go an look fur joabs an send me three that ye want tae apply fur, an I'll help ye. Awrite?'

He does a big, stupid pantomime groan, then gets up and storms out.

'Och, Jamie, wit's the matter?' I shout after him.

'You! You're the matter.'

'Me?'

'Fucking always oan ma case, man.'

'Don't fucking swear at me!' This is the first time I've shouted at him, screamed at him, since he was a wean. 'You need a joab.'

'Wit fur? Who's gonnae gie me a joab? How can ye no just leave me alane?'

'You need a joab and that's it. Awrite.'

His lip gets petted. He's trying not to cry; he does that when he's angry. I get a flashback to him doing this whole routine when I told him he wasn't allowed to go out, because he'd went missing for a few hours the day before. The angrier he got, the more he'd cry. A scared wee boy who can't control his emotions – that's all he still is.

'How, though? Wit's the point?' He slumps against the door frame and wipes tears from his eyes with the sleeve of his onesie.

'Cause you're nineteen. Wit wid you dae if, I dunno, if I died? Where wid ye go? Ye cannae live withoot money, withoot a joab.'

'Go tae my da's.' He spits the words at me.

'Well, you'll need tae go there if ye don't get a joab soon. I cannae afford the hoose maself. I stopped gettin money fur ye when ye turned eighteen.'

'So I get a joab, then wit? Just gie you aw ma money? Fuck off, man.' He storms away up the stair.

'Och, Jamie, ye know that's no wit a mean.'

But it's no use. He's away. I hear a sob from him as he goes up the stair, then I hear his room door slam shut.

The house is silent. I have no idea what kind of job he'd be able to do. There's no way he could work in a shop; he's not sociable enough. I imagine him trying to be all chirpy and help customers and sell stuff to them – no chance. A factory, maybe? Something easy, where he doesn't need to talk to anyone. Who knows. He'll find something eventually. Maybe he'll just grow out of this phase one day and stroll in, dressed in a suit from his fancy office job. Give me his dig money and tell me he's going to look for a wee flat of his own. Or is this going to be it? Me, barely making ends meet and no even able to retire, while my forty-year-old son festers in his room until I die.

I hear his room door open again, and he comes down. When

he enters the living room, he doesn't look at me, just slinks into the kitchen.

'Jamie,' I say.

No reply. He rummages about in the cupboards.

'Jamie, listen—'

He cuts me off before I have a chance to reason with him. 'There's nae crisps,' he says.

'I know, I—'

'There's never fuckin ANYTHING!' He slams the cupboard door and runs away again.

That look on his face. Neck craned towards me, eyes bulging out their sockets like even they want to fight me. To hurt me. He slaps his hand hard against the living room door as he leaves.

The words I've never wanted to say leave my mouth for the first time: 'You're just like your fucking da!'

I hear his footsteps stop dead halfway up the stair.

'Aye, well, I can see why he left ye,' he says back to me.

9

JAMIE

She's an absolute fucking nightmare. I thought maybe she'd follow me up the stair, but she hasn't bothered. It's like she doesn't care about me, like she just wants to make me miserable. I hate feeling angry like this and I hate that it's my maw that's making me feel angry. Whenever I get like this it feels like I'm going to burst into tears and like someone's got their hand on the back of my neck, squeezing me and forcing me down. It's fucking horrible. I can't get a job. Not now, anyway, not while I'm like this, in this state. She better get a grip soon and realise that I'll get one when I'm ready. I click on my da's name in my phone and send him a text. At least he'll be nice to me.

Awrite

HI SON HOW YOU DOING?

He always texts in full capital letters; he's mental. He's always on his phone and replies pure quick. I scroll up in our messages to see the last time we spoke. Three months ago.

> I'm awrite. No been up tae much. You?

JUST WORKING AWAY. YOU GOT A JOB YET?

Fuck sake, no him as well.

My maw chaps my room door. 'Jamie,' she says.

'Wit is it?'

'Can ye come oot here, please?'

'Naw.'

'Jamie, come oan.'

'Naw, just . . . Just go away, eh.' My phone starts ringing. It's my da.

'You need tae sort yerself oot,' she shouts. From the tone of her voice, she's the one who needs to sort herself out and calm down. She sounds pure stressed out, like a teacher.

'Am talkin tae ma da,' I say to her, then I answer the phone and say, 'Awrite.'

'If ye don't get a joab soon, ye can go an stay wi him then,' she shouts, and storms away.

'That yer maw shouting there?' my da asks.

'Aye. She's murder.' I sigh down the line.

My da laughs at this. 'Yer no wrang there, wee man.'

Wee man. That's the first time he's called me that since I was a wean. It feels nice. Nice to have someone talk to me who doesn't sound raging.

'Wit ye phonin fur?' I ask.

'Just a blether, son. Listen, sorry I missed yer birthday. Just been busy wi work an that. Ye know how it is.'

My birthday was fucking ages ago, but I don't say anything. I also don't know *how it is*, but I say, 'Aye, I know. It's awrite.'

'So ye've no goat a joab yet?'

'Naw.'

'Wit dae ye dae?'

How would I describe what I do? *Aw, I just sit aboot in ma onesie. Playin games, watching YouTube videos, the occasional wank, an talk tae ma only pal, who also happens tae be like this.* Maybe I should say I'm an incel now.

'Just sit aboot, I suppose.'

'Och, ye've only just left school, eh? It's only been a couple ae months. Ye'll find suhin.'

'I left school three year ago, Da.' He doesn't reply straight away, and I don't know what to say. I roll a plastic bottle back and forth under my feet, before remembering it's full of piss and back-heeling it under the bed. My da lives in his own world, and he's not good at remembering stuff like dates and all that. I don't mind, though. I can't work out whether the three years since I left school have flown by or dragged in.

'Fuck sake. Three year awready? Does that mean you're eighteen noo?'

'Nineteen.'

'Jeezo.' I hear the sound of a can opening on the other end of the phone. 'I better go. Gies a text an let me know how yer getting oan, awrite? An don't take any shite aff *her*.'

'I won't.'

'See ye later, pal.'

'See ye later.'

My maw and my granny always say that my da's a prick and that I'm better off without him and all that, but he's the only one who actually seems to like me. I wish my maw would even just act as if she cares about me. I wish she'd take into consideration what I'm like and not force me to do things I don't want to do. Just, I don't know, be *gentle* with me. She just seems to not have any emotions. Apart from being annoyed, if that's even an emotion. She's like a fucking robot. When I talk to my da, it's always just a laugh, like he's my pal. When I talk to my maw, it's just me getting a row. I can't really remember how she was with my da, like if she was moany with him all the time or no. She cried a lot; I remember that, obviously. And he shouted a lot, but maybe he was just annoyed at her. Two sides to every story and all that.

The house is in silence. I sit for a minute in the quiet and the dark and just think. I do need to get a job, I know that. I just don't want one. Lee sent me a meme ages ago, and it was a quote from some old guy who said something like, 'How can a man be expected to enjoy getting up in the morning, piss, shit, shave, get stuck in traffic for an hour, before going to a place he hates for eight hours?' It sounds awful, man. All people do is moan about their work. If I can just coast by for another wee while like this, my maw will give up and just let me do this forever. Well, maybe not forever, but just another couple of years. That's all I need.

I open up my laptop and brush off the crumbs and other

shit that's accumulated on it over the last while. I give the screen a wee wipe. It makes me feel a bit better.

Lee's online on Facebook. I don't want to message him first or try to talk to him, since he hung up on me, but I could be doing with somebody to talk to. I hate silence, and the house is like a morgue just now. Swear I can actually feel the quietness pressing on my ear drums.

Fuck it, I'm messaging him.

Awrite.

No reply, but he's seen the message. Prick.

I sit for another wee while before I check my messages again. He's typing this time.

Awrite.

PlayStation?

Aye.

I put on my headset and we connect. I can hear Lee shuffling about on the other end, the squeak of his chair as he moves and gets comfy.

'You calmed doon?' he says. He sounds like he's smiling, like he's taking the piss out of me.

'Mate, you hung up oan me,' I say.

'Och, I wis annoyed.'

'I know ye were.' I don't know how long me and Lee have

been pals for – it could be a year or two, maybe. We've never had a proper fight or anything, and even if we do sort of disagree or a joke goes too far, we just get over it and forget about it.

'Ye ready tae find oot if yer an incel?' A weird feeling erupts in my stomach as he says that. I think about my maw and how angry I got at her earlier. All the other times I've said something horrible to her or snapped at her. I think I might be one.

'Aye,' I say.

'Right. I've got a couple ae questions tae ask ye tae make sure, awrite?'

'Aye, wire in.'

'Right, first question,' he says, and clears his throat. This must be what a job interview is like. 'Are ye a virgin?'

'Aye, ye know I am.'

'Excellent, me tae. Second question.' His voice drops to be slightly deeper, like he's hosting a quiz show. 'Huv ye ever kissed a burd?'

'Naw.'

'That's good. I huv, when I wis in primary six.'

'Naw, ye didnae,' I laugh.

'Aye, I did! I swear doon!'

'So right away, am mair ae an incel than you?'

'It's no a competition, Jamie mate. Third an final question – huv ye ever held a burd's hawn?'

'Naw. If I've never kissed a burd, how would I have held their hawn?'

'Take it ye've never cuddled a lassie, either?'

'Naw.'

'Right, well – that makes you a kissless, handholdless, hug-less virgin. That's a proper incel.'

'Fucking hell.' I laugh. 'We're pathetic.'

'Here, it's no oor fault.'

It *is* our faults, I think, but don't say. We don't leave the house. At school, we didn't make any effort to make pals, never mind to try and find girlfriends. Why would people want us to be their pals or anything more? Who'd want to be pals with a pair of creeps like me and him? I suppose he's right that it's not our fault that we're shy, awkward, weird and ugly.

'Me and you, mate. Incels. How does it feel to have a diag-nosis?'

'*Diagnosis?* Fuck off. We've no got anything wrang wi us.'

'We've no got anyhin wrang wi us apart fae being genetically inferior. See aw the neds an that at school?'

'Wit have neds goat tae dae wi this? Is that the two types ae guy then? Yer either a ned or an incel?'

'Naw yer either an incel or a Chad. We're incels, geeks, losers – witever ye want tae call us. See, the neds an, like, aw the sort ae popular guys, the guys that were good at fitbaw an that, that aw the burds fancied, they're Chads.'

'Wit's a Chad? Am loast here, man.' My head is actually fried with this patter. It's quite interesting, though, I suppose.

'A Chad is somecunt who can shag any burd he wants. Like pure shaggin aw the time.'

'Right, I see.'

'Anyway. Ye know my mate Seb?'

'Aye, the mad American cunt,' I reply, trying not to sound

too disappointed. My stomach lurches whenever he mentions his name. Lee's all I have and I don't like the idea that I'm not all he has. I really hate Seb. I hardly know anything about the guy other than the fact he's American, but I hate it when Lee seems to choose to talk to him over me.

'He's been telling me aboot aw this. An he's a bit aulder and mega clever – like, really knows his stuff – and it just feels like he's pure opened my eyes tae how things actually are.'

He says this so matter-of-fact, like it's totally normal. I mean, I know to me, Lee is just a mad guy online, but this is different. My paedo alarm goes off in my head. Sirens, flashing lights, screams, everything.

'Here, you better be careful,' I warn Lee.

'Naw, listen,' he says. 'He stays doon in London. He lives in a mad flat wi loads ae guys like us.'

'How did ye even come across this cunt?'

'Oan that incel forum I was tellin ye aboot; ye should go oan it an huv a look. Just hunners ae cunts like us. There's a mad Japanese word fur us anaw.'

'So as well as incel, we've goat another word?'

'Aye. Hing oan, I'll look it up.' I can hear the sounds of keyboard keys being rattled by Lee. 'Hikikomorri,' he says after a moment.

'Wit does that mean?'

'So that's cunts like us. Cunts that don't dae anything, just sit in their rooms an don't have joabs or that. Don't go ootside.'

I look this up for myself. It's weird to think there are other people like us, like we're not the only people in the world that have made the choice to live like this. Suppose a year ago or

64

something, you'd have just called people like me and Lee and this Seb guy weirdos. Or hermits, or something. Can't believe I'm a hikikomorri incel.

'So wit's this Seb cunt sayin?'

Lee gets even more excited-sounding and animated. 'Aw, he's class, mate. So funny. Apparently, it's this flat somewhere in London. His da's loaded and bought it for him. He gets cunts like us tae stay there fur however long they want fur free. His da pays fur aw the food an that. He even gets in beer an fags an that fur everybody. Everycunt just sits aboot playin games an watchin films. It sounds amazin.'

'That does sound class, actually.' And I mean that when I say it, but I think the guy's definitely at the wind-up. It can't be real, surely. Lee's going to end up telling me he's running away to London to live with this guy.

'I was hinkin I could try an get doon there.'

There it is.

'I dunno, mate. Sounds too good tae be true.'

'It's real, mate. I'm no kiddin on.'

'I know you're no; I'm worried this Seb cunt is.'

'Nah, it's aw legit. I'll send ye pictures oan Facebook the noo.'

My phone vibrates a few seconds later as the pictures come through. The first one shows a living room with three wee guys who all look like me, sitting on a couch with their laptops in front of them and headsets on. They're smiling at the camera. The next shows the kitchen, along with more spotty, greasy-haired boys with twig-thin arms coming out of their T-shirts. There's some bigger guys as well, but you'd put them in the same category as me. The next picture shows a bedroom with four single beds and more wee guys sitting about and laughing. If they're sharing a room like that, how do they manage to have a wank? This looks horrific.

'That last picture is Seb,' says Lee. 'He looks sound, eh?'

It's a picture taken in a dirty toilet mirror. Seb has long, straight brown hair that looks sort of ragged. It hangs down and frames his red, acne-scarred cheeks. He looks more well-built, and is definitely older than us – maybe about thirty, I'd say.

'He looks horrible, man,' I say.

'Och, shut up man. He's sound as.'

'He's defo a beast.'

'How can he be a beast? I'm sixteen. He cannae be a paedo.'

'Just be careful. That's aw am sayin.'

'See if I go doon there, ye want tae come?'

If this was a few months ago, before my maw suddenly started to put me under all this pressure about getting a job, I would just have said 'naw' because I can do all that here and no have to go all the way to London.

But maybe this is my best option now. Heading down there means I can keep living like this without annoying anybody, and without upsetting my maw. She'll be glad to get rid of me, I think.

After a moment, and a deep breath, and despite knowing this is the worst idea anyone in the world has ever had, I simply reply: 'Aye.'

Fuck it.

10

FIONA

There was moments when he was a wee boy where I thought he could maybe be normal. Well, maybe that he'd *turn out* normal – eventually. Wee things he'd do, interactions we'd have that'd make me think everything would be okay. It's memories like the first Christmas we had without his da that keep me going when he's being like this. When he's being this horrible person.

He was about six years old. I had no money, and had got him stuff from charity shops and any other wee cheap things I could find. A bucket of green plastic soldiers was his favourite.

'Fae *Toy Story*!' he screamed when he ripped open the fag-paper thin wrapping to reveal the battered and bashed bucket. His wee face lit up like he'd just opened a PlayStation and every game ever made to go with it.

'Oh my god,' he screamed. 'There's HUNNERS!'

Some of the wee green soldiers looked like they'd just returned from war. Missing legs, snapped guns, some even had their heads missing, but he didn't care. He lined them all up, splitting them into battalions, giving them names, ranks and duties.

'Aw, I got you something,' he said, abandoning his large and powerful army. He shuffled off to his room, his wee slippers sclaffing on the wooden floor. He came back with his tiny hands holding the most badly wrapped present I'd ever seen.

'It's just a wee hing,' he said. 'I saved up fur it.' He blushed as he handed it over, avoiding looking at me and trying to stop himself smiling.

I still don't know what he was talking about; I've never been able to give him pocket money or much for his birthdays or Christmas, so I don't know how he had anything to 'save up'. I think my ma bought it, probably, and gave it to him to give to me. I still smile when I remember that kind wee lie he told me.

'I wrapped it myself,' he said.

'Aye, I can tell.' I laughed. Inside the parcel, which was held together with Blu Tack and Sellotape, was a bath set. A sponge, a couple of wee bars of soap, some shampoo and some bubble bath, all in a wee wicker basket.

'This is really nice,' I said to him. 'Thanks very much.'

'It's awrite,' he replied, and went back to his 50p army.

Other times, there were hints of what was to come. When he was eleven, we were sitting out the back garden. It's only small, but I've never been great at keeping on top of cutting the grass and the hedges, so it's always overgrown. It was the last day of the summer holidays, and I was watching him trying to find a cricket that was chirping somewhere in the grass.

'I cannae be bothered gawn the morra,' he said. He was topless, and his head was bowed forward as he stalked through the garden, looking for the insect. His shoulder blades jutting out through his skin as he moved among the washing on the line.

'Well, ye need tae,' I said. 'It's secondary school. The big school. Ye'll like it mair than primary.'

'Naw I willnae. It'll be so big. And hunners ae new people in the classes. I'm gonnae hate it.'

'Ye don't know that.'

'Aye, I dae. Just let me huv wan mair day aff, eh?'

'Naw.' I laughed.

'Sake.'

He squatted down, his bony knees meeting his even bonier shoulders, his eyes searching between blades of grass for the cricket.

'Wit wid ye dae wi wan mair day aff?' I asked.

'Dunno,' he replied. 'Play ma computer, sit aboot . . . It'd be brilliant.'

'So ye widnae help me oot wi the housework? Widnae go tae the shoaps fur me? Widnae make ma dinner?'

'Is that wit ye want?' He didn't look up at me. He cupped his hands and slowly reached down for the cricket.

'Aye, that'd be nice.'

'If I done that—' He lunged, but the insect hopped away. He stood up dejectedly. 'See, if I done that, could I stay aff the morra?'

'Naw, it wis a test. Ye failed.'

His eyes widened as he shook his head at me. 'Aw god SAKE, MAN!' He charged up the garden and away into the house, disappearing into his pit. I heard his bedroom window close.

When I looked up, he drew the curtains. They've been shut ever since. I let my head drop back and sighed the biggest sigh of my life, like I was the moody teenager. There was no winning with him; there never was.

'Fiona, just you *wait* till you hear what my Thomas is up to,' says my colleague Gillian. She sits across from me. Her desk has pictures of her husband, her son and her dugs stuck all around it. Mine has nothing on it but two snow globes that Gillian brought me back from her holidays last year. She went on two holidays in one year, and I've never even left Scotland in my life.

'Aw aye? Wit's he been up tae?' I ask, despite having no desire to hear of the boy's latest achievement.

She's got the smuggest look on her face you can imagine. I don't know what annoys me more: her face, her daft haircut or her constant bragging about her son.

'*Well*,' she continues, 'his work are sending him out to LA. Imagine being twenty-one and being flown out to America for work. Is that not just amazing?'

'Aye, it is. Good for him.' I go back to my spreadsheet. I don't mind my job here; it doesn't pay much, but it's easy, and I don't have to deal with customers like Gillian does. Although she likes doing that, as she likes to talk. I just process invoices and occasionally order in stationery. I've never been ambitious or wanted a really important job; I just want enough to get by and as little stress as possible. Thankfully, the real-wood furniture industry had just the job for me – admin work for a company whose stuff I can't afford.

My answer can't have been satisfactory. I can still feel her staring at me, her bobble-head peering round the computers.

'How's your Jamie getting on?'

'Aye, he's fine.'

Eyes locked on to the screen, just don't look up, I can end this conversation before it even starts by not engaging.

'What does he do? Does he have an apprenticeship or something? Is he at university?'

'Aye.'

'Oh,' she says. 'Okay.'

In my peripheral vision, I can see her head slide back behind the computer. She'll no doubt retell what just happened at lunchtime later, adding extra details to further the narrative that I'm a massive freak. The office weirdo.

It would be nice to be able to brag about Jamie and the things he does. To talk about how well he did in his exams, or how happy I am that he got into uni or got a good job or something. I can hardly turn to Gillian and say, 'Aw, well, if ye think that's impressive, wait till ye hear *this*. Ma Jamie ate *four* boxes ae Micro Chips for his dinner. He's such a high achiever. He can really dae anything he puts his mind tae. He played his computer for mair than twenty-four hours straight wan weekend. I found oot because ae the bottles ae pish sitting in his room. Int he amazing?! I'm so proud!'

'Fiona?' Gillian says to me later in the canteen.

I feel bad for being so awkward with her earlier; it's not nice when people do that. Makes them feel like you hate them. I need to stop it. It's not her fault she's got a lovely family and a nice life.

'Aye?' I say, trying to force a smile.

'Listen, please tell me if this is a bit . . . forward, or prying, or whatever.' Her fingers sweep over her blonde fringe, tidying it up. I can tell she's nervous talking to me. 'You know my Gary?'

Gary's her husband. I hope she doesn't want relationship advice or anything off me here.

I say, 'Aye,' again.

'Right, well. His best pal, Mark – best man at our wedding – he got divorced a wee while ago. His missus was messing about behind his back, right?'

I nod. Where on earth is this going?

'And he's no really been himself since. Well, he's doing better now, to be fair, but he was saying he fancies dipping his toe in the water with regards to seeing people again. He's so lovely; it's such a shame what happened. He's one of those people who've got a lot of love to give.'

She lets this statement hang in the air between us for a second or two while she studies my face. I think she's worried what my reaction is going to be.

'I'll show ye a picture of him, hang on,' she says, getting out her phone.

She shows me the Facebook page of the most normal-looking man I've ever seen. About my age, maybe a wee bit older. Dark hair, but going baldy. A beard. He's wearing golfing clothes and smiling a closed-lip smile at me.

'Now, I don't know anything about your love life, Fiona, but I'm assuming you're single?'

'Eh, aye. Aye, I am.'

I've never even considered trying to meet someone since I left Jamie's da. I don't know if it's a good idea. The thought of having a man in my home again freaks me out. But maybe Jamie needs a good role model; maybe I need someone normal and stable to sort me out.

Gillian looks at me expectantly. 'So?' she says. 'Would you be up for going for a wee drink with him, then?'

I don't want to be rude to her again. 'Aye,' I say. I immediately regret it.

'Okay,' she says, and smiles at me. She leans over and rubs my shoulder. I keep looking at where her hand has just been. I couldn't tell you the last time someone did such a thing to me. 'I'll tell him you're up for it. He mentioned this Saturday to me when I told him about you. I hope that's okay?'

'Saturday's fine. That'll be, eh, nice.'

'Aye, that's good. Is it okay that I told him about you though? I know you're quite a private person. I hope I've no overstepped any . . . boundary or anything like that?'

'Naw, naw, don't be daft. That was nice of you,' I say, and I mean it. It's quite strange to think of myself as existing in someone's thoughts when I'm not with them. This guy, Mark, must have told her that he wanted to meet someone and she's obviously thought of me. I hope that's a good thing. Probably best to just not think too much about it.

'Oh,' she says as she stands up. 'You better give me your number so I can send it to him.' She hands me her phone, and I dial my number in for her.

'There ye go,' I say.

She phones me right away. 'Now you've got mine as well,' she says, and smiles again, a really nice, lovely big smile. I feel bad for being so rude to her, to everyone in my work, all the time. She rubs my shoulder again and goes back to work.

11

JAMIE

My maw's been giving me the silent treatment. I heard her come in from work an hour ago or something, so I went down to see if she'd brought anything in, hoping for crisps, juice, chocolate spread and that. She was in the kitchen when I went down, standing with her back to me, putting the bags on the worktop.

'Awrite,' I said.

No reply. She just unloaded the bags and started putting the stuff in cupboards and in the fridge.

'You awrite?' I asked.

'Aye,' she said. 'I'm fine.'

That sort of 'I'm fine' response you give to people when you're not really fine. When you just can't be bothered with what would come after you explained what was up. 'I'm fine' just ends any conversation. The other person can take it to mean you're actually fine, or they'll go away and wonder what's really up.

I poured a big glass of cheap cola, grabbed a packet of

crisps and came back up the stair. I'll get something to eat later when she goes to bed.

'My maw's no talkin tae me,' I say into my headset.

'Aw aye? Wit fur?' Lee replies, while munching on crisps. The noise of it is crystal clear in my ears. It's horrible.

'Getting a joab. The usual. She's stopped nagging me, man. She's stopped talkin tae me aw thegither.'

'My maw's the same. Couldnae tell ye the last time I spoke tae her. Class, int it.' Another big crunch.

'Aye, I suppose.'

'Right, I was hinking,' says Lee, changing his tone a wee bit, sort of lowering his voice. 'It's mental we've never actually met.'

It *is* mental, I realise. I'd call this guy my pal, my best mate, and I've never met him. Never been in the same room as him, shook his hand or gave him a high-five or anything, man.

'You want tae come roon tae mine the night?' he asks.

'Eh, I dunno,' I reply, remembering the state I was in the last time I tried to go out the front door. 'Maybe if we're gonnae meet up then you should come here.'

'Aye, actually. That suits me better, aye.'

My stomach twists. I've never had a pal in my room before. What if I'm all weird? What if he gets here and I don't know how to talk to him? I can't remember the last time I spoke to another human being, one that wasn't related to me, in real life. If I just sit next to him and don't look at him, like, if we're playing a game or something, then I can just pretend we're talking on the computer like normal.

'I could be roon in like ten, fifteen minutes if that's sound?' he says.

'Aye, that's cool, mate.'

'Class, see ye in a bit. Text me yer address.' He clicks off.

I look around at the state of my room. Lee's room will be the same, maybe a wee bit better, maybe a wee bit worse, but it'll be the same – a tip. I clear some stuff off the bed so he's got somewhere to sit. I get up and practise what I'm going to do and say when he comes to the door. I whisper, in case my maw can hear me.

Awrite, mate. Wit's happenin? Then shake his hand. *Awrite . . . ma man.* Maybe do that thing where you shake with one hand and bring them in for a cuddle with the other. Nah, that's a bit cheesy. Maybe I'll just shake his hand, like a businessman or a drug deal. Is that weird? Too formal? Fuck knows. Maybe I'll just open the door, like a normal person, and say, *Awrite, moan in.*

Fuck, what if my maw hears the door going and goes to answer it before me? I text him to say he should text me when he's outside, just in case. I've never had anybody over, so I don't know how she'll react. I assume it'll annoy her. Or maybe she'll be buzzing that I've got an actual pal. Maybe she'd want to meet him and talk to him and ask him loads of stuff. Pure embarrass me.

My phone buzzes.

Am ootside mate

I run down the stair to let him in. My maw will hear me opening the door, but she'll just think it's me getting a takeaway

77

or something, maybe. It's only coming up for eight o'clock on a Friday night, but she's in bed already. She must be knackered from work or something. That's another reason I don't want a job, man. Folk that work are just always moaning about their jobs and how tired they are. Putting in mad hours at some place they hate.

'There he is,' Lee says as I open the door. He's holding a blue poly bag and wearing a grey trackie that looks too big for him. He has a backpack on. He's a bit taller than me and a bit more solid-looking. His ginger hair is short and the same length all over, so his head sort of looks like a tennis ball, I think.

'Awrite. Eh, moan in,' I say. I don't make eye contact with him. I'm weird-looking, and I always thought of Lee as being the same, but seeing him in the flesh for the first time, he's actually alright-looking – a bit spotty, but no bad. Like, if I looked like him, I'd be quite chuffed. He just looks normal. I'm three years older, but I'd say we look about the same age; maybe he even looks a bit older. I still just look like a wee guy.

'Thought we could maybe have a wee drink? Stole them aff ma da. You up fur that?'

'Aye,' I reply. 'Why no?' I've never drank before in my life.

He breezes past me and heads down the hall towards the living room and through into the kitchen instead of going up to my room. I hadn't anticipated him doing this. I watch the bag of cans swing at his side. I want to say something like, *Eh actually, my room's up here, mate.* But I can't say anything. I've got an actual pal in my actual house. Madness.

My maw's room door opens.

'Jamie,' she shouts down. 'Did somebody just come in?'

'Aye, it's ma pal,' I blurt out, without thinking. The excitement is overwhelming me.

'Aw,' she says. She obviously wasn't expecting this answer; she sounds genuinely surprised.

I can hear Lee rooting about in the fridge, and the rustling of the poly bag. I go in to see him.

'Your hoose is class,' he says, looking around the kitchen while he puts some cans in the fridge. I've not been in many other people's houses before, but I know ours is just a normal one. Quite wee I think, going by houses you see on the telly and in films and that. 'It's heavy tidy.'

'Aye, my maw's always cleaning.'

'Wish my maw wid dae a bit ae cleaning. Oor flat's a state, man.'

As Lee says this, my maw appears in the kitchen with us. 'Ye never told me ye were having somebody over?' she says.

'Aw, I know. Sorry.'

We all stand in silence for a few seconds, Lee on his knees with a can in hand next to the fridge, my maw in the doorway and me in the middle. My maw looks to Lee, then to me, and sort of nods her head at him. I've no idea what she means. She gives up trying to talk to me via mind-link and says to Lee, 'I'm Jamie's ma.'

'Awrite,' he replies, getting up. 'I thought ye were his sister!'

My maw laughs at this. I feel myself go red.

'I'm Lee,' he says. He sticks a hand out and my maw shakes it.

'You stay round here then?' my maw asks.

'Aye, just alang the road. Like a ten-minute walk or something.'

'That's good. With your ma and da, aye? Any brothers or sisters?'

'Just me, my maw and da. My da's a mechanic and my maw's a cleaner.' Lee looks around the kitchen before adding, 'But obviously no as good a cleaner as you.'

My maw does a wee laugh, then nods at the can in Lee's hand. 'Having a wee drink, aye?'

Me and Lee look at each other, not knowing what to say.

'That's fine, by the way. Rather ye were drinking in here than oot oan the street. How'd you two know each other, then? Did yous go tae school thegither?'

Me and Lee look at each other again and laugh this time.

'We met oanline,' I say.

'Aw, that's . . . nice,' my maw says. 'Right, I'll leave ye tae it. Have fun.' She disappears up the stair.

'Your maw's a legend,' Lee says. 'Bit ae a milf anaw.'

'She's a pain in the arse,' I say under my breath. 'A pure riddy.'

'Right, moan. Show's yer room. I want tae see if it's as bad as ye say it is.'

'I tidied it up a bit fur you coming. It's no that bad the noo.'

Lee hands me a yellow can of lager, and he follows me up to my room. As I open the door, I'm more aware of the foosty smell in my room than ever. Lee covers his mouth and nose with his hand as we walk in.

'Fuck sake, Jamie,' he says, laughing. 'It's fucking honking in here, man.'

'It's no that bad,' I reply. 'Ye get used tae it.'

He sits on the bed and makes a mad face while he opens his can. I open mine and hold it to my nose. It doesn't smell too appealing.

'Bit dark,' Lee says.

'Aye, the lightbulb's fucked.'

'Ye no change it?'

'I don't know how.' I take a sip from the can. It's not bad; not brilliant, either. I'd much rather just have a can of juice or something.

'You're like an alien, mate. Ye know that?' Lee says.

'How am I like an alien?'

Lee looks me up and down in the twilight with a smirk on his face. I'm wearing a pair of joggies I've had since I was like fourteen that are a bit too wee for me, a black T-shirt and a pair of my maw's fluffy socks that I stole off her cause I couldn't find any clean ones of my own.

'You're just so weird, man. It's class. It's like you've just landed oan this planet and ye just cannae figure it aw oot.'

I take another sip from my can. 'Aye, sometimes I dae feel a bit like that's wit I am.'

Lee looks around the room for a second, puts down his can, then pulls his laptop out his bag. 'Right, the reason am here is tae show ye something.'

I sit next to him and watch him log into his computer. In the glow from the screen, he looks like a hacker. His fingers move fast over the keyboard. His library of pictures flashes up, and he instantly closes it down. I only got a glimpse, but it looked like lassies. No porn stars or that: actual normal, real lassies around our age, maybe younger. I feel a bit weird after seeing that.

'Just ignore that. Wit's yer Wi-Fi password?' he asks.

I tell him and he types it in.

'So, as ye know, I've been talking tae Seb.'

I'd almost managed to forget all about Lee's incel carry-on. Seems like he isn't letting it go.

'Wit's he been saying?' I ask. I take a big gulp of my lager; it's starting to taste better. My head's beginning to feel a wee bit funny already. Am I drunk? Is this what being drunk is? It feels nice if it is. Lee turns and stares at me. He shows me his screen. There's a big, long email from Seb.

'He's asked if we want tae go doon.'

'Wit, fur real?'

'Aye, fur real, obviously. I was telling him aw aboot ye. He says we'll be a good fit.'

A good fit. I've never been a good fit for anywhere before.

'I dunno, man,' I say.

'Listen, this is probably the biggest an best opportunity two guys like us will ever get in oor life. I mean, getting tae move doon tae London, best city in the world, Seb says. At oor age, living rent-free, aw expenses paid, wi other guys like us. Mate, it'll be amazing. We'll never need tae worry aboot anything ever again. Ye need tae come.'

'I dunno, it's just . . .'

'Just wit?'

'Just . . . scary. Weird. I dunno.'

Lee's gaze returns to his screen.

'Let me think aboot it,' I say, rubbing the back of my head.

'Wit is there tae think aboot, man? This will be so class. Me and you.' Lee puts an arm around me. For a second, I imagine I'm his wee brother, or that he's my da. 'Oan the road. An actual adventure.'

I smile. 'It'd be good fun, eh?' I say.

'Mate, we'll have some fucking buzz. Aw the guys doon there seem dead sound anaw. Just like Seb says, we'll fit right in.'

'How dae we get there? I don't have any money.'

'I'm no sure. Moan, we'll go an sit in the living room an figure it oot. I cannae handle being in this room, mate. Nae offence. It smells like rotten totties.'

Three cans later, and Lee says Seb wants to talk to us over Skype.

'I don't know, man,' I say. This is all starting to feel a bit too real, if you get me. Like, it made me anxious just talking about it, but the thought of us actually going is giving me the fear. Drinking the cans has made me feel a bit better than normal, though. Like I don't feel so shy anymore.

'Stick the big light oan so he can see us,' Lee says. 'I'll get the computer set up fur the call.'

I do as Lee tells me, then sit down next to him.

'Why does he want tae talk tae us?' I ask.

'He's gonnae tell us how tae get doon. Like, how tae book the stuff an that.'

'Awrite. Cool.'

Both our faces pop up on Lee's computer screen as the call connects. We're grainy-looking. Still very obviously two wee guys, but a pure low-quality rendering of us, like an old computer game.

The words **NOW CONNECTING** appear on the screen for a second or two before Seb appears.

'Awrite, my man!' shouts Lee, giving him the thumbs-up. I awkwardly raise my thumb as well.

Seb just blinks. His chubby red cheeks fill the screen. His camera must be a belter, because I can see every single crater on his spotty face. He looks like Mars. His hair falls in thin strands either side of his glasses.

'Hey, boys,' he says. His voice is deep and extremely American. I've only ever heard Americans talk in films and that; it's weird having one talk directly to me. 'So, what's up?'

'No much, mate. No much,' says Lee. 'This is ma mate, Jamie, by the way.' Lee puts his arm around me and pulls me more into the frame. I'd started to drift out of shot without realising. Seb pushes his glasses up, as if to get a better look at me. I feel like some kind of lab sample under a magnifying glass.

'Say something,' Lee says to me, quietly.

I just wave at the camera.

'He doesn't say much, does he, Lee?'

Lee and Seb laugh at me.

'That's fine,' Seb says. 'There's a lotta guys just like you down here.'

'Right, that's the hing,' says Lee. 'How dae we get doon there?'

I see Seb is straining to understand what Lee is saying. Lee's talking to Seb like he's just a cunt from our bit. I drain the last of my can and go get another two from the fridge. I was feeling okay before we went on the call with Seb, but I'm all anxious again now. Another drink should make me better.

I come back to hear Seb say: '. . . just don't tell *anyone* where you're going, okay? I'm sure with Silent Bob there that won't be a problem.'

Lee laughs. I don't get the joke, but I force a laugh anyway so they don't think I'm any weirder than they already do.

Seb's got a pen in his hand. 'So, what's the closest bus station to you guys?'

I have no idea, so look to Lee to take the lead. 'Eh, Buchanan Bus Station,' Lee says. 'In the toon.'

'That's Glasgow, yeah?'

'Aye.'

'Okay, I'll get you two tickets down. They won't be under your names, okay? I'll send you a message with your new identities for the journey. When are you gonna come down?'

'Next week, I think,' says Lee.

Seb notes this down as well.

I'm a bit confused here. I nudge Lee and mumble for him to ask why this all sounds a bit dodgy.

'Eh, can I ask wit's wi aw the secrecy and fake names?' Lee asks on my behalf.

Seb sort of scoffs at this. 'This *commune*, as I like to call it,' he says, 'is for guys like you, like us. We're careful about who we let in; we have to be. That's why I select who gets to come. I don't like anyone that isn't like us knowing about the place: where we are, who we are, et cetera. It's a special place, and

I want to keep it that way forever. You'll be safe here, you'll
have fun, you'll have friends; it really is just great. And hey,
you know what? If you don't like it after you've completed
your initiation, then you're free to go.'

This all sounds rehearsed, like he's said it a million times
before. Like a pure sales pitch or something. It does sound
good in theory, chilling out with other guys like us, not having
to worry about anything. I'm getting bad vibes off him and
the whole initiation thing, though. But maybe it is all as good
as it sounds. Maybe I'd regret not going. Maybe I'd lose Lee
forever if he went alone. Lee looks completely sold on it as I
turn to look at him. He's nodding with his mouth open, pure
drawn right in by Seb's patter.

'We won't tell anycunt,' says Lee. Then he turns to me.
'Will we?'

I take a sip of lager and say, 'Naw.'

'You don't seem convinced, Jamie,' Seb says, leaning in close
to the camera.

I feel naked. I feel like I'm naked in front of the whole
world here. I've no said anything to suggest I'm no keen on
going down, or even said anything at all, and this cunt must
have been analysing my body language and has clocked that
am feeling apprehensive.

'Lee,' Seb says. 'Can you leave the room for just a sec, please?
I wanna talk to Jamie.'

'Eh, aye. I'll jump nip tae the toilet,' says Lee. He puts his
hand on my shoulder and stands up. Into my ear he says,
'You'll be awrite. Just be yersel.' Lee leaves the room, and I
hear the door to the toilet close over and the lock sliding into

place. I keep looking towards the living room door, willing him to come back.

'You're acting like a cop,' says Seb.

'Sorry, wit?' I say, turning to face the screen again.

'You're like a bad undercover cop.'

'Aw, eh, sorry.'

Seb smiles. 'It's okay. Can I ask you a question?'

'Aye, go fur it,' I say, trying to sound more positive. I don't want to be rude.

'Do you ever feel like the odd one out? Like you're different from everyone else?' Seb rests his elbow on his desk, his chin in his hand.

I nod and take another sip from my can. 'Aye. Definitely.'

He just blinks at me.

'Like, at school,' I say, feeling compelled to keep talking, 'I had no pals. Nobody liked me. Even the teachers couldn't remember my name.'

Seb says, 'Mmmm,' and nods.

'Lee's the only pal I've ever had. He's the only person who seems to get me, and—'

Seb cuts in and says, 'What about the girls at school?'

I just laugh. 'I had no luck with lassies. I don't blame them, to be honest.'

'Everyone here has a story about a girl. You have one, too, don't you?'

'What do you mean?' I ask.

'Who broke your heart, Jamie? You can tell me. I won't laugh at you.'

'Well, there was one lassie,' I say. My can's all warm and horrible now, but I don't care.

'There it is.' Seb laughs. 'Go on, tell me about her.'

'Well, eh, we were in first year. I was sitting in English and this lassie comes over to me and says her pal fancies me and asks if I want to kiss her at lunchtime.'

'Was she hot?' asks Seb.

'Aye, she was like the hottest lassie in our year. She'd never even looked at me before. I was getting bullied a bit and I thought this was, like, what I deserved after everything. Thought it'd be like I was in a film, and if I kissed her, then all of a sudden I'd be the most popular guy at my school and I'd have loads of pals.'

'What happened?'

'I said aye, and at lunchtime I went over to her outside the school. I felt about ten feet tall. All the guys that had been bullying me were watching. I went to kiss her, and then somebody came up behind me and just pulled my trousers and boxers right down. The lassie burst out laughing, and that was it. It was all just a big joke at my expense.'

'That sucks, man.'

'Aye, it was fucking shite.'

'Honestly – and I mean this, Jamie.' I like the way Seb always says my name. Don't know what it is; makes me feel like he really likes me or something. 'You need to come here. You'll be a lot happier here. There's no bullying or anything like that.'

I nod, but don't look at him. For some reason, I feel like I'm going to cry.

'I'll sort everything out with Lee. I can see you're worried about coming, but trust me, you'll be happy here.'

'Aye, I think you're right.' I look up.

He's leaning in close to the camera. 'No pressure, no stress, no worries *at all*. You can stay for as long as you like. Okay?'

'Okay.'

'One last thing. I take it you live with your parents?'

'Aye, with my maw.'

'You can't tell her where you're going, okay? I don't mind what you tell her, just don't tell her about this place.'

'She won't care. She probably won't even notice I'm away.'

'Whatever you tell her, make it plausible. Some guys here told their parents they had signed up for the military. Some said they were on a school trip or something. Just make it believable, and we won't have any issues.'

I hear the back door open, and in walks Lee. 'Everything awrite?' he asks, and sits down next to me again.

'Aye, man,' I say, rubbing my eyes to hide the fact I've been on the verge of tears. Lee hands me another can.

'I'll book the tickets for next Friday, alright?' Seb says. My stomach feels like it's going to fall out of my arse at the thought of going, but I think it's maybe in a good way. Like excitement.

'Class,' says Lee.

'I need tae go tae the toilet, back in a minute,' I say, and leave the room. I shut the toilet door, lock it, and just stand for a minute. I can hear Lee talking, but can't make out what he's saying. He sounds buzzing, though. I think I'm doing the right thing by going away. I get to go somewhere I'll be a lot happier, and get out of my maw's way. She'll be happy that I'm away, out from under her feet and all that.

When I go back in the living room, Seb's face has disappeared from the screen. Lee shuts his laptop over. 'Aw, eh, Seb says he'll see ye next week. Says yer gonnae fit right in.' He flashes a smile at me.

'I cannae wait,' I say, sitting back down and opening my can.

Lee picks up his own and clanks against mine. 'Easy as that. A whole new life starts a week fae the day,' says Lee.

'Class,' I say. And I mean it. This is going to be amazing.

'Wit you gonnae tell yer maw?' he asks, his tone not quite as excited as it was a second ago.

'Fuck knows. Wit you telling yours?'

'Dunno. I might just no tell her, in case she disnae let me go.'

'Aye, same here. My maw probably won't even notice am away.'

'Fuck it, it'll be fine. We'll figure it oot closer tae the time.'

'Aye,' I say. 'We'll think ae something.'

Lee rummages around in his bag for something. I sit back with my can and think about how much of a class guy he is. It feels like the lager has loosened me up. It's like my brain was all rusty, and the parts and components were all stuck together, and now it's all lubricated and working again. Feels like I can say anything I want now without holding back, without being scared of saying something weird or that'll make folk laugh at me. I can just be myself.

'You don't smoke, dae ye?' Lee asks, pulling out a packet of fags and a lighter.

'Naw, I've always wanted tae try it. But I've always been too scared.'

'Nothing tae be scared ae, man. It's lovely.'

'Gies wan.' I take the packet from Lee and turn it over in my hands. It's got a naked guy lying on his side on it, curled up like a baby. Underneath him, it says, *Smoking increases the risk of impotence.*

'Wit dis that mean?' I ask Lee.

'Means if ye smoke too much, you won't be able tae get a hard-on.'

'Fuck sake.' I slide a fag out of the packet and stick it in my mouth. 'Where's the lighter?'

'Ye cannae smoke in here, ya madman. Moan, we'll go ootside.'

'How no?'

'Trust me, mate. Yer maw will smell it an go tonto.'

We head out the back door with our cans. The cool night air skelps me in the face and I remember the mad freak out I had trying to get out the front door. Being out the back must not have the same effect cause I'm not actually leaving the house to go somewhere. Or maybe it's cause Lee's here with me. It's a full moon tonight. A fox does that mad scream they do sometimes, the one that sounds like a wean greeting.

I open my can. Lee plucks the fag from between my lips and sticks it between his own. He puts another one in as well, and lights the two of them at the same time. The ends glow like wee mini bonfires in the dark. He hands one to me.

I hold it up to my eyes, examining it. A small, bright ember burns round the paper like it's sliding down a helter-skelter slide.

'Don't be shy, mate,' Lee says. 'Take a draw.'

I put it in my mouth, then pull it back out. 'I'm scared in case I dae it wrang.' I laugh.

Lee laughs too. But it's not the way people in school would have laughed at me; it's nice. It's like he's laughing along with me, and not *at* me. Like he's laughing just because he's my pal.

'Just suck it, breathe in the smoke and blow it back oot, like this.' He closes his eyes and takes a drag.

I do the same, and immediately go into a coughing fit. He laughs again, and I copy him as he leans his elbows on the wall, overlooking the back garden.

'I love you, mate,' I say. It just comes out.

'Think you've had wan too many cans.' Lee laughs.

'Naw, I mean it. You're my best pal. First pal I've ever had, actually.'

'I cannae be the only pal you've ever had, surely?'

The two of us look out into the darkness for a few seconds. A siren wails in the distance.

'I think this might be the best night ae ma life,' I say.

'Aw we've done is have a few cans and talk tae a cunt oan Skype, mate.'

'I know, but it's been . . . nice.'

Lee exhales smoke through his nose as he does another wee laugh. 'Swear doon, you are the weirdest cunt I've ever met in ma life,' he says, still smiling.

I take another drag; this time, I manage not to cough. I can see some slugs glistening in the light from the kitchen.

'I love you tae, mate,' Lee says, breaking the silence. He flicks his fag away into the grass, pats me on the back and goes back inside. I watch my fag burn down to the filter before I go back in as well.

12

FIONA

Lying in bed, I can hear Jamie and his wee pal waffling away down in the living room. I'm stunned he has a real-life pal. I always wondered who he was talking to at night on his computer; I'd imagined he was talking to weird old American guys who live in their mas' basements. It's nice to know it was a real wee guy, just like him.

As his deep voice comes up through the floor, it reminds me of his da's. Sometimes, I'd come up the stair to get away from Danny when we were still together. Normally that was when he'd been drinking. I'd lie awake, wondering how I'd let my life get to that point. The deep baritone of his voice felt like it reverberated around the whole house as he ranted about me down the phone to his pals, or sometimes even just to himself. Sometimes I swore I could feel it in my chest, like it was making my ribs vibrate against each other.

Danny stayed in the flats across the road from my ma and da's. I used to see him outside, topless and tanned, cutting the grass for the old guy who lived in the bottom flat in the summer. Occasionally, he'd be hanging out his window having a fag. Sometimes I'd see him round at the shops. I never really thought anything of him; he was just another guy in the scheme. Just one of the same faces you'd see every day, as much a part of the place as the buildings, the shops, the waste ground, or the bus stops.

One day, from behind me in the queue at the post office, he made some daft joke about how long it was taking for us to get served. I turned round and gave a polite laugh.

He said to me, 'Aw, you're Tam Skelton's lassie, eh?'

'Aye, he's my da,' I replied, a riddy spreading across my face.

'Here.' He gently slapped me across the arm with his giro book. 'Know wit? We should go for a drink.'

'Aye,' I said, straight away, half flattered that someone would ask me out, half simply not knowing what else I could say; the thought of saying no and coming across as rude didn't seem like an option. I hadn't really had any luck with guys. Suddenly he looked handsome; he had kind eyes. 'That'd be nice.'

'I'll take ye somewhere nice. Gies yer number and I'll have a think aboot the best place tae go.' He handed me his big brick of a phone, and I punched my number in.

His idea of *somewhere nice* happened to be the pub along the road. I met him there the following weekend.

'You told anybody aboot me an you?' he asked, after his fifth pint.

'Naw, no yet. How come?'

'Right, well, see when ye dae? They'll nae doubt bring up ma ex-wife.'

95

It felt like my head was going to explode. Even though he was a good bit older than me, fifteen years, it was still weird to imagine that this man had an ex-wife. The words sounded almost foreign when he spoke them. *Ex-wife*. It made him seem so much older. I was probably in primary school while he was getting married.

'It's aw lies, by the way. She made up this big, mental story tae spite me efter I said I was leaving her. No many folk believed it, obviously; am no a bad guy at aw. But that kind ae . . . accusation. It sticks. Know wit I mean?'

My ma hated him before I'd even introduced him to her.

'Aw naw, no him,' she said, when I told her who the mystery older man I'd been seeing was.

'Och, wit's the matter wi him?' I asked indignantly.

'He's auld enough tae be yer da! An I bet he's no told ye wit he did tae the last woman he was wae?'

'He told me people would bring that up if I told them aboot me an him.'

My ma clamped her mouth shut and let her top and bottom lips crumple together. I've no doubt that she was also biting her tongue, hard.

'It's no true, anyway,' I added.

She rolled her eyes when I said that. 'See for yerself, then. Don't come greeting tae me when he slaps you aboot as well then.'

And I did see for myself. We were only together for a few months before I fell pregnant with Jamie. We put our name down for a council house, and got one just down the road from my ma. Nice wee two-bedroom terrace. Up and down stairs, front and back garden; it felt like I was moving into a mansion after living with my ma and da in their wee flat. Up until the wean was born, Danny seemed fine. He got a job as soon as I found out I was expecting Jamie, and suddenly I had this normal life, the same as other people had, after worrying that I was destined to just scrape by, living with my ma and da forever.

It wasn't perfect, but it would do for me. Danny drank an awful lot, but that seemed to be just the way guys were where we lived. They'd drink turps if they didn't know it would kill them. He could get a bit loud in arguments, and even during mild disagreements he'd lose the rag. He could be controlling as well, always going through my phone and quizzing me about where I'd been and what I'd been doing while he was at work. He loved to accuse me of having affairs. If the house was spotless, if his dinner was made and there was nothing for him to be angry about, he'd just make something up. He'd do this thing where he'd ask where I was or what I was doing at a certain time. I'd say, *I was here, cleaning, cooking, looking after the wean or at the shops*, the only things I ever did.

'You're a fuckin liar,' he'd snarl back at me. 'I fucking know wit you dae when ma back's turned, and if I ever catch ye, I'll fucking kill ye.'

I couldn't win. Having never been in a relationship before, though, and having grown up surrounded by other loud, angry men in the scheme, I thought it was normal. Just what men were like. Men apart from my da, I suppose. But then, he was with a loud, angry woman – maybe that's why. If I was more like my ma, I could have a nice, normal guy, but I'm just not that kind of person, so I had what I deserved.

Well, that was what I told myself. That's how I explained his behaviour. Or maybe 'excused' would be a better word for it now, looking back.

One Saturday, after coming back from visiting my ma and da with the wean – he was maybe three month old at the time – Danny was lying on the couch, steaming. It was five in the afternoon. He sat up as I came into the living room, holding Jamie.

'Where's ma boay?' Danny slurred, an idiotic smile on his face. He held out his hands, motioning for me to pass him this delicate wee bundle all wrapped up in a blanket my ma had knitted for him.

Empty cans lay on the floor. Danny always did this thing whenever he'd drained every last drop from his can. He'd squeeze the sides, then twist the top and bottom in opposite directions, then leave them all lying for me to pick up the next day. The noise of the metal crinkling under his grip used to go right through me.

'Gies him. He's missed his da.'

'You're drunk,' I said. 'You should go up tae bed.'

'Let me see the wee man.' He stood up and staggered towards me. 'It's fine, it's fine. I've only had a couple.'

'Naw, I'm scared you'll drap him.' I twisted my body like one of his cans so he couldn't reach for Jamie, putting myself between them.

Danny let his arms drop down to his sides. His face fell just as quick. 'Gie me the wean.' He didn't sound drunk now. Just angry. Exuding that sort of quiet, menacing anger that men sometimes do.

'I'm gonnae put him up the stair. He needs a sleep, anyway.'

His eyes widened. 'Is that how it is, aye?'

'Wit?' I said, laughing nervously. 'He's just tired. I want tae get him doon for a few hours before his next feed.'

'You think am some kind ae animal, dint ye? Think I cannae even hawd a wean right. Am no even drunk.'

I watched him sway back and forward slightly. Like a boxer before he goes down. He slumped back down on to the couch. I shook my head and went up the stair. He didn't follow me, but I could hear him mutter something as I left the room. He was still grumbling away when I came back down the stair.

'I didnae have anycunt up.'

'Wit?' I was confused here.

'You asked who I had up while ye were oot at yer ma's. I didnae have anycunt up.'

'Naw I didnae?'

He let out a big sigh. The same one Jamie does now.

'So yer calling me a liar noo?' he said, getting back to his feet. He towered over me.

'I'm no calling ye a liar,' I said. 'I just didnae say that.'

He pushed me. Not hard, a sort of playground shove, but it still scared me. I didn't fall, but I staggered back a wee bit. Then he got right in my face, the smell of drink pouring out of his mouth.

'If I say "Gie me the wean," you fucking gie him tae me. Awrite?'

I nodded. I couldn't say anything. He stood staring at me for a couple of seconds. His eyes darted around my face. Staring at me like he hated me, every single part of me.

I quietly said, 'I'm sorry.'

'Don't dae that again.'

I nodded.

He punched the door on his way out the living room.

Wee incidents like this would happen periodically. Him getting drunk and accusing me of something that either he'd totally misunderstood or that just hadn't happened at all, and me backing down and apologising for something I hadn't done. No matter what happened, it was all my fault.

I remember there used to be this advert for a domestic abuse helpline on the telly. It was a wee lassie happily playing with two dolls, a guy and a woman, while her ma stood and watched her from behind, looking close to tears.

'That's me home,' the wee lassie said, putting on a guy's voice. Danny used to say exactly that when he came in the door sometimes. I sometimes wonder if he picked it up from that advert, and did it to scare me. 'Get me a beer, will ye, hen,' the wee lassie added.

'Wit did yer last slave die of?' she said, her voice going all high-pitched.

'Wit?' she replied as the guy.

'Aw, nothing. It wis just a wee joke!'

'After everything I do for you?'

Then the camera cut to the poor woman standing with her hand over her mouth, tears in her eyes, while the wee lassie shouted 'I'm sorry! I'm sorry!' over and over again. The first time I saw it, I had to turn off the telly. It made me feel so sad about Jamie and what he thought was happening with me and his da. How the wee lassie in the advert must have thought that was a normal thing to act out with her dolls. The second time, I wrote down the number just in case.

He slapped me across the face a few weeks later. He'd decided the house wasn't tidy enough. He loved moaning at me and saying I was lazy, despite never lifting a finger to help me out with the cleaning, the washings, hoovering, looking after Jamie, feeding him, changing him. Nothing I ever did was good enough.

'Am oot working aw fucking day,' he said, right after he'd hit me. 'An I come hame, the dinner's no even ready, an the hoose is a fucking riot.'

'I'm sorry,' I said, cowering on the floor, my back against the washing machine. I could hear Jamie giggling away in the living room while he sat in his wee bouncy chair, watching the telly. Blissfully unaware. Or maybe he'd just become used to the shouting and the crying. My face was stinging. It sometimes didn't feel real when he hit me. It felt almost cartoon-like. Like I was living with some pantomime baddie.

After that, the house was always spotless. The dinner was made and ready for him getting in the door at twenty past five exactly every single night. Except Friday nights, of course – that's when he'd go to the pub. I always did extra cleaning on a Friday to make sure there was nothing he could pull me up for when he got home drunk. It was bad enough when he was sober, but while he had a drink in him, it was as if he lost any sort of veneer of civility he had towards me. Like any scrap of conscience left to stop him doing and saying things to me was drowned by the drink.

So that was me, until Jamie was about six. Just getting by, cleaning to keep my mind off the whole carry-on. It was like living with a human version of *Buckaroo!* at times. Walking about as if the floor was made of eggshells that I'd been instructed not to crush.

I'd told my ma about everything that'd been happening, except him hitting me, but she's no daft. She knew he was, and she knew I didn't want to tell her.

I'd lie, and think about the things my ma would say to me if I told her the truth. *Don't know how ye don't just kick him oot . . . Just come an stay here . . . Just phone the polis . . . Just get the locks changed and don't open the door or answer the phone.*

Every solution was prefaced with *just*. Like it was some trivial little problem that could be solved in a few minutes. I'd keep it together whenever I told my ma about him and the things he'd said to me since I last saw her. Projecting an air of togetherness so she'd think I could handle the situation.

A couple of days after Danny had given me a black eye, I went down to see her with make-up dappled on in an attempt to conceal the purples and yellows. I really didn't think she'd notice as it had faded slightly but she clocked it as soon as I sat down. Given that she suspected he'd laid his hands on me, she was probably always scanning and inspecting me any time

I visited. I still remember her expression and the way her eyes settled on the bruise. She narrowed them and I could see her jaw tighten.

'Let me go doon there an fucking sort him oot,' she said. I had to beg her not to do that.

'You're finishing wi him the night,' she said to me. I'd never seen her so angry. 'That's nae environment fur you tae be bringing a wean up in.'

'Okay,' I said. This felt like an accusation, like she thought I was *choosing* to bring up my son in this way. Like it was my fault. But I never said anything.

'If you don't phone me in a couple ae hours an tell me that you've kicked him oot, then I'm coming doon and I'll dae it fur ye.'

'Okay.'

'The wean's staying here. He's no gawn back doon there while that fucking arsehole's still there.'

'Okay. You're right.'

'Where's the wean?' Danny asked as I walked in. He had a can in his hand, but it must have only been his first of the night, because he didn't seem drunk.

'We need tae talk,' I said, fighting back tears. I don't know why I was so emotional. I hated him. I wanted nothing more than to just walk away from him. There were moments when I'd look at the time in the kitchen as it approached twenty past five, and I'd picture in my mind the way he drove home, and try and will him into having a car crash. A fatal one. I'd picture a lorry going right through the side of the motor as he pulled out of a junction without looking. Ploughing into him, smashing him into a paste. Then I'd feel guilty for having such thoughts. Then he'd walk through the door, and it was like my stomach twisted itself, like a facecloth being wrung out. I swear I could tell if he was in a mood just by the way he put his keys in the door.

'How? Wit's the matter?' He looked genuinely concerned as he turned down the volume on the telly.

I took a deep breath. 'I cannae dae this anymair.'

'Wit?' He stood up and I braced myself.

'I'm leaving ye. I'm gonnae go an stay wi my ma.'

He pulled me towards him, but not in a violent way or in an angry way. He just gently held me by the shoulders. 'I'm sorry,' he said, his voice croaky, kissing the top of my head. 'I've been horrible.'

I squirmed out of his grip like I was a wet bar of soap and pushed him back. 'Naw. It's went oan fur too long. This isnae normal. This is nae way fur me tae live.'

He ran his hands quickly back and forward over his shaved head, then dropped to his knees. He looked up at me. His bottom lip was petted, like a wee boy who's just been told his dog has been put down. 'Please, hen. Ye need tae gie me another chance.' He clutched both his arms around my lower legs. 'Please.'

'Why?' I asked, steeling myself. 'Why dae ye dae it tae me? Why dae ye hit me?'

'I don't mean it. I know I shouldnae. I just . . . I cannae control maself.' He began to sob, his shoulders heaving up and down. 'I've goat issues.' He looked so pathetic. This big hard man, whimpering at my feet.

I stepped out of his clutches. He got up and sat on the couch, reaching for his fags. I could see his hands trembling as he lit one.

'I need help,' he said.

I remember thinking to myself, *Aye, ye certainly dae.* I'd have said that if I wasn't so sure I'd have got my head kicked in for it.

'Wan mair chance,' he said, stabbing at the air with his fag. 'I'll show ye I can change.'

I knew then I wouldn't be leaving him that night. I didn't feel sorry for him, and I didn't believe he could change; I just couldn't go through with it. I think I was too scared to leave, scared of what he'd do. Maybe I was subconsciously clinging on to the hope that he'd go back to how he was when we'd first got together. When he didn't seem to have a temper, when I didn't seem to annoy him. I wished I could just say, *Naw. We're finished.* But the words wouldn't come out. While I tried to pretend that I was free to leave at any point, the fact is that I wasn't. I couldn't. I was a prisoner.

My ma told me I was stupid, and that anything that happened to me or, god forbid, the wean, would be my own fault now. She was that angry with me when I told her I wasn't leaving that I thought she was going to crack me herself.

As Jamie got older, he was still unaware of what was happening with me and his da. He was always quite happy in his room. Playing his wee games, drawing, watching films and reading. He seemed to have such a peaceful life. He always seemed so calm and never caused any problems. I was glad of it at the time, that what was going on wasn't affecting him, and I felt as if I was doing the right thing, just keeping him out the way. Making sure he didn't think, didn't know, that his da was a monster. But now I think about how sad it was that this wee boy lost most of his childhood, wasted it sitting in his room because he was encouraged to stay up there and out the way by me. I wish I could have told him that I loved him; I wish I could do it now, but I just can't. I wonder sometimes if I'm even capable of love or showing affection anymore, after everything. It's like Danny hollowed me out.

I remember one night, about a year after I'd tried and failed to leave his da, Jamie asked me about the 'poltergeist' in the house.

'Wit?' I asked him. 'Wit ye talkin aboot?'

'The poltergeist. The ghost. All the banging and shouting.' He reached under his bed and lifted up this big hardback book that used to be mine. He flopped it open across his lap while he sat up in bed, and pointed at a black-and-white photo of a kitchen that looked like it had been ransacked. Plates and glasses lying in smashed heaps on the floor. 'We've goat wan.'

His eyebrows were raised, concern etched right into his face. It clicked right away that he had put two and two together and come up with a ghost as the most logical explanation for the things he'd heard.

'Aye,' I said, ignoring the lump rising in my throat. 'That's wit it is. I'll get rid ae it.' I took the book off him and put it back under his bed. 'Don't worry aboot it.' I ruffled his hair and turned off his bedside lamp.

*   *   *

A couple of nights later, a Friday, Danny came home straight from work instead of going to the pub. He'd been in a stinker of a mood for the whole week. Something was happening at his work, some new boss had been on his case or something. I didn't really listen to him when he spoke anymore. I hated him. The sight of him, the sound of his voice, the smell of him on the bed covers – it all made me feel a kind of anger I'd never experienced before. I remember reading a term in a book I was reading once about a woman whose boyfriend had been battering her for years. She said she felt a *soul-shaking* anger. That was the term I'd been needing to describe how I felt. Every fibre of my being, every part of my very *soul*, hated the guy.

'Wit's fur dinner?' he said, standing in the doorway of the living room while I sat on the couch, flicking through a cata-logue.

I ignored him, not even looking up.

'I said, wit's fur dinner?'

'Look in the fridge,' I said, trying to sound calm even though my heart was racing. 'Make yerself something. I'm no hungry.'

Silence.

I glanced up. He had his hands on his hips and was shaking his head at me. His eyes were wide open in their sockets as he took a deep breath in. He wasn't used to me answering him back or being cheeky. I could count on one hand the amount of times I'd done it.

'That how it is, aye?' he said.

My eyes focused in on a set of Kitchen Devil knives on the pages of the catalogue. What would happen if I just plunged a knife right into him? Surely, I'd get away with it. If I could get him to hit me first, it would be self-defence.

'Aye,' I said. 'Dae wit ye want.'

I got up, breezed past him and went into the kitchen to empty the washing machine. Knives in the sink waiting to be washed, knives in the drawer just by my hand, scissors on the worktop next to me. Easy access to all of them. I remember thinking the same words over and over again: *hit me hit me hit me hit me hit me.*

'I've been oot working aw day, and noo I've tae make ma ain dinner?' he said, standing in the doorway.

I knelt down at the machine. 'Aye, that's how it looks, eh? Wit a shame.' I used to get so scared at the thought of being cheeky to him. It felt like some kind of impossible task, some unimaginable thing I could never do. I had nightmares about speaking to him like this, and would wake with a lump in my throat, feeling like I was going to be sick everywhere. Doing it then, that day, I felt nothing. I felt so calm, and like I could handle anything. I felt like no matter what he did in response, he couldn't hurt me, because I felt nothing.

'Never mind,' he said, after what was maybe ten seconds of standing staring at me, though it felt like hours. He went up the stair. I could hear from the creaking floor that he was in Jamie's room.

'How are you, wee man?' I heard his muffled voice say. I couldn't hear what Jamie said in response to him, because his wee voice was so quiet and soft back then, before it broke.

I pulled all the clothes out the machine and slammed the door shut. I looked at my distorted reflection in the shiny window. I looked a mess. Black T-shirt, black denims, black hair pulled back into a ponytail. Gaunt face. I left the bundle of wet clothes on the floor.

I got up and, without thinking, picked up the big pair of kitchen scissors from the worktop and slid them into my back pocket. Just in case.

In the living room, I picked up my phone. I was going to text my ma and see if her and my da would come down and pick up me and the wean. I was going to just run away, disappear from Danny's life without a trace. He wouldn't do anything to me if there was someone else there to see it.

But then he came in.

'Wit's the *matter* wi you, eh? Wit's wi the attitude?' he said, closing the door behind him. I still had my phone in my hand. I always used to pocket it whenever he came into the room and saw I was on it, but I didn't bother this time. He always thought I was cheating on him. Bit hard to do that when you never leave the house, and he's one of only two men you know, the other being your da.

The scissors dug into my bum as I sat down on the couch. I could feel how long the blades were. Would I just plunge them into him with them shut together, like a stake into Dracula's heart? Would I slash him across the face? Perhaps I'd open them up slightly, so he'd have two separate cuts, harder to stitch back together. Like when guys in the jail use two razor blades stuck in a toothbrush less than an inch apart to make an unfixable wound. Then I thought about how unfair it was that he'd had years to torment me, but I'd only have seconds, maybe even just a single second, to get back at him. It wasn't enough. I wished I could stop time and just go mental for years.

'Nothing,' I said. 'Nothing's the matter.'

He took a few steps towards me, and I felt my heart beating faster.

'Who ye texting?' he said, and lunged for my phone.

I jumped up and moved away from him, sticking my phone in my front pocket. My hand hovered over my back pocket. I was praying he'd go for me, try and grab me or something, so I could whip out the scissors.

'You're fucking mental,' he said. 'Ye know that?'

'*I'm* mental? Me?!'

'Aye, you. Look at the state ae ye.' He looked me up and down and sniggered. Then he took a step towards me and said, 'Gie me yer phone.'

I pulled out the scissors.

'Wit ye dain?' he asked, laughing at me. 'Ye gonnae stab me, aye?'

I held them out in front of me with both hands. Trembling, obviously. He shook his head and walked out the room, slamming the door shut behind him. I heard him going up the stair. I pulled out my phone and phoned my ma.

'Can ye come doon?' I asked her. 'I'm scared of wit's gonnae happen. I'm scared of wit I'm gonnae dae. I'm sitting here wi a pair ae scissors, ready tae stab him if he comes near me again.' I was frantic.

'Don't you fucking dae anyhin,' my ma said. 'I'll be doon in five minutes.'

Her and my da arrived just as he came back down the stair.

My ma came bursting right into the living room with my da following behind her. He was in suit trousers and a short-sleeve shirt, and still had his slippers on. My ma was wrapped up in a big jacket. I was sitting on the couch while Danny stood in the middle of the room.

My ma got right into his face. 'Hit me,' she said, so unbelievably calm it was sinister. 'Ye like hitting women, eh? Hit me, then. Go.'

Danny stared right into her eyes. My ma only came up to his chest, but I'd have backed her in a fight between them, no question. She told me soon after that she was desperate for him to hit her. She'd get him sent away for years, and get a few digs in herself in the process. But he didn't do it. He wasn't daft enough.

Then Jamie came into the living room. He looked scared.

'Get him up the stair, Tam,' my ma said to my da, without taking her eyes off Danny.

My da ushered Jamie away, all smiles, making him think nothing was wrong. 'Moan, you can show me yer room and we'll play a wee game, eh?' he asked Jamie on his way out, rubbing his wee back.

'Go an pack a bag fur this arsehole, hen,' my ma said to me.

Danny sat down on the couch as I got up.

My ma stared at him as I left the room. 'You're a fucking scumbag, ye know that?' she said.

I don't know what else she said to him after I left the room, but whatever it was must have worked, because I didn't hear a word from him ever again.

★   ★   ★

For days, weeks, after that night, I felt like a weight had been lifted. Like I'd been walking around with dozens of big, soaking wet towels around my shoulders for years, and now they were gone. All of a sudden, I didn't have to worry about the questioning I'd get after coming back from the shops, asking me if I'd been talking to other men. I didn't have to worry every time my phone buzzed with a text from my ma, as he stared at it and then me with pure and utter contempt. I didn't have to feel scared in my own house. I could just live again.

But now I'm wondering why I'm still not happy. How, after everything, I'm still in a fucking mess. How I can't look at Jamie without seeing his da. How I can't just be a real, normal ma. How I still fucked everything up, fucked Jamie up, despite being given a fresh start. Maybe all that wasn't Danny's fault. Maybe it was mine.

Maybe Jamie having a pal is going to fix him. But I'll still be here, existing like this.

13

JAMIE

When I wake up, Lee's away. I must have passed out. My head is pounding and it's sunny outside. I check my phone and see a message from him.

Ye fell asleep so I just boosted mate.
Left ye a cuppla fags. Talk tae ye later.

Two fags sit on the table next to my bed. The thought of smoking one makes me feel a bit sick. I think I'm hungover. I've heard guys on the PlayStation talking about hangovers; they always sounded horrible. If this happens every time, I don't think I'll ever drink again, to be honest. Although, I did like how I felt after the first few cans. I felt like I was able to actually be myself for a change – naw, actually, better than that, because being myself means being a freak. I felt pure cool and confident and funny. No awkward and shy and too scared to say anything in case people laugh at me. Hope I didn't say anything too mental the more I drank; I must have been actually steaming to pass out. Lee can obviously handle it better than I can.

Cheers mate. Class night.

You buzzing fur London?

Shit. We booked the bus to London last night. Every single thought I have about going is negative, it's a fucking obviously terrible idea, man. My phone flashes.

I cannae wait.

There's no backing out now, though. Lee will probably think I'm a pure shitebag for not going. What if he goes and it's amazing, and I'm left stuck up here with nobody, pure jealous of him and wishing I'd went? I can't not go; he'll be angry with me and fall out with me, probably. I take a deep breath.

Aye man, it'll be quality.

I can hear my maw walking about down the stair. Must be the weekend again if she's kicking about the house at this time. I'm about to roll over and go back to sleep when she comes up the stair.

'Jamie,' she shouts from the other side of my door. Her voice goes right through me. I swear to god it's actually stinging my ears.

'Wit is it?'

'I'm gawn up tae Granny's. You want tae come?'

'Naw, it's awrite.'

'Well, I'm gawn up there, then I'm gawn oot.'

Where the fuck is she going out? She's hasn't got any pals.

'Nae bother,' I say.

'I'll be hame later the night.'

'Fine.'

I hear her go down the stair and out the front door, locking me in. I wonder where she's going. Who knows, she'll be doing something shite and boring anyway. Away to buy some cleaning spray or cloths or something.

I wake up again a few hours later. I've got a missed call and a text from my da. Something must have happened. It's not like him to try and get in touch with me first. I phone him straight away.

'You alive then, wee man?' he says when he answers.

'Aye, wit's happening?'

'Just wanted tae see if ye fancied coming up tae mine later? I'll phone ye a taxi. We'll have a few cans and a smoke and that?'

'Eh, I dunno,' I say. I'm feeling more anxious than normal about having to leave the house, but I miss my da. He's never asked me to do anything like this before. Without even thinking, I say, 'My maw's away oot if ye want tae come here instead?'

He takes a second or two to answer. 'Ye sure?' he says. 'She'll go apeshit if she knows am in.'

'It'll be awrite,' I say. 'I won't tell her.'

'Eh . . . Aye,' he says quietly. 'Aye! We'll dae that. I'll be doon aboot half five then, awrite?'

'Aye, that's sound.'

'See ye soon, wee man.' He hangs up.

I defo shouldn't have invited him here; my maw will go mental if she comes home and he's in. But then again, my da will probably cancel on me anyway. He's like that.

I text my maw to find out when she plans on coming back.

Probably after 11. Keep the place tidy. X

I've no idea what she's up to, and I don't really care. If my da does come down, he'll be away by the time she gets home, so it's sound.

I've got the feeling I used to get right before Christmas: pure excited about seeing my da. It's been ages since I seen him, man. I've actually started to forget what he looks like. It's weird. Like, obviously I'll recognise him when I see him, but the image of him in my head is kind of fuzzy and vague.

I go for my first shower since I went to see my granny, the other day, or last week, or a month ago – I've no idea when the fuck it was. I don't want to be honking when my da comes down. I want him to think I'm normal.

When he used to come and get me, after him and my maw split up, he'd always be late. Was meant to be every Friday, and he'd take me to McDonald's or something, but sometimes I'd go out to his motor and he'd just give me a fiver and say he needed to go. Sometimes he just wouldn't turn up at all. My maw would always seem pure anxious about him being near the house, but he'd never come in; he'd just beep the horn and I'd run out. If he was late, my maw would be pure pacing about. She said she couldn't relax until he was away. Always thought that seemed a bit rude. She'd be up the stair in her room, watching from her window as I got in and we drove away. She wouldn't even wave.

The door goes at exactly half five. He rattles the letterbox so loud that I almost shite myself. I'm wearing a clean T-shirt and black denims. I think the T-shirt is my maw's; I found it on the clothes horse and it looked like it'd fit me, so I just fired it on. I worry my da will slag me for wearing women's clothes. I check through the spyhole, just to make sure it's him, then I open the door.

'Awrite, son,' he says, sounding all happy. He's wearing a grey jumper and blue denims. He looks older than I remember. Pure grey hair, cut dead short. He's got a blue poly bag and a black jacket swinging by his side.

'Awrite,' I reply. 'Eh, moan in.'

He walks in and looks about the hall like he's never been here before, even though this used to be his house. I shut the door behind him and follow him into the living room, his dirty white trainers squeaking with every step. Not in a weird way, but he smells pure nice. Just how I remember he used to when he got home from the pub. Smoke and bevvy. He sits down on the couch, in the same spot I can vaguely remember him sitting when I was a wee boy, and he cracks open a can. I kind of expected it to be like he's never been away, but it feels weird. Like he's pure out of place here. I don't remember him looking so bogging. It's like how clean the house is makes him look even worse.

'Ye want wan?' he asks and hands me a can.

My hangover has went away now, so I say, 'Aye,' and take it from him. I sit down on the other couch. My ma always wipes the couches down with some mad spray so they're always slidey. They squeak as me and my da both try to get comfy.

'First time we've had a drink thegither, eh?' he says.

'Aye.' I open my can and hope that if I drink it fast enough, I'll be less awkward.

'Ye were saying yer maw wis giving ye grief last time I phoned ye. Is she still at it?'

'Aye, man. She's murder.'

'Always wis,' says my da, then takes a big gulp of lager. 'Nightmare ae a woman.' His forehead is all crumpled and angry-looking.

'It's just aboot, like, getting a joab an that. I know I need wan, but I just . . . cannae be arsed.'

'Working's a mug's game anyway, pal. Ye'll get wan when yer ready, don't worry aboot it. She got enough money over the years aff me fur ye; if she had enough sense, she'd have saved it. Put it away fur ye when ye turned eighteen or something like that. But she didnae. Know why?'

I shake my head.

'Cause she's a fuckin idiot, that's why.'

I laugh, then we sit in silence for a few seconds. A text flashes up on my phone. It's from my maw.

Everything okay? x

I don't reply. I look over at my da, and he's looking at me with a daft smile on his face.

'Wit you been up tae then, wee man? Wit ye dain wi yerself?' he says.

'Eh, no much.'

Another couple of seconds of silence before he says: 'You no got a wee burd or anyhin?'

'Nah, no yet.' I don't know why I added 'yet', as if my lack of female company is just a small matter that I'm sorting out soon.

'I was oot shagging everything that moved at your age,' my da says, without looking at me. I don't know what to say in reply to this. I feel like I could be sick. 'You're auld enough tae go ae the pub noo, eh?' my da asks.

'Aye.' I drain the last of my can as I say this. He does the same, and does a big, manly rift before twisting his empty can and sitting it down. 'I've never been, though.'

'We'll go wan weekend then, right? Me an you. Couple a pints, watch the fitbaw; it'll be brilliant.' He flings another can at me, and I catch it.

The thought of going to the pub is genuinely terrifying to me. I can see from Facebook and that, I'm just totally different to other guys my age. Like, physically and everything. Even face-wise, they look pure better developed: big jaws, nice hair and beards and that. I'd look about twelve next to them all in a pub. Maybe it's just this mad incel stuff getting into my head. 'Aye, maybe,' I say.

My da's phone buzzes, and he picks it up and starts typing. I pick up mine for something to do, so I don't look weird. No one ever texts me, apart from my maw or Lee occasionally, so I just go into the calculator and type in some sums so it looks to him like I've got pals. I just zone out and smash numbers for a bit, and then my da does a big dramatic clearing of his throat.

'Am I boring ye?' he asks, and does a wee chuckle. 'Too busy talking tae wee burds tae talk tae yer auld da?'

'Naw, yer no boring me,' I say. I know he was joking, but I don't want him to feel like I want him to go or that I don't want him here or that.

'Where's yer maw away tae, anyway?'

'Dunno,' I say. 'She says she won't be hame till later.' I use the ring-pull on the can to clear some dirt from under one of my fingernails, then open it.

My da shakes his head and says, 'Well, fuck her,' then raises his can at me, like a cheers from across the room.

I raise mine as well, and then we drink at the same time.

'Is she still a weirdo?' my da asks.

'Eh, aye. I think so. Always cleaning even though the place is awready clean, and stuff like that.'

'Nuhin else fur her tae dae, is there? Goat tae make herself useful somehow; she's fucking hopeless at everything else.'

'She's good at moaning,' I say.

My da laughs at this. Makes me feel like a legend. He's got a nice laugh. 'Aye, she wis always good at that. Torn-faced cow,' he says. 'Does she ever ask aboot me? Or tell you stories aboot me?'

'Naw,' I say. 'My granny disnae talk aboot ye either. They just, like, kid on you don't exist, basically.'

'Fuck her anaw. Here, I bet yer maw's never told ye aboot when she came at me wi a big pair a fucking scissors?'

'Wit?' I say. I can't imagine my maw doing anything like that. She was always pure timid with my da cause he could be quite loud and angry at times. 'My maw did that?'

'Aye. She's a fucking psycho, wee man.'

I know it must've been my da's fault – like, my maw must have been provoked or felt threatened or something – but still, you can't just go at somebody with scissors, can you? That's not on.

'Fuck sake,' I say. That must be the first time I've swore in front of my da. My maw would definitely get annoyed and my granny would actually kill me if I said that in front of either of them.

'Aye, that's why I left. Cannae be dealing wi that, know wit a mean?' he says.

'Defo.' I take a long drink from my can and look at my da while he looks at the floor. I remember the night they split up. It's a wee bit fuzzy, to be fair, but thinking about it now, I'd say that my maw left him. It doesn't matter, I suppose, really. Or maybe I just remember it wrong.

My da's phone buzzes again and he jumps up. 'Back in two seconds,' he says, and taps his nose. I can hear an engine running outside, a fast motor by the sounds of it, with a loud and thundery exhaust. I get up to look out the window and see my da climb into the back seat. I worry for a second that he's had enough of me and how dull I am and just bolted, but he gets back out after a few seconds. I run back to the couch so he doesn't think I was watching him. I don't want to look pure desperate. I go back to my calculations as he comes back in.

'Noo it's a party!' he says, and flops down on to the couch, dangling a wee bag of white powder. The powder's in a wee ball, and the bag's been twisted pure tight around it.

'Wit's that?' I ask. I know what it is, obviously, but I don't want my da to know that I know.

'Wee bitta marching powder, son.' He takes out his key from his pocket, opens the bag and dips it in. He raises a scoop of the powder up to his nose and sniffs it. He flings his head back and makes a mad snorting noise, rubbing his nostrils as he does it. 'Woaft,' he says. 'That'd blow the heid aff ye.'

I laugh, nervously, and just study my can.

'Ye want some?' he asks me.

'Eh, naw,' I say. My stomach feels like it's going to either rise up out of my throat or collapse out of my arse with nervousness. 'Am awrite.'

'Ye sure?' he asks, but it's as if he's no really caring what my reply will be, just as if he's said it like a reflex response. He gets up and starts pacing about the living room, snorting. The noise is like as if his nose is full of bubbling sludge; it's bogging. His twisted cans next to the couch look like mangled fallen soldiers.

'Am awrite,' I say. I'm a wee bit scared; his eyes are pure bulging, and it's hard to describe, but I feel as if his whole mood's just changed. Like his energy has just went up a million per cent and he doesn't know what to do with it. Like it's needing to be used up or trying to burst out of him.

★   ★   ★

An hour later, and he's sitting perched on the worktop in the kitchen, just above the fridge. I mind him doing that when I was a wee guy. He'd sit up there in the morning with the paper spread out in front of him, circling horses to bet on. Whenever I sat up there after him and my maw split up, my maw would shout at me to get down.

'Wait tae ye hear this,' he says to me, still huffing the gear.

I've been standing listening to him talk non-stop. I've no even said anything in reply. He's just been talking forever, it feels like, like he can't even stop. He starts a story, then that goes into another one and another one. No ending to any of them. No point. This is horrible.

'There's this cunt in ma close, right, stays across the landing fae me,' he says. He started telling this story about half an hour ago, but went into a rant about Celtic instead, somehow. 'He's got this dug. Fucking crusty wee white hing. He lets it run aboot the close an it just fucking barks an pishes an shites everywhere, and he disnae bother his arse tae clean up efter it.'

I nod along, actually quite scared of where this is going, given how angry he seems. Pure spitting the words at me, as if *I'm* the dug's owner.

'Know wit I done?'

I shake my head.

'Noo, bear in mind I've asked the cunt tae clean up efter the dug, tae take it oot fur walks or witever, an he's no listened tae me. I've told him hunners a times that he needs tae deal wi it, but he's a fuckin stupit auld alky.'

'Right,' I say.

123

'I just fucking . . . Eh, hing oan,' he says, getting lost in his phone. His face goes vacant and almost calm-looking compared to the fucking mad intense stare he's had on.

He starts swinging his legs so his heels hit against the fridge. There's still wee dents in the fridge from when he used to do that.

'That's another hing aboot fuckin dugs,' he says, but again he trails off, looking at his phone. Mine buzzes in my pocket. I pull it out, and there's another text from my maw.

Home soon. X

Fuck. What does that even mean? She could be five minutes away, or she could be another hour. I wish she went out more so I knew what these things meant. Either way, I need to get my da out.

'Wit's the matter?' my da says, picking up on the fact I'm no listening to him anymore. He looks annoyed when my eyes come up to meet his. 'Yer looking at me the way *she* used tae,' he says.

'Eh, my maw's oan her way hame,' I reply.

'Ye wanting me ae go then, aye?'

'I don't *want* ye ae go,' I say, pulling my phone back out to look at her text again, trying to decipher its meaning. 'I just don't want any hassle.'

'Am yer da,' he says, sliding off the worktop. 'I'll never cause ye hassle.' He ruffles my hair and goes into the living room to put his jacket on. He kicks over an almost empty can, and the last of the lager comes out it. My maw will go mental if she comes home and sees that. I remember her screaming at me once when I was a wee guy after I spilled diluting juice in the kitchen.

'Sorry she's coming hame,' I say, standing in the doorway, unable to look at him, just focusing on the yellow puddle forming on the floor and thinking about how to deal with it.

'Yer awrite, wee man. Look at me,' he says. I do as I'm told. 'We'll have plenty mair nights like this. I'll no go that long withoot seeing ye again. I promise.'

'Aye,' I say. It's gave me a wee rush, hearing him say that. He's said that to me a million times over the years, but this is the first time in a while. Even if I don't believe him, it's nice.

'Right, I better be offski,' he says. He claps one of his big solid hands on my shoulder a wee bit too hard, and then heads for the front door. 'I'll gie ye a phone soon, pal.'

'Aye, that'll be nice,' I say, but I don't think he hears me, cause he just walks out the door. I watch him from the door as he walks down the street until I can't see him. I run back into the living room, grab all the empty cans, and then drop them into the bin in the kitchen. Using a single square of kitchen roll, I mop up the spillage. Job done. Don't know how this kind of thing takes my maw fucking hours to do. I lock the door, leave my key on the wee unit, and go right up to bed.

14

FIONA

I'm just sat with my hands still on the steering wheel outside the house. I feel fine when I'm driving; I can just forget about everything else going on, forget about the state of my life, Jamie's life, and concentrate on making sure I don't crash. Suppose if I said that to a therapist, they'd say it was because I feel like I'm in control when I'm driving. Or maybe they'd say I like it because it feels like I'm driving away from all my problems. That'd be good, wouldn't it? Just getting in the motor and driving away into the sunset, away from everything. I start to imagine what it'd be like to sit with a therapist.

'Tell me how you feel today, Fiona,' she would say to me. I'd be lying on a leather couch, facing away from her, in her fancy office. It'd be clean and tidy, but dark and filled with art and ornaments.

'The same as every day,' I'd reply. 'Nervous, stressed out and like I'm gonnae be sick.'

'I see, I see,' she'd say, and I'd hear her pen scribbling down everything I was saying. 'And you feel like this all the time?'

'Aye,' I'd say.

'Have you ever considered the fact that you might be completely and utterly mental?'

'Aye.'

'Because I think you are.'

She'd press a button, and a guy holding a straitjacket for me would come bursting into the room. 'This is for your own good, Fiona,' she'd say.

'Aye, you're right,' I would say, and just go quietly with the guy away to wherever they take mental people like me.

Tonight was horrible. The guy was fine, but I was just a freak. *Was?* I *am* a freak. Stuttering all over the place when I got the courage to speak. Just sitting there in silence when I couldn't think of what to say.

I can see the light's on in the living room. I don't really want to have to face Jamie tonight, to be honest. It's embarrassing that I even went on a date. Suppose he doesn't have to know. He won't care where I've been; he's not even replied to any of my texts. He's maybe been asleep the whole time I've been away. I wonder what he'd be like if he had a girlfriend – or a boyfriend, I suppose. Would he be like his da? Jealous and possessive, controlling? Or would he be nice and thoughtful? Sometimes I think it'll be all or nothing with Jamie. That the only outcomes are that he ends up like his da, or goes in the complete opposite direction.

A wee blue light flashes on my phone when I've got a text, and it's blinking at me now, in the dark. It's from that guy. I suddenly feel cold.

> Hope you got home okay. Thanks for a
> lovely night xxx

Maybe I wasn't such a freak after all. That seems like a nice, normal thing to text someone. Even if I never see him again, I just don't want him to tell Gillian that I was weird. I take a breath, my two thumbs practically vibrating as I type.

> Thank you. I had a great time x

I feel like I've got moths in my belly as I hit send. It makes me think of Danny again. How angry he'd get if he saw me on my phone. He'd have kicked me up and down the stairs if I'd ever dared to have so much as a conversation with a guy that wasn't him. Now here I am, just after going on a date with a new guy. A guy who probably won't ever have hit a woman, who has probably barely even raised his voice. He seemed so gentle, Mark, and shy in a way I've never really seen in anyone else apart from me and Jamie. Always smiling, looking down at the table instead of me sometimes, but still smiling.

We hadn't really spoken much since Gillian gave him my number. Just sort of sorted out the details for tonight, the when and where. I met him in this Italian restaurant in the city centre that he picked. I was late because I couldn't get parked near the place and had to walk, and I got all sweaty, maybe from the exertion of speed-walking but probably just from nerves.

I had a nice enough night, I suppose. He asked lots of questions about me, and it felt nice to sort of pretend to be a normal person. I couldn't help but think that the other people in the place thought we were an actual couple, or maybe even married, in just the way I looked around and thought that about them. Even though I was driving, I had two big glasses of wine. I barely ate any of my dinner.

He asked if I had any weans, so I told him a bit about Jamie – not everything, though – and he seemed really sympathetic. 'It's hard fur boays that age,' he said. 'Especially these days, but . . . he'll be fine.'

'Aye,' I said back. 'He will be fine.'

The wine started to kick in, and I asked him about his ex-wife, what she was like, and he was dead honest about it all.

'We just . . . grew apart, I suppose,' he said. 'We were together since we were aboot eighteen. Noo we're in oor forties. Completely different people tae who we were when we first met. Nae bad blood; I've no got a bad word tae say aboot her.'

I just smiled when he said that, and thought about how nice it was. I've wondered a few times what Danny will have said to people about me; it makes me feel like my chest is all tight and like I'm going to be sick. No doubt he will have cast me as the villain in his tales, twisting and distorting the truth to make himself look good and make me sound mental. The saving grace is that all his pals were just as horrible and scummy as him, so it doesn't really matter what they think of me.

I didn't want to tell Mark about what had happened with Danny, so I said that things just fizzled out between us as well.

He paid the bill and then walked me to my car. He laughed when I told him how far away I'd parked, as the busy streets in the city centre stress me out. 'Ye sure ye should be driving after drinking that wine? Ye don't want tae jump in a taxi wi me?' he asked. 'It's nae hassle. Where is it ye stay?'

'Och, I'm only ten minutes along the road. It's fine, I'm fine to drive. I dae this aw the time,' I added, for some reason. Word vomit tumbling out of my mouth.

He gave me a sort of mock-disapproving look when I said that. He told me to be careful and to text me when I got in, so he'd know I hadn't crashed or been arrested. I could see he was angling for a cuddle as he hovered about while I fumbled for my keys, but I just quickly got in the motor. I could see him smiling in the mirror as I drove away.

I think I've managed to get through the whole thing unscathed, but, as nice as he was, I don't want a guy in my life again. I can't take the chance that he'll end up treating me the way Danny did. He'd probably run a mile if I introduced him to Jamie. It's one thing to be told about someone like that; it's another when they're standing, stinking and torn-faced, in front of you. I'll just ask Gillian to tell him I'm no interested on Monday.

I grab my bag and step out the motor. The front gate's lying open, which means either Jamie went out – unlikely – or someone came to the door. Maybe he ordered a takeaway or something.

I open the door and turn on the light in the hall. There's a strange smell in the house. It smells like a man's lager breath. Maybe Jamie had his wee pal over again. Something doesn't feel right, though. I don't know how to describe it, but it's like there's bad energy in the air. Like if I go in the living room,

I'll find Jamie lying dead, or discover that we've been burgled or something. I can feel myself starting to get worked up. The anxiety-reducing effects of my wine have worn off, and now I'm experiencing life raw and unfiltered. I shouldn't have went out with Mark. I shouldn't have left Jamie in by himself. I shouldn't be allowed to be someone's ma. I shouldn't be a part of normal society.

I go into the living room after a few moments of hesitation and flick on the big light. It smells like Danny in here. I'd recognise that smell anywhere, stale smoke and B.O. and cheap lager. Peeking out of the bin in the kitchen is a can, twisted and crumpled. Just the way he used to leave them.

He's been in here.

Jamie's had his da in the house while I was out.

I can't do this. I run out the house and get back in the motor and just drive.

15

JAMIE

'Here, my maw went oot yesterday and she's still no back yet,' I say into my headset.

'How, where'd she go?' Lee asks me. His voice sounds too loud, so I turn him down a bit. It's eleven a.m., and I'm just up. I don't have as bad a hangover as I had the night after Lee was over, but I still don't feel great.

'Fuck knows. She text me last night saying she'd be hame soon, but she just hisnae came back.'

'Are ye sure? Have ye checked her room?'

'Naw, but she's always up and moving aboot by noo.'

'She might be lying deid in her bed, mate. Better go and check.'

'Hing oan, I'll go an look.' I take off my headset and go out into the hall. My maw's room is right across from mine. The door's shut – it's always shut, though. I chap it and don't hear any kind of response or any sign of life. What if she *is* dead? Fucking hell, what do you even do in that situation? Who do you phone? What if the polis think that I killed her or something? I get a feeling in my belly the same as whenever I have to try and go outside. Her room's painted white with white furniture, and with the sun coming in through the windows, it's bright as fuck. Like what your room would be like if you died and went to heaven. The bed's white as well, and the covers are pure pristine and unwrinkled. No sign of my maw. I run back through to my pit and put my headset back on.

'Naw, she's no in her room,' I say to Lee.

'Have ye tried phoning her?' Lee asks me.

'Naw.'

'Why would that no be the first hing ye dae instead of phoning me?'

'I don't know, man. You seem like ye always know wit tae dae.'

'Phone her the noo, and let me know what she says. It'll be awrite,' he says. Lee's got this tone to his voice, it's just dead calming and reassuring.

I take a deep breath and click on my maw's number in my phone and hold it to my ear. A robotic voice tells me my maw is currently unavailable.

'It's went straight tae voicemail,' I say to Lee.

'Fuck. That means her phone's aff,' he says.

'Wit am I gonnae dae?'

There's a couple of seconds of silence before Lee says: 'I'll ask Seb.'

'Dae ye hink she might be deid?'

'Naw, don't be daft. It'll be fine, man. Her phone will just have ran oot ae battery or something. Stay online, and I'll tell ye wit tae dae, awrite?'

'Aye, I will. Cheers, man.'

I take off my headset and flop back in my bed. My heart is pounding like fuck, and feeling it hammering away while I lie down is freaking me out. Every crumb in the bed is pressing against me and it feels horrible. I need to do something to calm down. I get up and head down the stair. The living room's a riot; you can see where my da spilled his can, the cushions from the couch are all squinty, and you can just tell I've had somebody in. If my maw saw this, she'd think it was just Lee I had over and no my da. Except I can still smell my da. He always smells like beer, fags and sweat that's been lightly covered with Lynx. It's like he's still here. I open the windows and the back door, and light a couple of candles. Job done. I run back up the stairs, two at a time.

'Ye hear me awrite, mate?' Lee says as I stick my headset back on. 'Right, Seb says yer maw's probably oot getting rattled aff some guy. I'm sorry tae say.'

'Fuck sake,' I say. 'Is there no a nicer way of saying that?'

'She's went oot wi him last night oan a date or witever, went back tae his, and she's still there the noo. She'll no be wantin tae talk tae you, obviously, wi a mooth full a boaby.'

I feel sick. 'I'll phone her again,' I say. 'It's probably nothing. Maybe she's just at work or something.'

'Aye, mate. Maybe she's at work. Oan a Sunday,' Lee says, although I can tell he's trying not to laugh.

'Ye hink I should phone ma granny?' I ask after a few seconds.

'Aye, maybe, man,' Lee says, but he sounds bored of me now.

'I'll talk tae ye later,' I say and take off my headset.

I try phoning my maw one more time. Straight to voicemail again. The robot woman says to leave a message after the tone and then hang up. I've never done this before.

'Hiya, it's me. Eh, Jamie. Just wondering where you are and if yer awrite. Eh, see ye later.'

16

FIONA

3 missed calls – Jamie
1 new voicemail – Jamie
10 missed calls – Mark
15 new messages – Mark

17

JAMIE

'Still nothing, mate,' I say to Lee.

'I'm telling ye, mate,' he says, 'it'll be fine. She'll be hame soon.'

'Wit if she disnae come back, man? Wit if she's deid?'

'Don't say things like that. She'll be fine. You'll be laughing aboot how freaked oot you've got when she comes back hame, man.'

'Aye, maybe,' I say. 'Right, I'm gonnae go and see if I can get a hold of her.'

'Nae bother, mate. Just stay calm, it'll all be sound.'

It's starting to get dark outside. This is fucking horrible. How can she no just text me and tell me where she is, when she'll be back, or even just that she's still alive.

My belly rumbles, so I go down the stair and see if there's anything in the fridge. Nothing apart from eggs and milk. I check the cupboard, and there's two slices of bread left in the packet. They feel hard and crispy, like they've already been toasted, but I drop them into the slots anyway.

The door goes.

I stand still and wait. My maw wouldn't knock, she'd just come in – unless I left my key in the door when I locked it. Running to it, all I can think is, *Thank fuck she's home.* I feel this urge to cuddle her as I yank open the door.

It's not my maw. It's a guy.

'Aw, you must be Jamie? Your ma's told me a lot about you,' he says. He steps towards me, and I instinctively shut the door over a bit. I want to say, 'Who the fuck are you?' but I can't say anything. My throat's closing up.

'I'm Mark,' he says. 'I'm, eh, a friend of your ma.'

The cunt sounds nervous. I don't like this. I slam the door shut and lock it. He rattles the letterbox. 'Is your ma there?' he shouts. 'I just want to make sure she's okay.'

'Naw,' I say. I feel like I'm going to burst out greeting. There's a big lump in my throat now, a big ball of fucking terror. I want to run up the stairs and just go under my covers until all this is sorted and done and my maw's back home and that cunt is away forever. I can't move, though. All my bones have turned into fucking jelly.

He chaps the door again. 'Jamie, have you phoned your ma? Do you know if she's okay?' He sounds as panicked I am. He rattles the letterbox again, and I bolt up the stair on all fours, into my room, slamming the door shut behind me.

'Lee? Lee, ye there?' I whisper into my headset. I'm going to have a heart attack.

'Wit is it, you awrite?'

'There's a guy at the door looking fur ma maw.'

'Wit? I cannae hear ye, why ye whispering?'

'There's a fucking guy at ma front door lookin fur ma maw. Wit am I gonnae dae?'

'Right, don't panic. It's awrite. Have you no seen this guy before?'

'Naw, never.'

'Try phoning your maw again.'

'Her phone's still aff.' I start greeting.

'Mate,' Lee snaps at me. 'Get yerself thegither. It's fine. Phone your maw again; I'll stay here.'

I take a deep breath and pick up my phone. I click her name and it goes straight to voicemail again.

'Fucking voicemail,' I say. 'He's fucking killed her, and noo he's came here so it's like he's goat an alibi or something.'

'Fuck, man.'

'He's gonnae boot the door doon. He's gonnae kill me noo.'

'Naw he's no. Right, let me phone Seb again. You got anybody else ye could phone? Yer granny or something?'

'Aye, I can phone ma granny, but wit if he kills her anaw?'

'He won't, mate. Is he still there? I cannae hear anything noo.'

'I'll check.' I go through to my maw's room again and look out her window, out the front. The guy's standing at his motor, looking up at me. He waves, and I duck down and scramble back to my room.

'Aye, he's still there,' I say to Lee. 'This is like fucking *Home Alone* or something. Am gonnae have to stab him.'

'Must've been him she wis oot wi last night, then. Fuck knows where she is noo if he's looking fur her anaw,' Lee says. 'I'll gie Seb an update, maybe he'll have an idea.'

'Should I phone the polis?'

'Naw, no yet, anyway. You phone yer granny and I'll talk tae Seb, awrite? We'll figure this oot, mate. Nae matter wit happens, you'll be awrite.'

'Cheers, man.'

'You can come stay wi me if she's deid.'

I phone my granny.

'Wit is it?' she barks at me, sounding panicked already. 'Wit's happened?'

'Eh, it's my maw. I don't know where she is.'

'Wit d'ye mean?'

'She didnae come hame yesterday. She's no answering her phone.'

'Oh, god. Are you awrite?'

'Aye, but there's a guy at the door looking fur her.'

'Oh my god,' she shouts. 'When did ye last hear fae her?'

'She text and said she'd be hame aboot ten o'clock last night, but she never appeared.'

'Right, something's wrang. I'll phone a taxi an be doon as quick as I can. Don't let the guy leave, I want tae talk tae him.'

'Awrite,' I say. 'Will I phone the polis?'

'No yet. Wait till I get there.' She hangs up.

I look out my maw's room window, and the guy's still hanging about outside. He looks up at me and then goes to the door again.

'Jamie,' I can hear him shout.

I go halfway down the stair and think about opening the door, but I can't.

'You there, pal?' he says through the letterbox, trying to sound all friendly and nice.

Pal. I'm not your fucking *pal*, mate.

'Where's my maw?' I shout back, my voice sounding the way it did when it broke when I was thirteen.

'I don't know, pal. That's why I'm here. Can I come in and wait for her?'

'My granny's oan her way doon,' I say.

'Oh,' he says, sounding surprised. 'Eh, well, if you hear from your mum, tell her to phone me.'

I want to be horrible to him, but I can't. I want to say, *You fucking cunt, you better no have fucking killed her, or I'll fucking kill you, pal.* But I can't say anything other than, 'Awrite.'

I hear the metallic clanging of the gate locking behind him, so I run up the stair and see him get into his motor and drive away. I know my granny told me not to let him leave, but what am I supposed to do? Go out and fight with him? Fuck that.

Five minutes later, a silver taxi pulls up outside. My granny gets out and rushes to the door. I run down and open it. She blows in past me like a big blast of wind or something; whenever she comes into a room she just, like, fills it up.

'You awrite?' she asks me, standing in the hall.

'Aye,' I say.

She chews on a bit of chewing gum for a second. 'She no back yet?'

I shake my head.

My granny looks at me. 'Where's the guy?'

'He drove away,' I say. 'I'm sorry.'

'It's no your fault, son,' she says, and goes into the living room. I follow after her. 'Have you ate anything?'

'I was making toast,' I say, nodding at the toaster.

She shakes her head and looks in the cupboard, then the fridge and the freezer. I just stand there and watch. This feels like in army films, when the sergeant's inspecting a new soldier's bed and that.

'There's fuck all here fur you ae eat,' she says. 'Nae wonder you're so scrawny.'

I don't know what to say, so I just look down at my feet. I get the vibe that she's no expecting me to say much here, anyway. She seems angry, but not at me.

'Wait tae I get a hawd ae her,' my granny says, putting on her glasses. She gets her wee black phone out of her bag and starts pressing buttons.

I swivel round as I hear the sound of the front gate opening and closing. My maw walks by the living room window.

18

FIONA

My ma looks me up and down as I open the front door. Jamie is standing next to her, looking terrified.

'Wit's the matter? Has something happened?' I say.

My ma bites her bottom lip, and then her expression seems to turn into a snarl. 'Are you fur real?' she says.

'Wit?' I reply, taking off my jacket. I look from her to Jamie, who's just looking down at the floor.

'Go up the stair, son,' she says to him. He tiptoes by me and goes up to his room, barely making a sound. He smells like toast. 'Get in there,' she growls, nodding towards the living room. I do as I'm told. I sit down on the couch as she paces back and forward. I plug my phone in to charge, anything to keep my hands busy here.

'Wit's the matter wi you?' she says. 'You've no been hame since yesterday. No answering yer phone. Yer son's in by himself, nae food in the fuckin cupboards—'

'Look, I'm sorry,' I say. 'I just needed tae . . . clear ma heid.'

'*Clear yer heid?*' she says. 'Are you huvin a fuckin laugh?'

I cover my face with my hands. She lets the silence grow between us for a bit. This is horrible. My ma always used to use silence against me when I was a wee lassie. No that I ever did anything bad, but if I ever did anything she deemed to be 'stupid', then I'd have to sit there and let her suffocate me with it – forcing me to admit that I'd been stupid, so that the silence could be filled.

'The wean says there was a guy here lookin fur ye. Wit's the story there?' she asks me eventually.

'I've nae idea. Guy? Wit guy?'

'Don't sit there acting like he's made it up. He phoned me, and I could hear the cunt chapping the door.'

'Could it no have been some salesperson or something? Double glazing, or—'

My ma puts her hands on her thighs and comes down to my level. I'm a wee lassie again.

'Dae you think am *stupit*?' she says. Her voice is a growl. 'The wean's been trying ae phone ye aw day. Poor boay's been terrified. Wit ye playing at? Where were ye?'

'Look,' I say. 'I was oan a date last night. I came hame efter it, I freaked oot, I had a bit ae a meltdown, and I went fur a drive.'

She just looks at me for a few seconds. Then: 'So while you're oot galavanting, yer son is in by himself, nae food an having tae deal wi a strange fucking man at the door? You think that's awrite?'

'Aw, come oan,' I say. 'I never go oot! I never dae anything! An he's nineteen; he's no a wee boay anymair, is he?'

'So who wis it ye were oot wi? Some other fucking scumbag

that's gonnae batter ye, aye? Some other arsehole am gonnae have tae come and get ye away fae?'

'Naw, he's no like that, but I'm no gonnae see him again anyway, so it disnae matter.' My phone comes back on, and flashes and vibrates with what looks like a million missed calls and texts. Mark's name flashes up again and again. I see Jamie's a couple of times, too.

'Jamie,' my ma shouts. 'Come doon here a minute, son.' I stare at the messages from Mark as they come through. They eventually stop, and the most recent one says he just wants to know if I'm okay. Can a woman not have a meltdown in peace? Jesus Christ.

Jamie comes into the living room and stands next to my ma. He looks like such a wee boy again. This feels like the night I finally left Danny, except I'm the baddie this time. Or maybe I always was.

'Tell yer ma wit the guy at the door looked like,' my ma says to Jamie.

He looks terrified, like he doesn't want to say anything.

'Tell her,' my ma says. 'It's awrite.'

'I dunno,' Jamie says. 'He had a beard and dark hair.'

'Wis that the guy ye were oot wi, then?' she asks me.

'Aye,' I say. 'Sounds like him.' I look down at my phone. There's another message from Mark, asking me to phone him.

'Right, son, away ye go,' my ma says to Jamie, and sends him back up the stair. She stands towering over me, arms folded across her chest. 'Sort yerself oot,' she says to me.

'I will,' I say, with my head in my hands. I hear her walk out the living room. 'Do you want a lift?' I shout after her.

'Naw,' she says, and the front door slams shut.

My phone rings. It's Mark.

'Fiona!' he shouts as soon as I put it to my ear. 'You're alive!'

'Aye,' I reply. 'Did you come to my house?'

'Eh, aye. Listen, aboot that. I was just worried aboot ye driving hame after a glass ae wine an that.'

'Jamie was terrified. That's no normal. You don't just turn up at somebody's door because they don't answer the phone. How did you even know where I stay?'

'Look, I asked Gillian for your address after our date. It was just so I could send you some flowers, I swear tae god.'

I feel like I'm going to explode. Like I'm going to have a heart attack, but my heart's a bomb.

'You've nae fucking right tae dae that,' I say. 'You're a fucking psycho.'

'Right, that's enough ae that,' he says. 'Calm doon, I was just worr—'

'Don't you dare fucking phone me or come to my door again.'

'Right, fine. Okay. I'm sorry, I'll let you calm down—'

I hang up the phone. The fucking cheek. Making me out to be the one in the wrong. I am so, so angry.

'Is everything awrite?' Jamie says, slinking into the living room. He won't look at me.

'Aye, I just feel a bit . . . overwhelmed,' I say.

'Are ye annoyed at me?'

'Wit? Why wid I be annoyed at ye?'

'Just, I don't know, cause I phoned Granny an that. I'm sorry she gave ye intae trouble.'

'It's awrite,' I say.

He rubs his eyes; he looks like he's been greeting. They're all bloodshot and there's dark circles around them. His voice is a wee bit croaky as well. 'Was that guy your boyfriend?' he asks.

'Naw, don't be daft. Ye don't need tae worry. He'll no be back.'

'Awrite,' he says, and goes back up the stair.

I give it five minutes, then go up to my room. I want to just crawl under the covers, curl up into a wee ball and die. I want to leave this house and never come back. Maybe I could; maybe I could get in the motor and drive away again. No one would care, again. Jamie and my ma would be annoyed, but they'd just be like, 'Aw, she'll be away having a meltdown, *again.*'

Every inch of this house makes me feel dirty and horrible. I swear no matter where I look, I can see a sort of ghostly silhouette of Danny. I can picture him standing in every spot, lecturing me and making me feel guilty for things I haven't done. Making me feel mental. I can hear all the horrible things Jamie has said to me sometimes. Now I can't stop picturing him alone while fucking Mark is trying to bang the door down. No matter how much I scrub, this house will always be full of horrible words and the residue of me being sad. It'll never be clean enough.

I think I can hear Jamie talking to someone, but he's keeping his voice down. Look at what my life has become – sitting in my room, alone, straining to hear what my son, who hates me, is saying.

I hate that I don't know what to do, or how to even begin fixing this mess. Fuck.

19

JAMIE

'She's back,' I say to Lee.

'Thank fuck, man,' he replies. 'Ye awrite noo? Ye calmed doon?'

'Aye, man,' I say, although I feel absolutely fucked. I'm hungover, I'm starving, I'm thirsty, I'm all sweaty and I'm knackered. I must have all sorts of mad chemicals, adrenaline and all that, pure pumping through me. I've not stopped shaking since that cunt came to the door.

'Where wis she?' Lee asks me.

'She said tae ma granny she wis oan a date wi the guy that came tae the door.'

'I knew it, mate. Don't take this the wrang way, but yer maw must be some ride if he was that desperate tae see her again so soon.'

'Aw, fuck off,' I say.

'Och, I'm only kiddin ye on, man. So where wis she when that guy wis looking for her? Surely wisnae oot wi *another* guy.'

'I don't know. She's no said. She's mental, I think. Like, actually mental.'

'That's foids fur ye, mate. They're aw mental.'

'*Foids?*' I ask. 'Wit the fuck is a foid?'

'A woman. That's wit Seb calls them,' Lee says proudly.

'I've never heard that in my life, man.'

'You'll pick up the patter soon enough. Aw here, Seb's just text me, actually. You want tae jump oan a call wi us?'

'When?'

'In, like, five minutes,' Lee says. 'He just wants tae have a chat. Just a catch-up and tae see how yer dain, especially efter the day you've had.'

'Tae see how *am* dain?'

'Aye, man. He wis worried aboot ye.'

'Aye, awrite, I'll jump oan wi ye.' I've never known anyone to be worried about me. I feel quite flattered.

'Right, he's gonnae jump oan wi us noo. Ye ready?'

'Aye, man. Wee bit nervous, but it's probably just wit happened earlier.'

'It's done noo, mate. Don't be nervous, awrite? Ye don't need tae be nervous.'

'Awrite,' I say.

'Hey, boys,' says Seb into my ear. 'How are ya both doing?'

'All good, my man,' says Lee. 'How's hings wi you?'

'Not too bad, either. How are you doing, Jamie? Lee says you've had a pretty rough twenny-four hours?'

'I'm fine, I think,' I reply. 'I was worried aboot her, mair than anything, but it's fine.'

'Don't worry about her,' Seb says, and I can hear him sort of like scoffing as he talks. 'Your mom's an idiot, and you deserve better than to be treated like that.'

149

'Defo,' says Lee, sounding angrier than he did when we were talking earlier. 'Has she even said sorry tae ye?'

'Eh, naw,' I reply.

'That's oot ae order, int it, Seb?' Lee says.

'Yeah, it is. And I'll bet she even did the classic foid trick of making *you* feel guilty? Am I right, Jamie?' He sounds like he's giving me into trouble.

'Maybe,' I say. This conversation is making me feel weird. Like, I'm glad my maw is alright and hasn't been murdered – Seb and Lee shouldn't be making me feel bad about that, surely?

'If I was you,' Seb says, 'I'd be giving her a piece of my mind right now. Stupid fucking slut.'

'Aye,' is all I can say. I feel annoyed that he's called my maw a slut, but I don't want to disappoint him or Lee.

'You should say something tae her, mate,' Lee says. He sounds different when Seb's around, more aggressive than he is normally. 'We're leaving fur London soon, so fuck it. Go mental at her.'

'I'm gonnae go an chill fur a bit,' I say, trying to get off this call. 'I don't feel good.'

'Okay, buddy,' Seb says, his voice softening a wee bit. 'You know we're just looking out for you, right?'

'Aye, I know. I'm sorry,' I reply.

'It's okay. Lee and I are gonna have a chat about you two coming down. I have some instructions, but I'll let him pass them on to you. That okay with you, Lee?'

'Sound,' Lee says.

'Eh, right,' I say. 'I'm away. Talk tae yous later.'

'Talk to you soon, Jamie,' says Seb, followed by Lee saying, 'Catch ye later,' but I click off before I say anything else.

I lie back on my bed again. I hate when people tell me how I should feel about things. It happens to me so often that I don't know how to tell how I feel about anything. I'm basically always wrong, though, I suppose, so it doesn't matter.

I hear a noise coming from through the wall. It sounds like my maw's pure sobbing. I immediately feel sorry for her and pick up my phone to text her, but then I remember I'm supposed to be angry with her. I feel like Seb can see me somehow, like he's watching me through a hidden camera, pure judging me.

The sobs seem to stop. I hold my breath so I can hear better, although fuck knows if that actually works. I hear my maw do that big sort of sniff thing people do when they're finished crying to try and compose themselves.

I open my bedroom door and look at hers. There's a dent in the cheap wood from when my da was meant to have punched it years ago. Although I never actually saw it happen, and given how mental my maw can be, maybe it was her. I give her door a tap a couple of times with my finger, so it's no too loud and she doesn't get a fright.

'Jamie?' she says.

'Aye, it's me,' I reply. Who the fuck else could it be?

'Wit is it?'

'Just seeing if yer awrite.'

There's silence for a few moments, and then she says, 'Come in.'

I don't think I've ever been in this room at the same time

as my maw before. She looks so weird lying in her bed under the covers. She looks so much smaller for some reason.

'Wit's the matter?' she asks me.

'Nuhin. I just thought I could hear ye greeting.'

'Aye,' she says. 'I wis, but I'm awrite noo.' She rubs her eyes. She doesn't look alright to me.

'I thought something had happened tae ye earlier.'

'Naw, nothing. I'm fine. It's done noo.'

I stand and look at her. I don't really know what else to say to her. I'm sure she feels the same.

'You can sit doon,' she says, out of nowhere.

'Wit, oan the bed?'

'Naw,' she says, with a smile, 'the flair.'

I take this as a joke, and perch myself on the end of her bed. It's mental how clean everything is in here. Smells nice, as well. Just the pure exact opposite of my room.

'Where did ye go?' I ask her.

'I just went for a drive,' she says. 'I did come hame last night, but only fur five minutes, then I went oot again. You must've been sleeping.'

'But ye were away fur ages,' I say. I pick at the grey blanket she's got over the end of her bed. I wish I had one of these; bet it'd be class wrapping it round myself while I play the computer.

'I drove aboot. Parked at the industrial estate and went tae sleep. I just didnae want tae be in the hoose.'

I can't really imagine wanting to be anywhere other than the house. Well, my room specifically. Nothing bad can happen to me in my room; anything could happen outside it.

'Why did ye no want tae be in the hoose?' I ask her.

She just shrugs her shoulders and looks down at the covers. She looks as if she's got something she wants to say, but can't. 'I don't know,' she says. 'I just felt weird.'

'I feel weird aw the time,' I say.

She looks at me and smiles. I wonder if this is what it'll be like when she dies. Like, her lying in a bed and me sitting talking to her, saying goodbye and all that; that's what this feels like.

'Everything will be awrite,' she says. 'We'll figure it oot.'

I don't believe her. If anything, everything's going to get worse. I pull some fluff off the blanket and roll it between my fingers into a wee hairy ball.

'Are you annoyed at me?' she asks eventually.

'I don't know,' I say.

'It's awrite if you are.'

I glance up at her, and she's not smiling anymore.

I want to say, 'Aye,' but I say, 'Naw,' instead. I think she can tell I am annoyed at her, though.

'Can I ask ye something?' she says. 'Wis your da in the hoose last night?'

I feel like all my intestines are twisting themselves into knots. A pure horrible, guilty feeling comes into me. 'Aye,' I say. No point lying.

She lies back and looks up at the ceiling. 'I thought so,' she says.

I rub my sweaty palm on the covers. 'I'm sorry,' I say. I feel like I'm going to cry, but I swallow it down.

'I don't want him here again,' she says.

I nod, but I start to feel angry. Now it feels like my intestines have all seized up so they're solid and hot. Maybe this is like the angry version of getting a hard-on.

My maw sighs. 'I hate the idea of him being in here,' she says. 'It really freaks me oot. It makes me feel sick.'

'Wit?' I say, standing up. 'I cannae see ma da, but it's awrite fur some fucking weird psycho cunt tae come tae the door, aye?'

She adjusts herself so she's sitting upright in the bed now. She looks pure stunned that I've got cheeky with her. 'You can see yer da whenever ye want, Jamie,' she says. 'Just no here. I don't want him here.'

My heart starts beating faster and faster. I look down and see my hands are balled into fists. Does my brain think I'm about to batter my maw?

'I fucking hate you,' I say.

She puts her head in her hands. 'Stop it,' she says. 'Don't say things like that.'

I know she's upset and that I shouldn't have said that, but she sounds calm, and it's making me feel even angrier.

'You don't gie a fuck aboot me,' I say. 'You've just left me tae fucking rot.'

She pulls her hands away from her face. 'I've done everything I can fur you! You need tae get a grip and sort yer life oot. It's no ma fault!'

'Aye, it fucking is your fault,' I shout back. 'You're a fucking slut.'

She shakes her head. 'Get oot. I cannae deal with this. I cannae deal wi you.'

I storm out, and slam her door shut behind me.

20

FIONA

My door slams shut, and then so does Jamie's. I hear the rustling of rubbish, something hitting the floor, and then the sound of a scream into a pillow. My hands are shaking, and I feel like all the blood has drained from my body. I wonder if it's his room that makes him act like this – all the bad energy or something. I imagine it's filled with all his negative, horrible thoughts, floating around like black smoke. All the bitterness and hatred he has towards me, pooling on the ground like sludge while his loneliness clings to the walls like mould. All of it seeping into him and making him even worse. My room's the opposite, empty and white and sterile, because I hardly feel anything ever.

I begin to feel something creeping up on me. Dread, probably; I have work in the morning. I'll have to face Gillian, but at least I'll be out the house. I wonder what would happen if I just didn't go to work tomorrow? It's the kind of thing you could get away with once, I think. If I didn't turn up, they'd phone me and I wouldn't answer. Maybe Gillian would send me a text. Maybe she'd tell Mark and he'd turn up at the house again. Jamie would freak out again, and get even angrier. He'd probably end up stabbing me. Jesus Christ, I'd be better off just going in.

I'm so tired of everything and everybody. I just want to be on my own. I wish I'd never met Danny. I wish I'd never had Jamie. I close my eyes and hope that when I open them again, all this, the last thirty-odd years of my life, will have just been a bad dream, and I'll be a wee lassie back in my bed in my ma's house.

There's another one of the few feelings that I'm able to feel coming up now . . . Oh, it's guilt! Now I feel guilty over wishing my nineteen-year-old son was never born. I roll over on to my side and curl up into a wee ball. Instead, I wish that I'll fall asleep and just fall out of existence.

My god, listen to me. How melodramatic can you get? Things aren't actually that bad, really. I've got a job, I've got a house, I've got a car. The job's rubbish and I hate going, but it pays enough to get me by, and it gets me out the house. It lets me pay the rent and put petrol in the motor. That's all I need, really. The problems in my life are caused by other people. It's not my fault Jamie's da was an animal. It's not my fault Jamie's turned out like this. It's not my fault my ma doesn't think I'm a good mother. If Jamie's the way he is because of me, then I'm only this way because of her. So it's her fault.

I start drifting off, soothed by the thought that all of this is actually my ma's fault, when I hear Jamie laugh. He used to have such a cute and sweet wee laugh when he was a wee boy;

now it's the kind of laugh that always sounds like he's laughing at you, even though you don't know what he's laughing at.

His voice is a drone, but I think I can make out what he's saying. He's definitely talking about me. Probably telling his wee pal how much of a *slut* I am.

21

JAMIE

My phone buzzes with a text from Lee.

You still up?

Aye.

Straight away, he phones me.

'Right, mate,' Lee says. 'Big news.'

'Wit is it?'

'We're gawn tae London in the morning.' He sounds excited, but I'm a bit confused.

'Thought it wis next week?'

'Aye, but Seb says it makes mair sense fur us tae just go doon as soon as. He's emailed me the bus tickets, and it leaves the morra at eleven in the morning. We'll get there fur aboot nine the morra night.'

'Fuck, mate. I've no even packed or anything.'

'Ye don't need much, mate. He says he'll get us witever we

need. Just bring clean boxers an socks, cuppla T-shirts and a pair ae joggies. Phone charger an that anaw. That's aw I'm taking.'

'Aye,' I say. 'I can dae that.'

'Class, my man,' Lee replies. 'Ye buzzing? I cannae wait.'

'Aye, I suppose,' I say.

'*Ye suppose?* Mate, this is gonnae be amazing.'

I'm absolutely terrified at the thought of this. The idea of just leaving the house is scary enough to me, never mind getting on a bus and going to a different country to stay with some American guy my pal met on some dodgy internet forum.

'Are ye awrite?' Lee asks me.

'Aye, man. I'm sorry, I just had a fight wi ma maw.'

'Mate, that's the hing – ye don't even need tae worry aboot her anymair. Yer away the morra. Ye'll never have tae see her again if ye don't want tae.'

Lee's right. It feels like a pure moment of clarity for me here. Everything that's wrong with me now is because of her, and she just doesn't give a fuck. Now I've got the chance to just fuck off away from her, cut her out completely and start again. Start a new life and be somebody else.

'Honestly, mate,' Lee says. 'This'll be good fur us. Especially you, man.'

'Aye, yer right,' I say. 'Fuck my maw.'

'Fuck yer maw! Fucking exactly, mate. Fuck her, and fuck mine anaw. We don't need anycunt. Women are bad news, mate. Look at how oor lives have turned oot. It's because oor maws are a pair ae sluts.'

'Aye, man,' I say, and I realise I'm smiling even though I'm still angry.

'They didnae even have the sense tae hawd oot fur anycunt better than oor das. We could've been taller and mair handsome if they'd opened their legs fur somecunt better. Then we'd baith have burds and joabs, or be at uni or something, but naw. Here we are, two virgins pure rotting away. London's oor last chance at having a good life.'

Lee's on a bit of a rant. I don't fully get the logic behind what he's saying, but I find myself agreeing with him anyway. It kind of makes sense, I think.

'Ye get wit am saying, mate?' Lee says, after he realises I've no replied to the last few things he's said.

'Aye,' I say, snapping out my trance. 'Eh, so wit's the plan the morra, then?'

'I'll meet ye roon at the shops aboot half-nine and we'll walk tae the bus station.'

'How long will it take tae walk there? Is it no ages away?'

'Aye, man. But Seb says it's safer that way.'

'Surely it's safer tae get a taxi or the train? We could get jumped or mugged or witever if we walk intae the toon.'

'Mate, it's a Monday morning, nothing's gonnae happen. It's just cause Seb disnae want CCTV picking us up, in case anycunt tries tae come and find us. Walking covers oor tracks, leaves nae trace.'

'Naebody'll be tryin tae find me, man. Naebody will even notice.'

'Same here, mate. Means we can stay doon there fur as long as we want wi naebody giving us any hassle.'

'Aye, man. That makes sense.'

'Right, mate,' Lee says. 'We better get packed an get tae

sleep. I'll text ye wit am bringin, an you just bring the same, awrite?'

'Aye. Cheers, Lee.'

'Nae bother, Jamie. See ye in the morning, mate.'

'See ye in the morning,' I say, and then hang up. I lie back on my bed. My maw must have fell asleep, as the house is totally silent. It's pitch black in my room. There's no point in me trying to pack a bag now, as I can't see, so I'll just get to sleep and sort it all out in the morning. The noise of me rustling about would wake my maw up anyway, and she'd ask what I was doing. I try and shut my eyes, but I don't feel tired enough to sleep yet. I pick up my phone again and go on the forum Lee told me about. The most popular post of the day comes up first and it's titled 'I hate my mom'. I click on it.

> My mom is never off my back. Always telling me I should go outside and get a job and all this other shit. 'Maybe you should take a shower?' Maybe you should fucking kill yourself you fucking bitch? Like taking a shower will make me attractive to girls? Like that'll get me a job? She calls me a freeloading bum even though she doesn't have to work because my dad makes buxx. Just wish I could LDAR in peace without some dumb fucking foid screaming at me.

I click on another few posts, and they're mostly all saying the same thing. I feel weird reading stuff like this, because the things they're saying and thinking and feeling are all feelings that I've felt as well. Everyone on these forums seems to be living the same life, more or less. The comments underneath the post are all guys telling him that he should kill and rape his maw. Seems a bit extreme to me. I get an image in my head of me taking a hammer to my maw, playing out in gory detail. My stomach lurches as I imagine caving in her face. I shut my eyes and try to make it go away. It's not normal to get so angry at your maw that you feel like killing her. Maybe I need therapy or something. Maybe I just need to be away from her for a bit, let her calm down and realise that she's the problem and not me.

I can hear a weird noise coming into my dream, but I've no idea what it is. It sounds like a phone ringing, maybe. It gets louder and louder, until I open my eyes and realise it's my alarm. I reach over and silence it. That's the first time I've been woke up by an alarm for years, I think. Feels weird to not just wake up naturally. It's mental to me that people have to do this every morning. I've got an hour to get packed and ready and get round to the shop to meet Lee. Sunlight comes pouring in as I pull the curtains open, so I can see what I'm doing. I can see all sorts of dust floating in the light that's coming through the window. I bet it's made up of, like, mites and fly eggs and viruses and fungus and germs and all that. It wouldn't scare me if it was, because I must be immune to all sorts of diseases, because of how bogging my room is and how long I've been in it without ever getting sick.

I've been wearing my maw's black T-shirt and the same pair of black joggies since my da came over. I grab my socks and pull them on. All my white socks went yellow at the bottom ages ago – I think it's cause of sweat – they've turned pure crispy. I can't find much else; a couple of pairs of crusty boxers, some socks that are even more bogging than the ones I'm wearing, and a black hoodie. I pull out my old schoolbag, which has been sitting untouched under my bed for years. I tip it upside down, and out come a couple of old books and jotters, all sorts of crumbs and a couple of dead woodlice, curled up into wee balls. There's still stains on the front of it from when someone flung an open bottle of Irn-Bru at me. I stuff everything in, along with my phone charger. And just like that, I'm ready to go and start a new life. My phone buzzes with a message from Lee.

You up and ready mate?

Aye.

Sound. Just jumping in for a shower,
then I'll be ready ae go.

I think about replying 'Me tae,' but then I'll either need to actually go for a shower or lie about having one when he'll be able to smell from a mile away that I've not.

I just need to get out the door now. I've done it before, and I can do it again. I remember seeing a mad inspirational quote on Facebook ages ago that said: 'Everything you want is on the other side of fear.' I don't know why that's pure stuck with me. How are you supposed to get what you want when you're scared of everything? I suppose being able to get out the front door might be a good start.

Before I attempt to get out, I go into the toilet. Should I brush my teeth? I've never really seen the point in doing it, since it's no like I'll be getting close enough for anybody to smell my breath, I'm hardly going to be kissing anybody or anything, but this is a special occasion, so I'll do it. I've had the same toothbrush for years, but it still looks brand new. My maw's is lying on the sink, and the bristly bit is all flattened out. She must go to town on her teeth, man. I stand and look at myself in the mirror above the toilet. I should've had a shower, but I look reasonably clean, I think. My hair's a bit greasy, but I did only wash it a week ago. My teeth and gums start to hurt from brushing, so I spit the foam out into the sink. It's got red streaks of blood running through the white stuff. I wash it away and take a drink from the tap before I take one last look at myself. I don't look good – I'll never look good – but as long as I just look normal, then that'll do me. None of the incels on the forums post pictures of themselves, so I don't know if I actually look like one. Maybe I'm decent-looking compared to them, or maybe I'm worse.

I go out into the hall and stare at the front door. I start to get sweaty and dizzy again. If this was a film, the door would start pure moving away from me and the hall would be miles long. I'd run towards it, and it'd keep getting further away.

My heart beats faster as I walk towards it. If I just don't react to the mad feelings my body is forcing me to feel, I'll be able to do it. I can get outside. People do it every day. I used to be able to do it, and I can still do it. One thing at a time: get to the door, turn the key, open it, step out, shut it behind me. That's it. Five wee tiny steps. It's no a big deal. I reach my hand out, pure shaking as I go for the key. I stop midway and have to rub my hands up and down against my thighs. I try again. Fuck it, I can do this. I turn it and open the door with my eyes shut, step out and shut it behind me. I lean back against the door and realise I've been holding my breath. I open my eyes and I start to pant like a dog. It's so fucking bright out here, Jesus Christ. The shop's just right round the corner, and it'll only take me like a minute, so I've got plenty of time to get myself together. That thought seems to calm me down. Just another wee tiny step. I walk up to our front gate. I can't feel my feet hitting the ground; it's like I've went totally numb. I reach out to unlock the gate, but my hands aren't working right, either. It's like I've got the most intense pins and needles ever. My hand's just all limp as I touch the rusty metal, but I get it open, and now I'm on the street. Nobody's about. I look up at my maw's room window, and her blinds are still down. I look up and down the road to see if Lee's about, but there's no sign of him. My maw's motor sits across the road. Shit, she's meant to have left for work by now. If I want to do this, I need to go now in case she sees me. I stare down at my feet as I walk, my stomach churning with every step. Motors rumble by on the main road at the end of the street. It's weird feeling wind against my face and pure whistling into my ears, man. I look up, and there's the shop. I want to say that was a piece of piss, but my belly's in turmoil, I can't feel any of my limbs, I'm dizzy and my heart's beating like fuck.

An old woman I recognise from living on our street comes out the shop, and I look away. The door makes a sort of electronic ding-dong noise when it opens. I've no heard that noise for years. It seems slower now, like the battery for it is dying. The old woman looks like she's dying. The whole place seems to be dying. I recognise another woman, who breezes by me and goes in. The same people still doing all the same stuff in the same place. I'm glad I'm leaving.

'There he is!' says Lee, as he comes running towards me, his bag bouncing up and down behind him. He jumps on me with his arm round my neck, and I can't help but smile. 'Wit's happening, wee sacks?'

'No much, man,' I reply. He ruffles my hair and gently punches me on the arm. 'It's weird seeing you ootside, oot in the real world,' he says, looking me up and down. 'Ye look . . . smaller.'

I don't know what to say to that, so I just smile and look down at my feet.

'You're nervous, int ye?' he says.

'Aye,' I reply.

'Don't be, mate. I'm here wi ye. We're in this thegither, awrite? It's gonnae be class.'

I look back up at him, and he's leaning his head towards mine.

'Moan, mate. We better get moving,' he says, and starts walking. I walk beside him, matching his speed. 'I know where am gawn, don't worry.'

We walk in silence for a bit. We come to a wee park I used to cut through to get to school. Bits of broken glass and dog shite cover the path. Somebody's bike has been dumped in the wee burn. A pair of trainers dangle above us from a lamp post.

'Did yer maw see ye leaving this morning?' Lee asks me.

'Naw, man,' I say. 'I don't hink so. Did yours?'

'Nah. My da wis awready away tae work, and she wis still in bed when I left. Just shut my room door and snuck oot.'

We come out the other side of the park, and in the distance I can see my old school. I start to feel weird again. The feeling in my legs goes again, and I start to feel dizzy. There's a mad stabbing pain in my chest.

'You awrite?' Lee asks me.

'Feel like I'm gonnae have a heart attack,' I say.

'Fuck sake, man. Ye wantae stoap fur a minute? Catch yer breath?'

I can't speak. I'm hyperventilating. I crouch down and try to will my heart to stop beating so fast.

'Here, a hink yer having a panic attack, mate,' Lee says.

I feel like I'm going to be sick. The pain in my chest is throbbing, and with each throb I get a flash in my vision like a camera going off. I think my eyeballs might burst as well. I look up at Lee, and he's typing something into his phone.

'Don't phone an ambulance,' I say between breaths.

'I'm no, ya madman. I'm trying tae see how tae help ye.' He kneels down next to me and gently slides my schoolbag off. He rubs his hand between my shoulder blades. 'Right, ye need tae focus oan yer breathing, try an slow that doon first,' he says. 'In an oot, mate. Nice an slow. When I rub yer back up the way, breathe in, and when I go doon, breathe oot.'

I do as he says, and my breathing starts to slow.

'Right, it says ye need tae count suhin as well. Eh, how many dug shites can ye see?'

I'd laugh if I didn't feel like I was dying. I focus on the

furthest-away dug shite I can see on the path, and then count them as they get closer to me.

'. . . three . . . four . . . five . . .'

'Keep trying tae slow yer breathing anaw, mind.'

The pain in my chest starts to subside, and the flashes of light stop. Before I know it, I'm breathing normally and I've counted twelve dug shites. At least I presume they're from a dug.

I stand up straight and exhale deeply.

'Says here if ye can name some hings ye can see, touch an taste, that helps anaw. Don't saw ma baws,' Lee says, laughing.

'Am awrite noo,' I say. 'Fucking hell, that wis mental.' I start walking again. My old school is dead ahead, a big, horrible and depressing grey building. I swear it must have been built on some kind of cursed land, given how mental it made me go.

'Wit caused that?' Lee asks me.

'Think it wis seeing the school, mate,' I reply. 'Just freaked me oot.'

'Ye never need tae go back there, mate,' he says. 'Yer too auld noo.'

'Naw, I know that. I don't know, it just makes me feel weird seeing it. I've no been doon this way since I left school.'

He looks at me with a half-smile, then looks away. I can tell he thinks I'm mental. He thinks he's going to be stuck helping me all the way through all of this. Looking after me like I'm a wean. I think about the hierarchy of types of guys I saw on one of the forums. How it said Alphas are at the top, and Omegas are at the bottom. Lee's an Alpha. At least in our hierarchy, at least to me. I'm at the bottom and always have been. The Omega in every hierarchy. The weird wee guy nobody likes to even look at, never mind talk to.

'Arse oan that,' Lee says, after we've been walking in silence for a while. He nods towards a lassie in shorts up ahead of us. She looks younger than I do, and I look younger than nineteen. 'Wit a wee slut,' he says.

I don't make eye contact with him. I don't know what to say.

'Wit is it?' Lee says. 'Wit's the matter?'

'Nothing,' I reply. 'I never said anything.'

'Ye no like the look ae her, naw?'

He seems angry. Fuck knows why. Sorry for no perving on a wee lassie, I suppose. That's what I want to say, but I'm too scared he'll get annoyed at me. I've never heard him take this tone of voice with me. He's got an air about him that reminds me of my da just now. Volatile.

'It's no as if she'd ever even go near us, mate. There's nothing wrang wi saying stuff like that if she disnae hear it.'

'I'm sorry,' I say, and we overtake the lassie. Lee seems too angry at me to notice.

We're walking down a main road. I think I've been here before, but when I was a wee boy. The roads are getting busier with people heading to work. Lorries and vans park outside shops, and guys in hi-vis vests unload boxes and pallets of stuff. I get a whiff of smoke in my face from an old woman as we squeeze by her. Even above the engines and shouting, I can hear her walking stick clacking off the pavement.

For the next half an hour or something, Lee doesn't say a word. I just walk slightly behind him, having to do a wee jog

169

every couple of seconds to keep up. I'm scared that he'll go too far ahead and I'll lose him. I wouldn't know how to get back home from here.

'Bus station's just roon that corner, mate,' he says. When he adds 'mate' on to that sentence, it makes me feel a wee surge of butterflies in my belly. It's like he likes me again. He turns round to look at me, and he's smiling. 'Ye awrite?' he asks.

'Aye, I'm fine,' I say. I'm out of breath, not because of another panic attack or anything, just because I've never walked this far in my life.

'Hawd oan a minute,' he says, stopping dead and putting a hand on my chest. He reaches into his pocket and pulls out two fags. They're bent and crumpled.

'Sorry I snapped at ye earlier,' he says.

'It's sound,' I say. 'Don't worry aboot it.'

He sticks both fags in his mouth and lights them at the same time, then passes one to me. 'I never had anything tae eat this morning,' he says. 'This is ma first fag anaw. That's why I wis in a mood.'

'It's fine,' I say, taking a draw.

'We've still got fifteen minutes till we need tae be oan the bus.' He tilts his head back and exhales. I watch his smoke mingle with mine in the air above us before it disappears. 'Did wit I said aboot that lassie, like, annoy ye or something?' He's no saying it in an angry way, more like he's just curious.

'I don't know,' I say.

'You always say that,' he says with a smile. Then he does an impression of me saying it.

I laugh a wee bit and look down as a bit of fag ash drops to the pavement.

'I'm only kidding ye on,' he says. 'I think Seb's got intae ma heid, man.'

'Wit d'ye mean?'

'Like, honestly, mate. I was never bothered aboot no bein able tae get a burd or that until I started talkin tae him. Noo I feel like I *hate* burds. Cannae even have a wank withoot getting angry noo. You feel like that? An don't say, "I don't know."'

'No really, mate,' I say. 'I just don't really care aboot burds, I don't think.'

'Look at they two,' he says, pointing across the road to two lassies, older than us. 'When I first see them, I'm like, "I want tae shag them." But then I hink, naw, I don't. They've probably been rattled aff hunners a guys, but they widnae even gie me a chance. Then a just hink how much I hate them an hope they fuckin die.'

'Fuck sake,' I say.

'I never used tae be like this, mate.'

I wonder if he's having second thoughts about going down to stay with Seb, but then he says, 'Still, I'm glad he showed me the truth.'

I flick my fag on to the road. I can feel the life draining out of me, through the soles of my shoes. I want to go home.

'Let's go, mate,' Lee says, and he puts an arm around me. He guides me towards the bus station, where I can see a big blue bus with LONDON on the front of it in lights. I start panicking, and I can't hear anything. Lee puts his hand on my back, and when my hearing returns, I realise I'm sitting down next to him and the bus doors are closing. No going back now.

22

FIONA

My phone keeps ringing, and I keep ignoring it. I just hold it in my hand and stare at it. I switch it to silent and slide it under my pillow. I've never phoned in sick to work, or even been late, so they must think I've died or something. I go down the stairs to the toilet to see Jamie's left me a brown surprise in the pan. Delightful. I shut the lid and flush it away. Why does he have to be so fucking horrible all the time?

I go back up to my room and consider just getting ready for work. It would get me out of here and away from the house and Jamie, but I really can't interact with anyone today. I can't look at another human being, and I can't listen to any words coming out of anybody's mouth. My brain won't be able to handle it, and I'll end up killing someone. I reach under my pillow and pull out my phone. The last missed call from my work was ten minutes ago, so they must have given up trying to get hold of me. I quickly click on their name in my phone and hold it to my ear. I can get this done and over with, and have a relatively stress-free day as soon as I hang up.

'Hi there, Gillian speaking. How can I help?' Her sing-songy phone voice makes me tense up. It's far too early in the morning for someone to be so cheery.

'Gillian, it's me, Fiona.'

'Oh,' she says, sounding surprised. 'Is everything okay?'

'Aye, I'm just . . . no feeling too great.' I cycle through the different maladies I could say I have, but decide not to elaborate. 'I won't be in.'

'Oh, okay. Eh, no problem. I'll let Suzanne know, and I'll give you a wee text later on to see how you're doing, okay?'

'Okay,' I reply, and hang up before she can say anything else or ask me anything. I climb back into bed. It feels weird being home at this time on a Monday. I try to get comfy again and see if I can fall back asleep, but I can't. I imagine what my ma would say if she could see me right now, and the thought of her standing over me and giving me a lecture makes me get out of bed.

I immediately start stripping the bed, almost as if I'm on autopilot. Something clicks in my brain; a big clean of the house will make me feel better. Like a reset. This happens to me every so often – I get depressed and the house starts to get into a bit of a mess. At some point, it gets too much for me, and I start feeling as if I can see flies and maggots everywhere, and wee beetles crawling all over my bed and the floor. I strip the bed, open my windows and put away the clothes I've left on the floor. I feel lighter and cleaner already. My brain feels like it's been power-washed.

I go down the stair and into the living room. The smell of Danny seems to have gone by itself, but I still want to disinfect every single possible place he could have sat, and everything he could have touched.

After a few hours, the whole place is spotless again. Well, apart from Jamie's room, but that's his problem to deal with, not mine. I've no seen him yet today. Maybe he snuck down while I was hoovering and I just didn't hear him. Maybe he's avoiding me. Maybe he's just still asleep.

Gillian's name flashes up on my phone. I click on the notification immediately, without thinking, and then feel annoyed at myself for it. Now she'll see that I've opened it, and that I'm available to talk to her.

How you feeling?

I want to send a message back to her that says:

> I feel absolutely mental and depressed,
> and I feel like I've lost all control of my life.
> My abusive ex-partner was in my house
> my son called me a slut and you sent me
> on a date with a complete freak . . .

But instead, I just say:

> I'm okay. Thank you x

Suzanne says you've to let her know
in the morning if you'll be in, there's no

pressure. How did it go on Saturday night,
and did you get your flowers ;)

That winky face is making me want to snap my phone in two. Saturday made me feel terrible about myself – and no, Gillian, I didn't get any flowers. Instead, the man came to my house because I didn't answer his texts, and he terrorised my son. I take a deep breath and realise that none of this is Gillian's fault. I want to tell her that Mark was out of order and made me uncomfortable, and that she should have a word with him or get someone else to, but I feel a pang of guilt for some reason. How can all this happen, how can a man do that, and I'm the one sitting here thinking that I'd be in the wrong for just telling someone?

All good. See you tomorrow x

I get up from the couch as I hear someone opening the front gate, that metal-on-metal squeal. A red-headed woman walks by the window and I hear the sound of her knuckles on the door. It'd be funny if it was Mark's wife, I think, coming to confront me and accuse me of being his mistress. *Oh,* I'd say if it was, *he told me he'd just got divorced.* And then maybe I'd end up best pals with her, and she'd also be really rich and generous. It'd be good if life worked like that.

'Sorry,' the ginger woman says as I open the door. 'Is Lee there, by any chance?' She's about my age, lots of freckles and frizzy hair. I'm sure I've seen her at the shop a few times. She looks flustered.

'Aw, Jamie's wee pal. Aye, he was here the other night, but I don't think Jamie's got anyone in just now,' I say.

'Aye, he said he wis pals wi your Jamie. It's just I cannae get a hawd ae him. His phone's aff. I've been up an doon the street lookin fur him, and I saw your name on the door and thought it'd be worth a try.' She looks really worried, and I feel sorry for her.

'I'll ask Jamie if he knows where he is,' I say.

'That'd be brilliant, ta,' she says. 'I'm sorry tae be a pest. I'm just worried.'

'Boays, eh?' I say, and try my best to give her a reassuring smile to make her feel like it's all going to be fine. 'Two seconds.' I shut the door slightly and run up the stair.

'Jamie,' I say. 'You there?'

Silence.

'Jamie, have you heard fae Lee? His ma's wondering.'

Silence.

I push his door open a wee bit until the smell hits me. It's pitch black, but I can just about make out the shape of him on his bed. I shut the door back over, scared that if I wake him up, then Lee's ma will hear us have a fight. I go back down the stair.

'I'm sorry, he's sleeping. I think he's nocturnal,' I say.

'Can I leave ye ma number?' she says, ignoring my joke. 'Please just gie me a quick text or a phone an let me know if he hears fae him, eh?'

'I will,' I say, handing her my phone. She puts her number in and hands it back to me. She's saved her number under 'Jacqui LEES MA'.

She puts her own phone to her ear and walks away, her other hand clenched tight around her ponytail.

I shut the door and give Jamie another shout, but to no avail. I should just leave him; he had a difficult weekend, I suppose. His keys lie on the unit next to the front door, the metal still shiny and untarnished. They're never really used as he never goes anywhere. I'll leave him until I hear him moving about, then I'll ask him about Lee. No doubt the wee guy will turn up soon, anyway.

23

JAMIE

'Mate,' Lee says, as his elbow digs into my side. 'We're nearly there, I think.'

I remove my head from his shoulder and sit up straight. I wipe my hand over my chin to remove the slabbers that have dribbled out of my mouth. I must have been proper out cold.

'How long was I sleeping fur?' I ask.

'Aboot six hours, mate. Gonnae let me oot fur a pish,' he says, clambering over me with his arse in my face.

I woke up a few times, but fell right back asleep every time. That panic attack or whatever it was must have fucking knackered me. Maybe my brain just went into, like, a mad power-saving mode once we sat down on the bus.

This must be the furthest away from my house I've ever been. Lee disappears down the stairs, looking unsteady on his feet. I look out the window at the buildings flashing by in a grey blur. It just looks the same as anywhere else I've been. I thought London was full of skyscrapers and Big Ben and all that. So far, I've seen fuck all.

'Where are we?' I ask as he comes back.

'Fuck knows,' he says. 'Still ootside London, I think.'

'Sound,' I say. I can't believe how far away from home I am – and there's nothing I can do about it. I can't get off this bus, and even if I could, I don't have money or even any of the required knowledge to get home.

Lee flops back down into his seat. 'Choking fur a fag,' he says. 'I tried tae light wan up in the toilet, but I shat it when I saw the smoke alarm. Fuck getting kicked aff the bus here in the middle ae England.'

I look past him and out the window again. We might as well be on the moon. Pure uncharted territory. An alien environment.

'I'm starving,' I say.

'Me tae, mate. We'll get something when we get tae Seb's, though.'

'How long till we get there?' I ask.

Lee looks outside, then turns to me and says: 'Another hour or two, max.'

I think about going back to sleep again, but when I shut my eyes, they just want to ping back open. I wonder if it's some kind of survival mechanism. Like, now I'm in a weird new place, miles away from home, so my body's like, 'Naw. Stay awake and stay alert.'

'Is this furthest you've ever been?' I ask Lee.

'Wit d'ye mean?' he replies, not looking at me. He pulls a fag out of its packet, then slides it back down again.

'Have you ever been this far away fae your hoose before?'

'Eh, naw, I don't hink so. My maw said wance that she

took me tae Disneyland when I was a wean, but I just don't remember it. I think she was talking shite. There's nae pictures or anything.'

'This is mental,' I say.

'Wit is?' Lee replies.

'Just this whole thing. Running away tae London. It's mental.'

'I know, man,' he says, turning to me and smiling. 'It is, but it's class. I don't know anycunt apart fae us who'd have the baws tae dae this.'

'Aye, I suppose,' I say, and look down at my thumb. I've been picking it again without realising.

'Don't go aw weird and moody,' he says, and taps me on the thigh. 'We're nearly there. I'll always make sure yer awrite as well.'

'Cheers, mate,' I say.

He smiles at me, then turns away to look out the window.

As we pull into the bus station in London, Lee looks noticeably more nervous. He's played with a fag so much that it's became soggy and floppy from being rolled around in his sweaty hands. He sticks it in between his lips and it droops down below his chin instead of sticking out, pure proud and erect.

'Let's go, mate,' he says. I get up and stick my schoolbag on, and squeeze out between the other passengers. We make our way down the steep stairs. I can smell the hot fumes and the stink coming out the toilets. I bet I must be stinking as well, but Lee hasn't said anything, so maybe not.

I don't feel as anxious as I normally would about going from inside to outside. I think it's cause I feel like me and Lee and everybody else are part of one big sort of river of people spilling out of the bus. No one's looking at me, I don't think; they'd just look over and see a group of people coming off the bus, not one individual weird-looking wee guy. I feel safe as part of a crowd actually. This is weird.

I watch the other passengers wait for the driver to hand them their luggage from under the bus. I pull my phone out to check the time, but it's dead.

'You boays waiting oan bags?' the driver asks us.

'Naw, mate,' Lee says, without looking up at him, as he rummages in his bag.

'Make a move, then,' the driver says, sounding annoyed. 'Ye cannae be stawnin aboot here.'

'Fuck sake,' Lee mutters under his breath, and we follow an Indian family into the bus station and outside until they disappear. The sky above us is a dark orange colour as the sun gets ready to set. There's people everywhere. Just millions of people, all walking pure fast, overtaking each other, talking on their phones, cunts on bikes and scooters. Everything moving at a million miles an hour. We duck into a bricked-up doorway to stay out the way while Lee figures out our next move. He turns his phone on, his eyes darting around as he waits for it to boot up.

'Right, I've goat it,' he says and switches off his phone again. He lights the cigarette with his green lighter. He takes a long drag, then passes it to me. I do the same. 'Basically,' he says, 'we just walk in a straight line from here, doon that way. Should take us aboot an hour.'

'Sound,' I say.

'Your phone turned aff, aye?' Lee asks, and I nod while I take another draw. I start to get that light-headed, dizzy feeling again as I hold the smoke in my mouth. It feels amazing.

'Cannae believe we're actually dain this,' I say to Lee, as we walk side by side.

'I know, mate,' he replies. 'I thought you'd have shat it and left me tae go maself.'

'Aw, fuck up,' I say with a smile.

Lee smiles back. 'You feelin awrite? You no gonnae have another panic attack or that?'

'Naw, I feel fine here fur some reason.'

'It's a weird feeling, int it?' he says, with his brow furrowed. 'It's class that naecunt here knows who we are.'

'Aye,' I say. 'Like back up the road, there's always a chance I'd see somecunt fae school or that. And they'd laugh at me or something. Or I'd feel pure, I don't know, inadequate seeing them.'

Lee nods but doesn't look at me. I presume he feels the same. It's starting to get dark as we walk along a never-ending main road. There's all sorts of mad smells and new sounds here. Pure sensory overload: it's amazing.

'You awrite?' Lee turns round and asks me after a few minutes of silence.

I do a sort of half-jog to catch up to him. 'Is there nae chance ae getting a taxi or something, mate? This is a cunt ae a walk.'

'I know, mate, but we cannae. Seb's rules, man. Cannae have anycunt knowing where we're gawn.'

'My feet are killing me.'

'Mine anaw. Ye wantae stoap fur a bit?'

'Aye,' I say. I'm out of breath here. This here is now the most walking I've ever done in my life.

We walk a wee bit further up till we get to a bench, and we sit side by side and watch motors roll by.

'We're no in a rush, by the way,' Lee says. 'Take as long as ye need.'

I lean forward with my head almost between my knees and spit on the pavement. I feel like I've just ran a marathon. I sit up and lean back, my bag providing a nice cushion against the metal bench. Lee pulls out his packet of fags and hands me another one. He lights his own and then hands me his lighter. I spark mine and keep a hold of the lighter. He leans forward with his elbows on his knees.

'I'm starving,' I say. 'Can we go fur a McDonald's or something? There's wan back there.'

'Naw, we better no,' he replies. He sounds a wee bit sort of annoyed that I've asked that. 'Seb said he'll order us something when we get there.'

'You awrite?' I ask him through a puff of smoke, my voice cracking a wee bit.

'Just nervous, mate,' he says.

'Wit fur?' I ask.

'Och, nothing,' he says, leaning back again. 'Natural, int it?'

'Aye,' I say, trying to sound reassuring, despite the fact that him saying he's nervous has made me feel nervous again. I notice he's bouncing his leg up and down.

'How long you want tae stay doon here fur?' he says.

'Dunno, man,' I say. 'Suppose it depends.'

'Depends oan wit?'

I use the index finger on my left hand to peel back a small flap of skin around my left thumbnail until it starts to sting. 'Wit the place is like. Wit Seb's like.'

'Aye,' he says, looking dead ahead, his tone giving nothing away.

'It'll be fine,' I say.

'It will be, aye. Let's get gawn,' he says, standing up. 'There's nae turning back noo, anyway.'

I take a second, and sit and watch him walk for a few steps. Then I relight my fag and catch up to him. I go to pat him on the back, but I stop myself, as I don't want him to think I'm being weird.

We walk in silence for the next hour or so. It's dark now, and the streetlights have came on. My feet feel like they're on fire, and my knees feel like they're all seized up.

'We must be nearly there, eh?' I say, feeling like I could collapse at any moment.

'Aye,' Lee says. 'Should be roon aboot here somewhere.'

'Wit is it we're looking fur?'

'I've only goat an address, but fuck knows where it is. It's defo somewhere here though, wan ae these buildings. Looks like a picture he sent me.'

All around us are fucking enormous high-rise flats. Bigger than anything I think I've ever seen, man. It's like this whole city is on steroids. A couple of people zoom by on scooters and bikes. Two boys in puffer jackets eyeball us from a distance, and I start to feel all sweaty. It's not as busy here as it was when we get off the bus and for nearly all the walk. Instead of just being part of the crowd, we look like exactly what we are – two scared and lost wee guys.

'Phone Seb,' I say to Lee. 'Maybe he can come and get us.'

'I'm no allowed to turn ma phone oan, man. He'll go mental and tell us tae just go back hame.'

'Surely no, mate,' I reply. 'How ye meant tae find somewhere withoot a phone?'

'Fuck knows, man. I thought this wid be easy.' He kicks an empty Capri-Sun pouch and sends it skidding across the road. 'Fuck.'

The two boys in puffer jackets are looking at us and laughing.

'We should move fae here, I think, mate,' I say. 'We'll end up getting battered or mugged or something if we hing aboot here fur too long.'

Lee pulls the last two fags out of the packet and hands one to me. 'We'll look a bit harder if we're smoking,' he says.

I toss his lighter back to him that I pocketed earlier. He catches it no bother. He lights his and tosses the lighter. I fumble it and it falls to the ground. I hear him mutter, 'Fuck sake,' as he keeps walking.

'Let's just sit here and wait,' Lee says, after we've done five laps around the high-rises. 'Maybe he'll see us fae the windae and come doon.'

'Maybe we should just ask somecunt fur directions,' I say.

'Nah, man,' he replies. 'Too risky.'

'I don't like this, mate,' I say. 'It's getting dark, we don't know where the fuck we are, or where this cunt is. Wit if he's made aw this up?'

'It'll be fine, mate,' Lee says. 'Just calm doon.'

'Sound,' I say, and sit down on the pavement next to him. There's no one around now, just me and Lee, sitting under a streetlight. Most of the lights are out in the flats that tower over us. They're so big, they look as if they're going to topple over and flatten us. Two foxes look over at us and freeze before disappearing into the dark.

Lee looks down at the ground between his feet. I hate when he gets cheeky with me. I don't know what to say to him when he gets into these moods. I feel like he'd have preferred to come down here without me, and that he only asked me because he felt sorry for me. I'm a fucking idiot for agreeing to this in the first place.

'I think it's that wan there, maybe,' Lee says, nodding across the road. 'Or maybe it's the wan behind it.'

Out of nowhere, an American voice shouts, 'Hey!'

A figure across the road comes jogging towards us.

'Fucking hell, mate,' Lee says, turning to me. 'That's him. That's Seb.'

We both stand up, as if a teacher has just came back into the classroom and we have to behave. Lee runs a hand through his hair and zips up his trackie top. I feel the urge to try and sort of make myself look a bit better as well, but I can't think of what could possibly work, so I don't do anything.

'You guys coming?'

'Awrite, mate!' Lee shouts, and runs across the road. I follow behind him, doing that sort of half-walk, half-jog thing. The meagre contents of my schoolbag jump around and rustle as I do it.

'Lee and Jamie, here at last. I've been watching you both trying to find this place, laughing my fucking ass off!' Seb says. 'Anyway, how was your journey?' He looks us up and down. He looks a bit more normal in real life, and not quite as weird as he did on the video calls. He's taller than I expected. He's wearing black denims, white trainers and a black T-shirt. He's bigger than both of us, with a bit of a belly.

'It wis fine, mate,' Lee says to Seb. 'Cheers fur sorting it oot fur us.'

'It's no problem, great to have you here. You okay, Jamie?'

I presume he's asking me because how I feel on the inside must be reflected on the outside. I must have turned green or something.

'I'm awrite,' I say, but I can't hear my own voice over the mad staticky noise that's filled my ears, so I'm not sure how it's came out.

'Just help me get him in,' I can hear Lee say as he puts an arm around me and helps me into the close. 'He's having another panic attack.'

I look at Seb to see he's laughing at me.

I'm on autopilot now. Lee helps me up the stairs; my legs are moving, but I'm not asking them to. I try and will them to take me in the other direction, to make me run back home, but instead I feel myself going limp, my body just giving up.

When my eyes open again, I'm lying in a bed that feels pure close to the floor. It's still dark. I shut my eyes and assume the last twenty-four hours has just been a mad nightmare. Then I hear Lee's voice from just outside the room I'm in.

187

'. . . aye, man,' he's saying, over and over again, in response to Seb, whose voice isn't coming through as clear as Lee's. 'I'll check oan him.'

The door creaks open and I sit up as the light from the hall comes pouring in. There's nothing in the room except me, the bed I'm lying on and my schoolbag. The floor is wooden, and there's a small window behind me. The room's about the same size as my own. A lightbulb is hanging directly over my head, tethered to the ceiling with a dodgy-looking wire. At least the light in my own room back home has a shade on it.

'Ye awrite, shagger?' Lee says.

'Wit happened?'

'Hink ye had another panic attack, and then ye fainted. Had tae carry ye in here. Good thing ye only weigh aboot two stone, man.'

'Fucking hell.'

'I know. Ye awrite though, aye?'

'I feel starving, mate. Need a drink anaw.'

I kick the covers off myself and try to get up, but Lee tells me to lie back down and says he'll get me a drink and something to eat.

'Wit's he like?' I ask.

'Seb? He's sound, man. He's wanting us tae dae something fur him, but he wants tae tell ye himself the morra, wance you've had a rest an that.'

'Sound,' I say and lie my head back down on the pillow. 'Wit's the other guys like? Where's everybody else?'

'Aw, it's just us, mate,' Lee replies. 'People just come and go, he said. Better this way, just us.'

'Aw, sound,' I say again, but it's set alarm bells ringing for me. I'd feel a bit safer if there was other wee guys here apart from me and Lee. I don't like this.

'We've goat a McDonald's in the living room,' he says. 'I'll bring ye some stuff in.'

The door shuts, and the room goes dark again.

24

FIONA

'Jamie,' I say, as I stand outside his room door in my pyjamas. 'Jamie, are you there?' I hear some rustling coming from his room. 'Can you text your pal, Lee? His ma's worried aboot him.'

No reply, as usual. I hope he's not still angry with me. Although sometimes it feels like he's been angry at me for the last almost twenty years, so what difference does it make? I go into my room and collapse on to my nice clean bed. I stare at the ceiling for a bit, replaying the day's interactions in my mind – between me and Gillian, and me and Lee's ma, Jacqui. Could I have been a bit nicer to Gillian, or should I have been angrier? Should I have just went into work? No, I needed a day to sort my head out. Should I have tried to do a bit more to help Jacqui find Lee? What would I do if it was Jamie who went missing? Maybe it'd be good if he just took off. I'd never need to worry about him again, and I could just start my life over in any way I wanted. And then I'm hit by the deep shame – what an awful mother I am.

I pick up my phone.

You alive? X

One tick next to my message says that it has been sent at my end, but the second tick confirming it's arrived on his phone hasn't appeared yet. I'm sure it's fine, and turn off the light, but find myself tossing and turning. My brain is going at a million miles an hour, flipping through all the different reasons Jamie's phone might be off. It's like one half of my brain is going, *He's just exhausted after an emotional and intense weekend, and is asleep and/or ignoring you,* and the other is going, *He's lying dead in there, he's killed himself because of you.*

Maybe I should just go in and wake him up and see if he's okay. I'll do that. I get up and put on my slippers, along with my housecoat, and go and chap his room door one more time.

'Jamie,' I say. 'I'm gonnae come in, is that awrite?'

No reply.

'Jamie,' I say, opening the door now. I reach for the light switch in the darkness and turn it on, but nothing happens. I pull out my phone and turn on the torch, and shine it into his room.

What I thought was Jamie earlier was just his twisted covers. My son isn't here.

'Jamie!' I shout. The rational part of my brain says he's just down the stair in the toilet. The irrational one says my son is lying dead somewhere. I hear that rustling sound again as I sweep the light around his room, and a mouse, I think, runs out from under a mound of crisp packets.

I run down the stair. His keys are still by the front door. The toilet door is open and the light is off. I turn it on and pull back the shower curtain, feeling stupid as I do it, but telling myself I have to check everywhere to make sure. I run into the living room, then the kitchen, then check out the back. Nothing.

He's gone.

Fuck.

What do I do? What the fuck do you do when your child disappears? The calm half of my brain says, *He'll be back home tomorrow, or at the very least he'll answer his phone and let you know where he is. He's probably either with his wee pal or he's at his da's.* One of these situations is far more desirable than the other. I hope to god he's not with his da. The mental, irrational part of my brain is saying that he's dead, and I'm somehow going to be accused of killing him and his pal, and that my life is over.

I'm going to be sick everywhere. I stand with my hands on either side of the kitchen sink. I try to slow my breathing, and stare straight down the plughole.

It's going to be fine. I'm overreacting. I'm being mental. I'm in a heightened state of anxiety after the weekend. Boys do this kind of thing. He's nineteen, and I don't need to know his whereabouts at all times. It'll be fine. He'll be fine. I catch my reflection in the kitchen window. I look mental. Hair all over the place, wide eyes.

I turn off the light and head back up the stair, unlocking the front door en route just in case I lock him out. I have another look in his room. It's such a state that it feels loud and noisy to look at, like it's overloading my senses. Not just messy, but actually *dirty* as well. The pile of crusts is unbelievable; no wonder he has mice. I should clean it for him. It's too much of a mess for one wee guy to sort out on his own. I'll do that tomorrow. When he's back. Of course he'll be back. It's mental of me to think that he's been stolen or something. That doesn't happen in real life – not to normal people like me, anyway. It's just some misunderstanding, some miscommunication, and he'll be back tomorrow, and it'll all be fine. He'll sneak in during the night while I'm asleep, and I'll be woke up by the front door shutting, or his footsteps on the stairs, or his room door creaking as he opens it. *Get to bed and he'll come back.* I repeat that to myself over and over again. *Just get to bed and it'll all be fine when you wake up.*

And on the off-chance that he's not back by the morning . . . Well, it won't come to that, surely.

25

JAMIE

I wake up on my side, looking at the back of Lee's head, his ginger hair close enough to tickle my nose. We're both wearing a T-shirt and joggies. I sit up a wee bit and see his bare feet sticking out from under the covers. I can feel that I've still got my socks on, while his are draped over the greasy McDonald's bag on the floor. I'm bursting for a pish, but I don't want to get up and wander about a strange place looking for the toilet. I can hear Seb playing the computer in another room. I think I can smell weed as well, but I don't know where it's coming from. I turn my back on Lee and face the wall, conscious of the fact that we're now arse to arse, but that feels preferable to spooning him, I suppose. My top rides up, and I feel crumbs sticking to my back; it's just like being back home. I'm sure when Lee sent me pictures of this place, there was more than one bed.

Lee shifts his weight and wiggles around a bit. When he comes to a stop, I can feel his breath on the back of my neck.

I try and force myself to get back to sleep by screwing up

my eyes as tightly as I can but the need to pee is overriding everything else. I roll on to my back.

'You up?' I say quietly.

Lee grumbles in reply. I think he's half-awake but still kind of sleeping.

'Where's the toilet, mate?' I ask.

He opens his eyes and looks at me, then rolls on to his back as well. 'Aw, fucking hell,' he says. 'Ma heid's poundin.'

'You awrite?'

'I'll be fine,' he says, sitting up. I sit up next to him. He looks at me and smiles. 'Sure I gave you a spoon during the night, mate. That means you're my burd noo.'

'Fuck off,' I say. 'When I woke up I wis spooning you.'

'Aww, so that's wit wis jabbing me in the arse, then?'

I laugh and almost say to Lee that I wish I could lie here in bed with him all day. No in a gay way, but this is nice – just two pals lying about and having a laugh. I stop myself, as something tells me it's a bit of a weird thing to say.

'Where's the toilet?' I ask again.

'Just oot there, mate.' Lee nods towards the door. 'Just turn left.'

'Sound,' I say, feigning confidence. I get up and head for the door. I hear Seb crystal clear, talking as he plays the computer, but I can't see him or pinpoint where he is. I remember when Lee was showing me pictures of this place, way before we came down, and there was loads of other wee guys here, but it seems totally different now. I open the door to the toilet and slip inside. Seb keeps talking as I pull the door shut, so I don't think he's heard me.

I pull the cord hanging from the ceiling, and horrible orange light pours out of the bulb above me. It's like something out a horror film in here. The toilet looks smaller than a normal toilet, and the shower is in the corner, a cubicle with, like, frosted glass. I can see there's stuff piled up inside it. Maybe it's the bodies of all the wee guys that came here before me. The white tiles under my feet reflect the orange light in slightly different shades, depending on how dirty or cracked each one is. I step only on the ones that look semi-clean. I lift up the lid on the toilet pan and stare in total awe at the black water at the bottom. Never in my life have I seen anything so mental. This is what my house would be like if my maw wasn't there and it was only me. I feel self-conscious pulling out my dick to piss. It's one thing doing it in my own bogging room back home when I have a wank or get changed or pish in a bottle or whatever, but that's my mess there; I know where it all came from and what it all is. Here, I don't have a clue what diseases are just circulating around about me. Dead flies lie on the window ledge.

I've got to just get it over with. My piss shoots into the black water, but I don't get the noise I was expecting. If you piss into a pan normally, it sort of tinkles and splashes, and the noises are light and cheerful, but this is like pishing into tar or something, man. It sounds fucking grim. Whatever's in the water must be acting like a silencer. I tuck my cock back in without shaking off the excess; I don't want it exposed to the cursed air in here, in case it gets infected and falls off or something.

The sink smells like something, but I don't know what it

196

is. It smells sweaty, kinda. I run my hands under the cold tap for a couple of seconds and look about for a towel. There's one on the radiator, and I can tell it used to be white. I opt to just wipe my hands on my joggies and get out. I open the door and slink back to mine and Lee's room. Lee is sitting on the edge of the bed, pulling his socks back on.

'Wit's the plan?' I ask Lee.

'Fuck knows, man,' he replies, standing up and kicking the McDonald's wrappers and boxes under the bed. 'We'll go an see Seb and take it fae there.'

I sit down on the bed. I feel anxious again.

'Wit's the script wi these panic attacks ye keep having, mate?' Lee asks me.

'Nae idea, man,' I reply. I wonder if he can read my mind or something. Maybe because we slept in the same bed, our minds are now synced up.

'Ye know wit I hink it is?' he says.

'Wit?'

'I hink it's your body being like, "Here, we're meant tae be a shitebag, we're no meant tae be dain shit like this." But you're no listening tae it, and just dain the shit that yer body disnae want ye tae dae, like coming doon here.'

'Maybe,' I say. I think he could be right.

'Right, ye coming?' Lee says, standing up.

I nod, take a deep breath and stand up as well. He pats me on the back and motions for me to follow him out of the room. I follow behind him like a wee dog who always does what he's told. We go down the narrow hall, and it gets darker as we walk. Seb is sitting topless in the living room with the blinds and curtains shut. A massive telly sits on the floor, leaning against the wall behind it. Seb turns round and takes his headset off as we enter, leaning back in his gaming chair.

'Morning, boys,' he says, standing up. 'I thought you'd died in there!'

'We were just having a lie-in, mate,' Lee says. 'This place is class, I slept like a log.'

'Good to hear, good to hear, how 'bout you, Jamie?'

I feel his eyes on me and snap my gaze back to meet his, away from the mess and filth of the living room. 'Aye,' I say. 'I slept fine.'

'That's good, I was worried about you, y'know? Especially after your little *episode* when you got here.' He looks at Lee with a smirk, and it's like they're both having a laugh at my expense. Quite openly in front of me, as well; it's as if they think I won't notice or won't understand what's so funny. Maybe they think I've got something wrong with me. I decide it's best to not be cheeky.

'I'm fine,' I say, and offer them both a smile.

'I'm so stoked to have you boys here,' Seb says. 'I've got some really good things lined up.'

'Aye,' Lee says, looking at Seb. 'I was gonnae tell him last night, but I hink it's best coming fae you, big man.'

'*Big man*. You crack me up, Lee, you really do. Well, I have some little tasks for you. A few, sort of . . . initiation rituals.'

I turn to Lee. He looks at me, smirking.

'We're up fur anything, mate,' Lee says.

'Good, that's what I like to hear,' Seb says, and then his phone starts to ring. 'Sorry, I need to take this.'

My heart immediately starts thumping. Seb looks me up and down while he says, 'Mmm hmm,' a few times into the phone, and then turns around. 'Yeah, just leave it outside my door. I'll leave the cash under the doormat.'

I look at Lee and he nods back towards the bedroom. We take Seb turning his back on us as our cue to leave. Seb sits down in his gaming chair but then hangs up.

'Jamie, can I have a word with you real quick?' he says. I watch him put his phone down, and then I turn to Lee, who smiles and pats me on the back. He sort of pushes me forward at the same time, and leaves me alone with Seb.

'Awrite?' I say, walking round to stand in front of Seb.

He looks me up and down again. 'You're weird,' he says.

I feel my face flushing and turning red. I know I'm weird, but I like telling myself that no one notices how weird I am, because no one notices me at all.

'Aye,' I say.

'Don't be shy,' Seb says. 'Sit down.'

There are no other places to sit in the room. I go for the floor, sitting in front of Seb while he reclines back, feeling like he's my granda or something and he's telling me a story around a campfire – not that I've ever been in that situation, but you see it in films and that.

I notice how dirty the soles of my socks are, and move my hands to cover them. Why, in this palace of filth, am I suddenly so self-conscious about my own hygiene? I should be in my element.

'Why did you come here, Jamie?'

'I'm no sure,' I say. 'Cause Lee invited me, really.'

'I thought you were having problems back home? I thought your mom was giving you a hard time?'

'Aye, well, that anaw.'

Seb's eyes are going all over my face and body. I can tell he's trying to suss me out. I feel like he already knows too much about me.

'Do you *want* to be here?' he asks.

'Aye,' I say, trying to sound cheerful so he doesn't think I'm ungrateful.

'Good,' he replies. 'Actually, would you mind coming with me for a little walk?'

'Eh, aye,' I say.

'Go and get your shoes on, and meet me at the front door, okay?'

I do as I'm told again.

I go into our room and shut the door behind me. 'Seb wants me tae go fur a walk wi him,' I say to Lee who's lying on the bed.

'Just the two ae yeez?'

'Aye, I think so.'

'That's weird. How am I no invited?' Lee says.

I can't tell if he's joking or not, so I just shrug my shoulders and go to put my shoes on.

'Where yeez gawn?'

'I dunno, man,' I say, to no reply. I turn to Lee, and he's lying back, looking up at the ceiling. 'You awrite?' I ask him.

'Aye, fine,' he says. 'Have fun.'

I stand still for a moment, feeling sick, waiting and hoping

Lee will kill off this tension he's created, or that I've maybe imagined.

'See ye later, then,' I say. 'I'll no be long.'

'Sound,' he replies, not looking at me.

I'm not expecting a cuddle or anything dramatic like that, but a goodbye of any form wouldn't go amiss. I leave the room and shut the door behind me, leaving Lee to stew in the horrible, awkward air.

Seb stands with his hands in his pockets, waiting for me in the close. 'Come on, buddy,' he says, his voice echoing around the stairwell.

I trot along behind him until we emerge outside. In the brightness of the day, it hits me just how far away I am from home.

'You okay?' Seb asks me.

'Aye,' I say, trying to keep a panic attack at bay. I take a couple of deep breaths and shut my eyes. I can feel the warm sun on my face. The panic attack seems to go away. I open my eyes and look at Seb, who smiles at me and starts walking.

'You know,' Seb says, 'I read this article once that said it's easier to have deep and meaningful conversations with someone when you're walking side by side. Something about the way you and the other person are moving towards the same destination makes the true feelings come out.'

'Eh, cool,' I say.

'Maybe not then,' he laughs. 'Smoke?'

I nod and he hands me his packet. On the front is a wee guy reaching for the fag in his maw's mouth. I pull one out and stick it in my gub and Seb lights it for me. I get an up-close look at his dirty, yellow fingernails. With my free hand, I instinctively reach to my pocket to check my phone while Seb lights his own fag. I realise it's still in the bedroom, turned off.

'You miss your phone, huh?' Seb laughs.

'Aye, sorry,' I say, smiling.

'It's just for safety. Mine and yours. I don't want anyone knowing about this place.'

'Aye, it's awrite, I get it.'

'We can't go too far on this walk, either. Just in case. Let's just walk around the courtyard for a bit.'

I nod and we walk side by side in silence, puffing away. I look down at the ground as we walk, trying to trick my brain into thinking that I'm back home and just walking down my own street. If I look up and I see the flats or the surrounding area, my brain will go into panic mode again.

'Jamie?' Seb says suddenly, causing me to flinch. 'My god. You have got to be the most nervous boy on the planet. You're like a fucking chihuahua!'

I laugh and then suck too hard on my fag. I inhale too much and start coughing as it burns the back of my throat. Seb is pissing himself laughing.

'You're alright, you're alright,' he says, rubbing my back. I can feel his fingers as they go over my ribs and backbone. 'Fuck, you're skinny.'

I spit on the ground and then move away from him slightly. 'I know.'

'Look at that,' Seb says, pointing across the road. A guy and a lassie are walking hand in hand. 'Doesn't that make you feel sad, Jamie?'

'I dunno,' I say. 'Not really. Maybe. Kinda.'

'He gets to walk around with a girl. Okay, she's maybe only a six, a seven at a push. But you just get to walk around with me.'

We stop and watch them as they walk away from us. 'Suppose it'd be nice to have a girlfriend,' I say.

Seb scoffs. 'Come on, man! I mean this with no disrespect, but look at you! You won't get a girlfriend unless you go through a second or third puberty.'

I notice I'm trying to make myself look and feel smaller for some reason.

'But him?' Seb says, nodding at the guy. 'Look at how big his arms are. The V-shaped back. The slick haircut. He'll be fucking her brains out tonight while you rot away in bed with your friend. Hey, maybe you could jack each other off!'

I turn and look at him. I want to say, 'Wit the fuck?', but think better of it.

'What?' he says. 'I'm joking. But seriously, it's bullshit. Women just don't give a fuck about guys like us. They won't even look at us, but they'll suck the dicks of guys who won the genetic lottery. And that's all it is, a fucking lottery. Some people win, but we certainly lost. We lost the second we were born, my friend.'

'Aye, maybe,' I say. I realise I've given this guy nothing but pure shite answers to any questions he's asked me and I feel even more self-conscious.

'Tell me about your dad,' Seb says. 'What's he like? Is he still on the scene?'

I feel like I'm being interrogated. 'Aye, he's fine,' I reply. 'Him and my maw split up when I was younger. He was quite bad tae her, I think. He had a hard time growing up. A lot of unresolved issues, maybe.'

'How often do you see him?'

'Just once every few months, really. No very often.'

'You miss him? You wish he was still around?'

'I don't know.' I drop my fag to the ground and stand on it. 'Sometimes.'

'You don't give much away, do you, Jamie?' Seb says, laughing. 'I like that. Cards close to your chest.'

I like that he likes that about me. I like that he seems to like me. He looks at me in a way that's different to other people. Most people, when they talk to me, I feel like I can tell that they don't want to be talking to me. But it feels like he's interested in me. Lee's like that too; well, he was up until right before I came on this walk.

'We should head back,' Seb says and starts walking. I follow. 'So, about this task I have for you and Lee. You wanna know what it is?'

'Aye, please,' I say. It's weird that I've said 'please', I think to myself. Like, *Please give me this task that's almost certainly going to make me anxious as fuck.*

'Well, tonight you'll do a dry run, a practice attempt. I want you and Lee to go out and follow and scare a couple of foids, okay?'

'Wit d'ye mean, *follow?*'

'Follow them a little,' he says, while laughing. 'Nothing bad. Just make them feel uncomfortable, the way you're made to feel uncomfortable.'

'And then what?' I feel like I'm going to be sick.

'That's it – for tonight, anyway. I just wanna see how you are at following instructions. I've had a few boys come down here, and they've mostly all let me down. I had to send the last batch away, but I've got a good feeling about you, Jamie.'

I'm torn between complete terror at the thought of what I'm going to have to do later, and feeling chuffed that he thinks I'm capable of doing something for him.

'Let's go back upstairs,' Seb says.

We head back to the flat without saying anything else.

I lie across the bottom of the bed sideways while Lee is passed out with his head on the pillow at the top, so we form a sort of right angle. I hear Seb rummaging about outside our room, and the clinking of bottles. I don't know what he's up to, and I don't really want to know. I don't want to get up.

Listening to Lee's breathing, I try and work out whether he's still going to be weird with me when he wakes up. Occasionally, he does a deeper inhale, followed by a long exhale that sounds like someone sighing, the way they'd do if they were annoyed at you. Sometimes, he makes a wee humming sound, which seems happy and cheerful and like he's sort of singing. I close my eyes. I try and imagine my room, the shape and size of it, the feeling of my bed and every single bit of rubbish, and hope that when I open my eyes I'll be back there, in amongst it all.

Lee moves his feet and kicks me softly. 'Fuck ye dain doon there?' he says, causing me to flinch like I'm being attacked.

'I didnae want tae lie up next tae ye in case I woke ye up,' I reply.

'How wis your walk? When did ye get back?'

'Ages ago, man. I've been sleeping anaw. Why am I so tired?'

'Same, mate. It's been a big couple ae days, I suppose. We've travelled the whole length ae Britain and walked a fucking marathon anaw.'

He doesn't seem annoyed at me, which is nice. I sit up with my back against the wall and watch him as he lies with his eyes still closed.

'We should get up,' he says. 'Go an talk tae Seb. See if we can get something tae eat.'

'Aye, man.'

He gets up and stretches. His T-shirt rides up as he does so, and I can see that even though he's skinny like me, he's got what looks like a six-pack. I immediately feel like I'm less of a guy than him.

'Stoap eyeing me up,' he says, laughing.

'I'm no,' I say, and look down at my hands. My finger automatically starts picking at the skin around my thumb again.

'Your mission,' Seb says, pacing around the living room while we sit on the floor in front of the telly, 'should you choose to accept it, is to find and follow a foid.'

I turn to Lee, who's nodding. I feel like running and jumping out the window.

'You don't need to do anything to this foid when you find and follow them, but your task is to make them *run*. Bonus points if they scream.' Seb looks at us and smiles. 'You ready?'

Lee nods again and turns to me, looking excited. I force my mouth into a smile.

I am fucking shitting myself.

'This is where it all happens,' Seb says as we turn on to a busy street. 'The bright lights of London.'

Loads of takeaways line the street on either side, with their orange and yellow signs flashing brightly. People mill around; people charge by us. There's loads of taxis and guys on scooters and bikes. There's lassies, but they're all in pairs or groups.

'Wit aboot her,' Lee says, pointing at a lassie, maybe about our age, across the road.

'Yeah, she'll do nicely,' Seb says.

'Who's gawn first?' Lee says, turning to me.

'I think it's gotta be Jamie,' says Seb.

Fuck. They're both staring at me with their eyes wide, pure grinning.

'Let's go,' Seb says, ushering us across the road. I have to do a half-jog to keep up with him and Lee. A guy on a wee motorbike thing shouts something at me in another language. Or maybe it was just his English accent I couldn't understand.

We speed up until we see the lassie again. She has her hair in a ponytail and earphones in. She turns back, and I look anywhere except at her. I don't want to do this.

'Ah, this is good,' Seb says, as she does a sharp right and goes into a newsagent's. 'Okay, Jamie – you wait here. We'll cross the street and watch you, and follow you from a distance to see how you get on, okay?'

Before I can answer, him and Lee are across the road. I look around and see everyone else who's just standing about is either talking to someone or looking at their phones. I do neither and just stand and stare off into the distance, wondering how the fuck I've ended up in this situation. I wonder if I could just run away again. Fuck knows what I'd do, though, with no phone, no money and no idea where I am. I cross my arms, then uncross them and put my hands in my pocket. Then I take them out again and hold my face in my hands. I can just tell something bad is going to happen.

The lassie comes out and carries on in the direction she was going. I look across to see Seb and Lee grinning and giving me the thumbs-up. I start following behind her.

I keep my head down and only glance up occasionally. Every time I glance up, it's as if the lassie starts walking faster. I can feel myself getting light-headed, and a stitch in my side starts to scream at me.

She turns round and looks at me, then looks across the road and keeps walking. There's less people around now, and I can hear my own footsteps. I can hear the contents of her bag jangling and bouncing as she speeds up. I look across, and Seb has his arm around Lee, laughing as they watch me. Seb does a sweeping motion with his arm, as if to say *hurry up*. It's getting darker as we seem to get off the main street and more houses appear.

The lassie turns right, and now we're both on a quiet street, just the two of us. I start to panic even more. I think I hear Seb say, 'Oh fuck,' but I don't know if my mental state is making me hear things. I swear the lassie must be able to hear my heart beating now, it's so quiet.

'Are you following me?' she shouts at me.

I stop dead and don't know what to say.

She stops as well. 'I'll just phone the police right now if you are,' she says, holding her phone out in front of her. She sounds like she's off the telly; she has a lovely voice. I feel myself turning red.

'Naw, am sorry,' I say. I feel like I'm going to burst out crying. 'Please don't phone the police.'

'What are you doing?' Her voice crackles and her eyes are wide open. I can see loads of white. Her chest rises and falls quickly, the way mine must have when I was having my panic attacks.

'I don't know,' I say. 'I'm sorry. I'm really sorry.' I turn round and start walking the other way. I glance back to see if she's phoning the police, but she's jogging away.

I turn left, and Seb and Lee are standing at a bus stop.

'What happened?' Seb says. 'Fuck, are you *crying*?!'

'He's greeting!' says Lee, laughing. 'Fucking hell, mate. You're such a fucking pussy.'

I lean against the bus shelter and take some deep breaths.

'Right, okay,' says Seb, quieter and calmer now. 'Did she say anything to you?'

'She said she wis gonnae phone the polis,' I say.

'And did she?'

'Naw, I don't think so. She ran away.'

'Okay, that's fine. You made her run, then?'

I nod.

'Well, you've got that look about you. You look scary some-times. I'd run away from you, too. You've got the eyes of a killer. You're like a fucking school shooter!'

Lee bursts out laughing and pulls out a fag.

'Okay,' Seb says. 'Lee, you're up next.'

We head back the way we came. Seb and Lee laugh and joke in front of me, while I hang behind. I can't get the way that lassie looked at me out of my head. She looked like she totally hated me. No one's ever looked at me like that before, I don't think. Maybe my maw, sometimes. Most of the time in school, people looked at me like they were either disgusted by me or they felt sorry for me or they thought I was funny-looking, but never like they hated me. I feel disgusting. I hope the lassie is alright, but I know she's almost certainly not.

'You awrite, mate?' Lee says to me, as we stop outside a takeaway that looks like a knock-off KFC. Seb looks around silently.

'I'm fine,' I say, visibly, obviously, not fine.

'It's awrite. It's just a game, mate. We're no gonnae dae anything.'

'I want tae go hame,' I whisper.

Lee doesn't reply. I look up at him and he rolls his eyes. 'Don't be a shitebag,' he says, after a moment.

'Her,' Seb says quietly, as a lassie goes between us and him.

I look at Lee and try to say, 'Don't,' but my mouth isn't working. It's all dried up.

The lassie is talking on the phone and doesn't hear him. She's laughing.

Lee goes to walk after, but Seb puts his hand out. 'Wait till I say go.'

Lee looks like a boxer getting ready for a fight, puffing out his cheeks and bouncing slightly on his toes.

'Okay, go,' Seb says, and Lee goes after her like a dug that's been let off its lead. He's got a swagger about him, like the cool guys at school had. Like he knows he's the man.

'We'll stay on this side for now,' Seb says, but doesn't look at me. 'We'll cross over further down. Let's go.'

I feel hatred towards him for the first time. Like I wish I was double my size and weight, so I could just fucking attack him and batter fuck out him for making us do this. For turning Lee into the guy he's becoming.

I walk behind him as we follow Lee. Lee turns back to look at us as the street gets quieter. He doesn't look as bold now. For some reason, this makes me feel more nervous. If he gets scared, I worry he might do something daft. I just get that feeling from him.

The lassie is still talking and laughing on her phone. I don't think she's noticed him yet. I can see puffs of smoke coming from her as she puffs on a vape. She uses it to gesture some-times as she's talking, waving her hands about, the blue light from the vape leaving wee trails in the dark.

We get to where the lassie I followed turned right, and now a couple appear, walking hand in hand towards us on the other side of the road. The guy looks at the lassie, looks behind her to Lee, then says something to his girlfriend as Lee speeds up.

'Oh my god! Rachel!' the girlfriend shouts. 'How have you been?' The couple cross the road, and the guy makes a move towards Lee, who stops dead. I turn to Seb, who looks terrified.

The lassie takes her phone away from her ear and looks around, confused. 'Sorry, do I know you?' she says.

'It's me, Charlotte,' the other lassie says, taking her arm. 'From, um, school.' She then nods towards Lee. 'Rachel' turns round and looks at him, and then us. Three guys standing behind her in the dark. It feels like the whole city has just been put on mute.

'You lost?' the boyfriend says to Lee. He looks like he could quite easily take on all of us. 'Haven't seen you round here before.'

'Be careful,' his girlfriend says to him, quietly.

Lee turns on his heels and walks towards us, wide-eyed with panic.

'Shit, fuck, let's go,' says Seb, breaking into a light jog. Lee goes by me, and I'm left frozen on the spot.

The lassie and the couple stare at me for a few seconds, and I stare back at them, not knowing what to do or say, wishing I could fall through the pavement and into the sewers below.

'Fuck off,' the guy shouts.

I do as I'm told.

26

FIONA

'Ma,' I say down the phone. 'Right, don't panic.'

'Wit is it?!' she shouts in reply, very much panicked. 'Wit's wrang noo?! Wit's happened?!'

'Nothing, well, it's just . . . I cannae find Jamie.'

'You've goat tae be joking me, Fiona. Honest tae god, hen.'

'I checked his room last night, an he wisnae there, an I thought he'd be back this morning an he's no – an his phone's aff, an I don't know wit tae dae.'

'Have ye phoned the polis? Have ye done anything?'

'Naw, I've just woke up. I thought he'd have been hame by noo.'

'So the wean goes missing, an you just go ae your bed, aye? How'd ye no phone me?'

'I didnae know wit the right thing tae dae wis, am sorry.'

'Right, I'll come doon. Try an phone him again, an have a think aboot where he might be, awrite?'

'Aye, okay.'

She hangs up the phone on me, but not before I hear her

say, 'Fucking hell.' I go up to check his room one more time, hoping that, somehow, he'll have just materialised. I pull back his curtains. His room looks even worse in the light of day. The amount of dust in the air looks like snow as it passes by his window, stirred up by me swinging the door open. His covers and mattress are covered in creamy yellow stains. Piles of stuff – in fact, it's really one big pile of clothes and rubbish – fill the whole room. Bottles filled to the brim with piss, rotting food, flies, wrappers – it's like a dump. My ma is going to go ballistic at me when she sees the state of this. I don't think she's seen the inside of his room since he was just a wee boy, and I was able to keep it all neat and tidy before he decided to stop letting me in.

My phone buzzes and I reach for it, hoping it's him, but it's not. It's a Facebook friend request from Jacqui. I click on her profile. Her picture is her, and someone who I presume is Lee's da, and Lee at what looks like Ayr Beach. I feel sick as I imagine something happening to that wee ginger boy in the middle with sun cream on his nose. I click on her profile. She's already posted about him.

If anybody's heard from Lee please let me know as he's missing and I'm worried sick. He was wearing a black trackie the last I saw him and white trainers.

A picture underneath shows Lee, sitting on a couch with a wee baby in his arms. About a dozen people have commented, asking if she's phoned the police or saying they'll keep an eye out for him, or just saying they're really sorry but they're sure he'll turn up. I'm going to have to do this for Jamie if I can't get a hold of him soon. Oh god, I don't even know what the most recent picture I have of him is. Probably his last school picture. I check his Facebook just to see if he has any – maybe he's taken a selfie recently or something – but no. His profile picture is something from a game. He's also unfriended me.

I shut his door and go to walk back down the stair, but my legs are like jelly and I have to sit down. I sit on the top stair and my head falls between my legs. I grab the back of my head and start pulling at my hair. I can't believe this is happening.

I feel like I'm going to be sick all over myself. I wish I could just go back to bed so I don't have to deal with this. I start to cry. That's twice in twenty-four hours; I'm going mental. I hate crying, I always have. It feels to me like something people only do for attention, or maybe it's like an evolutionary thing to let other people know you're in distress from before we could talk. It doesn't feel like something that should happen to you on your own, but here I am, sobbing like a child. And any moment now, my ma will come in through the front door and rant and rave and scream and shout at me about how useless I am at everything. I let out a scream and I go numb.

'Fiona!' my ma shouts as she comes in the front door. I hear her footsteps going down the hall and into the living room. '*Fiona!*'

I almost run into her as she comes back out.

'There you're there,' she says softly. 'I thought *you'd* went missing anaw.'

215

'Naw, I'm here,' I say.

She puts her arm around me and we go into the living room. 'Ye awrite?' she asks, making me sit down on the couch.

I rub my eyes and clean the snotters from my nose with the sleeve of my jumper. I look up at her and concern is written all over her face, in every one of her wrinkles, instead of the anger I was expecting. She frowns and snarls when she's angry; this time, her eyes are wide and her face is neutral. I can tell she's worried, but she's holding it in.

'His wee pal is missing as well,' I say. 'His ma told me.'

'Does she know that Jamie is tae?'

'Naw, no yet. Should I tell her?'

My ma takes a minute, looking deep in thought. She's very logical and breaks things down into steps, trying to work things out so they can be done in the simplest way possible. Maybe she's just working out how best to pin this on me.

'Well, they're probably thegither, int they? Wherever they are,' she says, walking over to the window.

'Aye, you're right.'

'Have ye goat this woman's number?' she says after a few moments, turning round and biting her nails.

'Aye.'

She spits out a fragment of fingernail and says, 'Phone her, or gie me yer phone an I'll dae it.'

I pull out my phone and navigate to Jacqui's name, but I can't bring myself to press the call button. I hand it to my ma without saying anything. She grabs it from me and holds it to her ear. I wish I had even half the confidence she has.

'Hiya, listen,' my ma says, turning away from me and

walking to the window. 'Am Fiona's ma. Oor Jamie's missing anaw.'

She says, 'Mmm hmm,' in reply a few times, and then, 'I know, I know. Right, aye, we're in, hen. Just come roon.'

She turns to me and says, 'It's gonnae be fine. We'll find him.'

I nod and hold my head in my hands again. I feel my ma breeze by me, and then hear the sound of the kettle clicking on. I stand up and catch sight of myself in the mirror above the fireplace. I take out my bobble and put my ponytail back in tighter. I look slightly less dishevelled and slightly more presentable now. Except for the snotters glistening on my sleeve.

'Can I have a coffee?' I shout in to my ma.

'Naw,' she says. 'That's the last hing ye need. It'll make ye aw jittery.'

She rattles the spoon around each cup, then picks each tea bag out with her fingers and drops them into the sink with a wet thud. A third cup lies waiting – for Jacqui, I presume. Or maybe she made one for Jamie without thinking.

'I hope he's no done this tae get back at you,' she says to me as we sit down in the living room.

My stomach flips. I hadn't thought of that. I don't know what to say in response, but she doesn't seem to be wanting one anyway.

We sit in silence until the door goes. My ma gets up straight away to answer it. 'Hiya, hen,' I hear her say. 'Aye, come in, come in. Through there.'

Jacqui walks into the living room. She's wrapped in a

housecoat. Tartan pyjama bottoms cover her dirty white trainers. I can smell smoke off her.

I meet her gaze and give her a half-smile, but it's as if she's looking right through me.

'Cuppa tea, hen?' my ma asks her.

'Naw, I'm fine,' she replies. She sits next to me on the couch. My ma stands in front of us.

'Any word?' I ask Jacqui.

'Naw,' she says. 'His phone's still aff. Polis urnae being very helpful, either.'

'I thought Jamie was just sleeping,' I say. 'I never realised he wisnae here until this morning.' Jacqui looks at me and I think I can see suspicion in her eyes. I hope she doesn't think I've got anything to do with them disappearing.

'Right,' my ma says. 'I don't know how much we can dae here, but I'll phone the polis an see if I can get their arses intae gear. Have they gave you a number or anything?'

'Aye,' Jacqui says, pulling out a card. She hands it to my ma. 'That's the guy I spoke tae.'

My ma hands the card to me, along with my phone. The card is all worn around the edges already, as if Jacqui has been constantly holding it. The Police Scotland logo looks so big and important and angry. Graham Fitzpatrick is the man who I'll have to ask to find my son. 'Put that number in yer phone, Fiona, so I can talk tae him.'

I do it, and hand the card back to Jacqui. She slips it into her housecoat pocket.

'I better get gawn,' she says. 'I'm sorry Jamie is missing tae.'

'Thank you,' I say. 'We'll find them.'

218

She looks at me, but I can't read what she's thinking; her face is blank. She leaves and my ma goes after her to see her out. I hear my ma say something to her, but it's so quiet I can't make it out. Immediately I think it's cause it's something she doesn't want me to hear, but then I think maybe my ma's just being gentle with her.

'This is fucking tragic, int it?' my ma says as she comes back into the living room. 'Two wee boays just disappearing.'

'It's horrible,' I reply.

'They'll no have went far, surely. Jamie disnae have a clue. Has he ever been oan a bus or a train by himself?'

'Naw, I don't think so.'

My ma looks deep in thought as she sits back down. She starts biting her nails again. It's weird seeing her look worried. 'I wonder if he's spoke tae his da,' she says.

'Maybe,' I say.

'Gies yer phone,' she says, standing up and looking ready to go to war. 'Ye still goat his number?'

'Aye.' I bring up his number on my phone and hand it to my ma. She presses the button and holds it up to her ear. She holds it away from her slightly and says, 'I'll phone the polis efter this.'

I nod.

'Listen,' she says into the phone as the ringing stops. 'Is Jamie wi you?'

'Eh, naw. How?' I hear Danny reply. Hearing his voice makes me feel instantly sick. I feel my shoulders tense up. Like a dog raising its hackles.

'Ye sure?' my ma says. She can sound aggressive at the best of times, but this is something else. I think I'm terrified of her.

'He's no here. Has something happened?' Danny says. He sounds scared.

'Naw, never mind,' my ma says and hangs up. 'Arsehole.'

I sit on the couch, staring down at the rug. My ma stands at the window, keeping an eye out for the police. This is absolutely mortifying. The idea of other people seeing the motor pull up and police coming to my door makes me want to go up the stair and jump out the window. I'd rather they saw me getting taken away in an ambulance than that. I can just imagine their curtains twitching, and how they'll gossip and speculate at why they're here.

'Think that's them,' my ma says.

I jump up and look out. I can see a black motor through the hedge. Thank god they've no came in a proper police motor with the lights on and all that. The heads of two tall guys appear over the hedge. One is baldy and maybe my age, the other is younger with a haircut like a presenter off the telly. They're smiling as they walk down the path. We both move away from the window and head for the front door.

'Hi, Police Scotland,' the baldy one says as my ma opens the door. I hang back a little bit.

'Come in,' my ma says to them.

I turn and walk into the living room. The sound of their shoes on the wooden floor of the hall is so loud as they come in behind me.

'Right,' my ma says. Her voice seems slightly deeper than normal, like she's trying to intimidate the guys. 'Tea or coffee or water or anything?'

'No, we're fine, thanks,' says the baldy guy. He turns to me, smiles slightly and says, 'I'm Graham, by the way.'

'Fiona,' I say.

'And it's your son who's missing, is that right?'

'Aye, that's right.'

'What's his full name?' He pulls out a notepad as he asks this, and sits poised with his pen. The guy with the hair hasn't said a word.

'Jamie Skelton.'

'And how old is he?'

'Nineteen.'

'Nineteen,' he says. 'Difficult age.'

I don't know what the fuck he means by that, but he looks at me smiling again, so I force a smile back, in case he thinks I'm mental – or worse, have done something. Please just think I'm normal.

'I telt ye aw this oan the phone,' my ma chimes in.

I can tell the guys are doing that thing where they change their accent to sound more professional. My ma's thick east-end accent sounds even more pronounced amidst their stupid voices.

'Aye, it's just to make sure we've got everything correct,' he says.

My ma puts a bit of chewing gum into her mouth and then crosses her arms. She's standing while we're all sitting.

Graham turns his gaze back to me, clears his throat and says, 'We need a description of him. Height, weight, hair colour and what he might be wearing.'

'Em, he's maybe five fit seven, five fit eight. Skinny, eight stone or something. Dark hair, messy, wee bit curly, longish. He's probably wearing black. Black joggies and a black T-shirt.'

'Great. And when was the last time you saw him?'

'Sunday night. I didn't realise he was gone until last night, though.'

'And why didn't you phone the police last night?' he asks, not looking up at me.

'I just assumed he'd be back by the morning,' I say.

He nods. 'Has he done this before?'

My stomach flips. 'Naw.'

Graham turns to his colleague, then writes something down. I look to my ma. She looks angry at me.

'Is his father on the scene?'

'We split up a while ago. I've already phoned him; well, my ma did. He's no wae him.'

'Any thoughts on where he'd maybe go? Any other relatives or friends he may be in touch with.'

'Naw, I doubt it. Well, I think he's maybe wae his pal, Lee. He's missing as well.'

Graham looks at the other guy again, and scribbles something else down. One of their radios crackles with static, causing me to flinch.

'Has anything happened recently that might have upset him? A death in the family or something?'

'Naw, nothing like that. Me and him have had a couple of arguments recently, but nothing major.'

'Do you mind if I have a look at his bedroom? Have you looked to see if he maybe left a note?'

Fuck. I really don't want men in my house full stop, never

mind two policemen. And I especially don't want them poking around Jamie's room. I don't want my ma to see the state of his room, either.

'Aye,' I say, trying my best to not sound apprehensive. 'Up the stair.'

I get up and they follow me. My ma mutters something under her breath, but I don't know what. I get to the top of the stairs and pull my own bedroom door shut. 'In there,' I say, nodding at Jamie's door.

Graham goes in first, with his colleague trailing behind. The two of them stand in the path through the rubbish and other detritus Jamie has made. They look massive in his tiny room.

I cover my face with my hand. 'Sorry aboot the mess,' I say.

'Jesus Christ,' says my ma, poking her head round the door-frame.

'We've seen worse, don't worry,' says Graham. He'll be telling all his pals at the station about the state of this wee boy's room. *How can his ma let him live like that?* is what he'll say, I'll bet. I can tell they think I'm a terrible, feckless mother.

'We'd be here aw day looking through this,' the other officer says quietly. I assume he doesn't mean for me to hear it, but the house is so quiet. Graham nods.

'Does Jamie have any medical conditions? Mental health problems?' he asks.

'Eh, well, he's never been diagnosed with anything, but I suppose he's been quite withdrawn the last few years.'

'He's goat suhin wrang wi him, I'll tell ye that,' says my ma.

'I see,' says Graham, making another note. 'Can we just have a quick look in your bedroom as well?'

He walks by me as he asks this, so I have no time to protest. He walks into my room and stands at the foot of my bed, looking around. The other guy skulks in after him and opens my wardrobe. I feel sick.

'Aw, fur fuck sake,' shouts my ma. 'Ye gonnae check under the bed anaw, aye? Ye want tae check her poakits?'

'I'm sorry,' says Graham. 'This is all standard procedure. You'd be surprised where people turn up.'

My ma shakes her head. She looks like she's going to explode.

'We'll just check the back garden now,' says Graham, and they both head down the stair ahead of us.

Me and my ma stand at the kitchen window, watching the two guys walk around the back garden. I wonder if they think Jamie will pop up out of the ground. Jesus Christ, maybe they think I've buried him out there. Why else would they be checking out there? I break out in a sweat.

'Fucking hopeless,' my ma says. 'The fucking state ae them.'

The guys come back in, and my ma says, 'Did ye no find him oot there then, naw?'

Graham chooses to ignore her, and instead he asks me, 'Do you have any pictures of Jamie?'

'I don't have any actual photies. Just an auld school picture, but I don't know where I've put it.' If you could see shame, it'd be dripping off me right now.

'Well, if you find it, or if you've got any on your phone, then just email them to me as soon as you can,' he says, handing me the same card he gave to Jacqui.

'I will,' I say, knowing full well that I'm not going to have any.

'Is that it?' says my ma. 'Ye turn up, ask a few questions, look in the fucking wardrobe and away ye go?'

'I know this is a . . . difficult time,' says Graham. 'But I can assure you we'll do our best to get Jamie back. Most missing people turn up within forty-eight hours, so try not to panic. We'll be back in touch soon. In the meantime, keep trying to phone him, and keep an eye on his social media profiles, if he has any. And remember to send us some pictures as soon as you can, okay?'

'Aye,' I reply. 'I will. Thank you.'

'We'll be making some inquiries with your neighbours too, to see if anyone saw him leave, where he was heading, things like that,' Graham says, and then he takes his leave, along with his pal.

My ma makes a point of slamming the door shut after them. 'Fucking pigs,' she says, coming back into the living room.

27

JAMIE

'Fuck,' says Seb, as we all stumble through the front door. 'That was a fucking *disaster*. You two are *fucking* idiots, honestly.' He takes off his jacket and throws it down.

'Och, it wisnae that bad,' says Lee. I can tell he's just trying to act hard and confident, as his voice sort of croaks a wee bit.

'Especially you, Jamie,' Seb says, ignoring what Lee just said. 'You were fucking crying earlier. What's the matter with you?'

'I'm sorry,' I say, looking down at my feet.

'Look at you! You're like a child! Fucking look me in the eye when I speak to you.'

I look up. Seb has his hands balled into fists. I turn to Lee, hoping he'll be on my side.

'Shitebag,' Lee says to me. He then looks to Seb for approval.

Seb looks at each of us then sighs. He puts his hands on his hips and looks up at the ceiling, biting his lip.

'One more chance,' he says, a bit calmer now. 'If you fuck up again, you're on the first bus back to your shitty little lives in fucking Scotland. Okay?'

'We won't,' says Lee. He looks me up and down.

Seb heads through to the living room while we stand in the hall. I hold Lee's gaze, trying my best not to burst into tears.

'Are you pussies gonna come in here and have a beer or what?' Seb shouts.

'I'm gonnae go ae bed,' I say.

'Naw yer fucking no,' Lee replies. 'I didnae come aw the way doon here fur you tae fuck this up fur me.'

'Wit?'

'This is the best place fur us. If we cannae stay here, then we need tae go back hame and deal wi aw the fucking shite back there. Am no fucking gawn back, awrite?' He says it in that mad half-whisper half-shout thing people do sometimes when they're annoyed.

'Things urnae that bad back hame. Better than this, anyway – this is fucking mental.'

'You don't know wit it's like fur me back up the road. Noo, don't fuck this up.' Lee grabs the back of my hoodie and pushes me forward towards the living room.

'Okay,' Seb says, as I stumble into the room. He holds a can of lager at his mouth and takes a big drink from it. 'I've calmed down. I'm sorry for yelling at you guys.' He picks up his game controller and puts on some music. I don't know much about music, but I know this is shite. It's just guitars and some guy with an American accent moaning about something.

'It's awrite,' says Lee. I look at him, and he smiles at me and winks. I can't handle all these mixed signals, man. I feel like I'm going mental, being pushed and pulled in opposite directions.

'You know what I think it is?' Seb says.

'Wit wit is?'

'I think being around foids is bad for guys. Bad energy and bad vibes. They make us act all weird. If they don't make you want to fuck them, they make you want to kill them.'

'Fucking too right, man,' Lee says. 'If am around my maw fur too long, I feel pure angry.'

I sit down on the floor. I'm knackered and I want to go to bed, but I don't know what'll happen if I do. I don't trust Seb, and I worry what will happen to Lee. That Seb'll poison his brain more than he has already.

'How did that chase make you feel, Jamie?' Seb says. He turns the music down a little bit.

'I don't know,' I say, picking at the carpet.

'*Ah don't know,*' Seb says, copying my accent. He sounds like he's talking with his nose pinched shut. I hope I don't actually sound like that. Lee bursts out laughing.

'Hey, you don't sound much better, my friend,' Seb fires at Lee, but it seems friendly and Lee just laughs again. 'Jamie, give me a proper answer. How did it make you feel?'

I sigh and say, 'I don't know,' again.

'You know,' Seb says. 'I think you're a pretty selfish and rude person, Jamie. You never engage with conversations, you never ask any questions.'

'Naw, it's no that. I'm just shy, I'm just quiet. I don't really like talking.'

Being called selfish or rude is one of the worst things you could say to me. I was always told at primary school by the teachers that I was really polite and nice, and I always got good report cards and all that. My teacher would always say how nice I was to my maw at parents' night and stuff like that. Once I got to secondary school, it turned out that being quiet wasn't allowed. I'd get into trouble for not participating in the class, for not answering questions, or for not asking for help if I was stuck on something. I just hate having to talk to other people in case they think I'm weird or I say something wrong and they laugh at me. It's just easier to stay quiet.

I want to say all that to Seb, but I can't. Instead, I say, 'I'm sorry.'

'Well, to be fair,' says Seb, 'that's what most incels are like.'

'Am no shy,' says Lee.

'No, you're certainly not.' Seb laughs and leans back in his gaming chair. 'Jamie, ask me a question. Lee and I are the guests on your chat show or your podcast or whatever. Ask us anything.'

Lee sits down next to him. Seb hands him a can.

'I don't know,' I say, and I turn my attention back to picking fluff from the carpet and rolling it into a ball between my fingers.

'Oh, come on!' Seb shouts. 'Lee, get him a beer. Let's see if we can loosen him up.'

Lee gets to his feet and scuttles to the kitchen. I look to Seb, who's smiling at me.

'You *can* talk, you know,' he says. 'You don't have to be afraid of me.'

'I'm no scared or anything like that,' I say, but I know he knows I'm lying. I know he knows I'm fucking terrified; not just at the thought of speaking, but at the idea of being here, a million miles from home.

'It's okay if you are,' he says. 'Most of the guys that come here are like you. Some have been a lot worse.'

I nod.

'It's good that you have Lee, you know? I hear you talking to him with no problems.'

'Aye,' I say. 'It's different with him.'

'How come?'

Lee comes back into the living room and hands me a can. It's a kind of beer I've never seen before. Maybe it's American like Seb, or maybe it's English. I don't want to answer Seb's question while Lee's in the room.

'I don—' I stop myself from using my new catchphrase. 'Eh, it's just cause he's my pal, I suppose.'

'That's fair,' says Seb. 'Anyway, I get that you're quiet. I won't push you any further. I want you to be happy and comfortable here.'

I nod.

'Here, see that lassie I followed?' Lee says, looking worried all of a sudden, with his brow furrowed and voice lowered. 'She won't, like, phone the polis or anything, will she? I won't get in trouble, will I?'

Seb laughs. 'This is a big city, my friend. You can get away with anything here. No one knows we're here. No one knows our names, or where we came from, or anything. Don't worry about that.'

'Sound,' Lee says, looking relieved. He looks at me and smiles, then opens his can. I do the same. It smells and tastes bogging.

★   ★   ★

'Wit's the plan for the morra?' Lee says, lying on his belly on the floor.

'I'm glad you asked, Lee,' says Seb, standing up from his chair with a groan. I pull my knees up to my chest to keep out of his way. 'Now, you know I got you boys down here to do a job for me, right?'

'Aye,' says Lee. I nod.

'As you can appreciate, it cost me a lot of money to get you down here, and to get you away from your lives back home. So this is how you guys can pay me back.' He looks at both of us in turn. I get a mad tingly feeling in the back of my neck. It's one of those moments you hope lasts forever, because you're scared of what's going to come next.

Seb leaves and I hear him rustling around in another room.

'I don't like this,' I whisper to Lee.

'Don't worry,' he replies. 'It'll be awrite. It won't be anything mental.'

His words don't reassure me in the slightest. Seb comes back into the room holding a white plastic bottle, about the size of a bottle of Coke.

'You boys know what this is?'

I look at Lee, who is looking at Seb with his eyes narrowed. He shakes his head.

'It's a very powerful acid,' Seb says, holding it aloft. 'Sulphuric acid.'

My brain immediately tells me that the safest course of action to take right now is to run and jump out the window, head first, or I'm going to be dissolved.

'Wit the fuck,' says Lee. He looks as rattled as I feel.

Seb throws the bottle in the air so it spins. I flinch as he catches it, imagining the lid coming right off, and it all coming out and covering me.

'Don't worry,' says Seb. 'It's not for you.'

'How'd ye get that? Where dae ye even get a bottle ae acid?'

'I can get anything. You name it and I'll get it for you – if you do this job for me.'

'Wit we meant tae dae wi that?' asks Lee, nodding at the bottle. 'You goat a deid boady yer wanting rid ae or something?'

'Yeah, because a litre is all you'd need to get rid of a whole fucking body,' Seb says, sarcastically. 'Well, maybe it would be if it was Jamie you were getting rid of.'

Jump out the window, man, just jump out the window and all of this is over, my brain says to me.

Lee nods at me and says, 'Ye don't want me tae kill him, dae ye?'

'Jesus Christ,' Seb exclaims. 'Nobody's killing anybody!'

'Right, that's awrite then,' Lee says. He looks relieved. We're about to be given some kind of job involving a litre of sulphuric acid, and he looks relieved. I am in a flat in London with my pal and an American guy he met on a forum who's convinced us we're incels and who is holding a bottle of acid, and Lee looks *relieved*. I feel like my head is going to explode.

'There's this fucking foid who I *absolutely* hate. She's the most fucking *vapid* and self-obsessed creature who's ever walked this earth, and I wanna teach her a lesson. This,' Seb says, holding the bottle towards us, 'is how we're gonna do it.'

'Wit d'ye mean?' Lee asks.

I don't care what he means. I don't care what he's got against this poor lassie, or what he's going to do. I just want to go home.

'You just throw some of this on her. It won't kill her, it'll just leave her with some burns. Some scars. Only superficial damage. Then she'll get to see what life is like when no one wants to look at you, never mind fuck you. She'll get to see what it's like to be like us.'

'I don't know, man,' Lee says, sounding nervous. 'Is that no a bit much? Could we no just . . . chase her, like we did wi the other lassies?'

'What?' Seb says. His face turns sort of angry-looking, and he seems even more raging than when he was talking about the lassie he wants to melt the face off of. 'Are you some kind of fucking pussy? An ungrateful pussy at that?'

'Naw, am sorry,' Lee says. He looks all sheepish, like when you back down from a teacher who you were being cheeky to at school.

'We're doing it tomorrow, so I suggest you get real cool with it real quick,' Seb says.

'Aye, you're right,' says Lee. 'Am up fur it. You are tae, int ye, Jamie?'

Say no. Say this is the worst, most disgusting thing you've ever heard in your life. Say there's no chance you're doing this and you're going home right now to your maw and you're never talking to Seb ever again in your entire fucking life and you hope he rots in the fucking jail.

'Aye,' I say.

Jesus fucking Christ. I'm an even worse guy than Seb,

because at least he has the balls to do and say evil things. I can't even say no.

'You still up?' Lee whispers to me. I don't know what time it is, but it's pitch black and the house is silent. I don't know when we went to bed. It could've been half an hour or three hours ago. Everything feels weird. I feel like I exist outside of time now. Like I'm just stuck in this horrible day forever.

'Aye,' I whisper back.

'I cannae sleep.'

'Same.'

We're lying side by side on our backs. I turn on to my side and face him.

'I want tae go hame,' I say. 'I cannae throw acid over some lassie.'

'I know, man,' he replies, turning to face me. 'Wit we gonnae dae?'

'Fuck knows.'

It's dark, but I can just about see that his eyes are open. They're glistening.

'Wit's stopping us leaving right noo?' I ask.

'He's goat oor phones. And wit if he catches us sneaking oot and throws that shit oan us?'

'This is a fucking nightmare, int it?'

'Aye.' Lee sighs. 'Maybe we can just dae wit he asks, then he'll let us go.'

'I'd rather no, tae be honest.'

'If he said tae us right noo, "Ye can throw acid oan somecunt and then ye can get the bus right back hame," I'd go oot an dae it right noo. I'd dae anything.'

'You seemed pure up fur it earlier,' I say. 'When we had tae chase they lassies.'

'I know, man. I just goat caught up in the heat ae the moment. Ye know how it is.'

I feel bad for Lee. I can tell he's the kind of guy who'd do anything to impress people.

'An you did it, anaw,' he says suddenly.

My stomach lurches. I feel like I'm going to shit the bed.

'Just don't go aboot thinking yer better than me,' Lee says.

'I don't think am better than you,' I say. 'I'm just saying, that's aw.'

Lee does a big sniff, as if his nose is running. I don't think I could ever be better than anybody. I'm scum.

'I'm sorry,' I say.

'It's awrite. We'll get oot ae here the morra an go back hame, somehow.'

'I wonder if my maw even knows I'm away,' I say. 'Will your maw have noticed?'

'Will she fuck,' he replies. 'Too busy worrying aboot my da. Worrying aboot how they're gonnae afford fags and bevvy.'

'I think my maw will be worried. My granny anaw.'

Lee doesn't say anything for a moment; he just sighs and then yawns. 'Maybe they will be missing me,' he says, his voice softer this time. 'Maybe things urnae that bad back up the road.'

'I think I miss my maw,' I say.

Lee is quiet and doesn't reply right away. Then he sniffs again and whispers, 'Same.'

28

FIONA

I was so sure I heard him come back home during the night that I got up and shouted his name. Thinking, in my still half-asleep state, that all of this was over. I checked his bedroom, then ran down the stair and checked the toilet and the living room – but no, nothing, and I had to slink back to bed. I stand, looking at the mess of his room again, leaning against the doorframe. Where would you even start to clean something like this? I hear a rustle from under the pile of rubbish and close the door, not wanting the mouse to explore the rest of the house. I stand at the top of the stairs, and my hand flies up to the back of my head without me even thinking. It grips hard, and when I pull it away and look at it, it's covered in my hair. I rub my fingers together and let it fall to the floor, then run my hands through my hair, feeling more strands breaking and ripping out of my scalp. I don't know if it's because of stress, or if it's the fact I haven't ran a brush through it, never mind washed it, in days. I imagine there are big bald patches, but I'm not checking. Another problem for another day.

I emailed the police last night with the most recent picture I have of Jamie, which was his last school picture. I found it in a box in my wardrobe. I have loads of him as a baby and up until he was maybe five or six, then nothing. They emailed back, asking if I had a more up-to-date one, and I just had to apologise and say that I don't take many pictures. Every single thing about this is making me feel like an even worse mother. Who doesn't have a relatively recent picture of their own child? Lee's ma had one of him that could've been taken a week ago for all I know.

I open my phone and check Facebook, only to see that picture straight away. I feel a lurch, immediately assuming it's a news article announcing their deaths. Then I realise it's a post from the police.

Police Scotland is appealing for information to help trace two teenagers missing from the east end of Glasgow.

19-year-old Jamie Skelton and 16-year-old Lee McGonigle were last seen in the Springboig area on Monday morning.

Jamie is described as being 5' 8", slim build, with dark brown medium-length hair, and possibly wearing black jogging bottoms and a black hoodie.

Lee is described as being 5' 10", slim build, with red short hair, and wearing a black tracksuit and white trainers.

Inspector Graham Fitzpatrick said:

'We are growing increasingly concerned for the welfare of Jamie and Lee, who have not been seen since Sunday.

'Officers are carrying out extensive searches and reviewing CCTV in an effort to trace them both, but there have been no confirmed sightings of them.

'I would urge anyone who has any information on the where-abouts of Jamie and/or Lee, or who has had contact with them, to call Police Scotland on 101.'

Jamie looks at me from my phone screen. He didn't like smiling in pictures as he got older, as he didn't like his teeth. I've never noticed how he had the dark circles under his eyes, even back then. Comments underneath the post say things like *Shared in East Kilbride, Shared in Motherwell,* and I think, why on earth would he be in East Kilbride or Motherwell? Other people say things like *So sad* and *Hope they're found soon.* Some people leave just the emojis for prayer hands and sad faces.

I should probably share it. But then everybody I know from work and from school and all the other semi-acquaintances I've accumulated throughout my life will all see that my son's gone missing. They'll maybe feel sorry for me. Or maybe they'll think, *Didn't even know she had a son.*

I hit the share button, and it gives me the option to write something to go with it. I write: *Jamie is missing, please can everybody keep an eye out and get in touch if you know where he is or if you hear from him. I'm really worried.*

I throw my phone on to the couch. I get up and look out the window to try and zone out. Focus on the clouds as they float behind the flats across the road and reappear out the other side. Deep breaths. Nobody's around. No noise. Everything will be fine. He'll appear at the front door soon, and everything will go back to normal.

Two policemen emerge from the close directly across from

me. I want to move away as they look at me, but I worry that that'll look dodgy, so I just look in a different direction. When I look back, they're going into the next close. They must be asking people around the scheme if they've seen Jamie and Lee. I wonder what they'll be saying about me and Jamie. I don't think I want to know.

I go into the kitchen to make a coffee. I pour a teaspoon of the granules into my cup, then remember my ma saying to me it'll make me feel worse. I pause for a moment and decide that I don't care – I can't possibly feel any worse than I do just now. The kettle shakes as it boils, and I start to feel angry at Jamie for doing this. He'll come back and everything will be fine for him, but I'll be left with the terrible guilt and shame. The kettle clicks off and I snap out of it.

I sit back down on the couch and pick up my phone, realising it's on silent. What if he's been trying to phone me and it goes to voicemail, and he thinks that I haven't even noticed he's away, or worse, that I have and I don't care? I stare at my phone: no notifications. I turn it on loud, set it down next to me, and sip my coffee. Immediately it buzzes. It's Gillian from work.

Hi Fiona, I'm so sorry to hear about Jamie. Are you okay? Have you heard from him at all?

Shit, I forgot to even phone my work and tell them what was happening.

> No news yet. I'm so sorry for not phoning in,
> I'm all over the place just now.

I am a walking disaster. I'm going to get sacked. I'm going to lose the very little that I have.

> Omg don't worry about that at all.
> Everything will be okay. I'm here if you
> need me, just give me a wee phone and I
> can go to the shops for you or drop round
> some dinner later. Anything you need at
> all, just phone me.

That's a nice gesture. She really is nice to me, Gillian. I feel bad for the times I've been short with her in work or just not wanted to speak to her.

> Thank you. X

I put my phone down and it starts ringing again. It's my ma.

'Am oan ma way doon, hen,' my ma says as I put it to my ear. 'Ye want anything in?'

'Naw, I'm fine,' I reply. I'm starving, but I really don't feel like eating.

'Have you even ate anything?'

'No yet, bu—'

'Fuck sake.' She sighs. 'Right, I'll bring ye something in. Be doon in hawf an oor.'

She hangs up without saying goodbye. I take a deep breath.

What can I do? How can I get this nightmare to be finished and over, and everything to go back to how it was? Should I go for a drive and see if I can find him? Is that just an excuse for me to get away from everything for a bit again? There are so many things I should be doing that I don't know where to start, and I just feel paralysed.

'Look at the state ae ye,' my ma says as she comes into the living room, carrying a blue poly bag. 'Go an brush yer hair an wash yer face. I'll make ye something tae eat.'

I sit and stare at her. I don't know what to say.

'Fiona, hen. Get it thegither. Come oan, wan hing at a time. Move, get in that toilet and sort yerself oot.'

I do as she says. I feel like I'm floating out of the room. I think something's snapped in my brain. I don't know why it's happened this morning, when nothing's changed since yesterday. I close the door and lock it behind me, then sit on the pan. I can hear my ma banging about in the kitchen, the sound of plates being stacked and cutlery being dropped back into its drawer. I don't feel like any of this is real. This doesn't happen to people like me. I'm supposed to live the most dull and boring and uneventful life, with nothing extremely bad happening. Nothing extremely good, either. I'm just supposed to exist quietly, minding my own business.

I stand up and grab my toothbrush and scrub away at my teeth, then splash my face with warm water. I quickly brush my hair and tie it up out of the way. My face looks different to how I remember it. Not like I've got a spot or some of my wrinkles have deepened or something; I just don't know who that woman is looking back at me. I've never seen her before. I take another deep breath, then drink some cold water from the tap and look back up. Back to normal. I need to get a grip.

I walk back into the kitchen, and my ma is buttering some toast. Two eggs are frying in what looks like a litre of oil on the hob. I could be sick at the thought of eating my ma's greasy eggs. She spins round and gives the pan a shake, then flips the eggs over with a wet splat.

She carries the pan over to the plates and slides the two eggs on to the toast for me. Yellow splashes dot around the plate. 'Here,' she says. 'Get that doon ye. It'll fill a wee hole.'

I stand and stare at the plate.

'Go an sit doon,' my ma says to me, as if I'm a wee lassie again.

I carry my plate into the living room, feeling like I'm back at school and carrying my tray to my table, alone, at lunchtime.

'Right,' my ma says, sitting on the other couch. 'I take it you've no seen anything oan that Facebook?'

'Wit d'ye mean? The thing the polis put up?' I cut off a corner of my toast and ignore the rapidly congealing egg.

'I was talking tae Helen next door, ye mind her?'

'Aye, eh, hingmies ma?'

'Aye. She was asking if I'd saw wit folk were sayin oan there aboot you and Jamie.'

'Wit? Who wis saying anything?'

'I don't know who they are. Helen showed me them oan her phone.'

I grab my phone and check Facebook. I find the post from

the police and check the comments. It's just a flurry of con-
dolences and people talking as if he's dead.

'It wis in a *group*,' she says. 'I don't know wit that means.'

I search for the Springboig page on Facebook. At the very
top, a post reads:

*Anybody had the polis at their door aboot they wee boys that
are missing?*

It has forty-odd comments, and it's only been up since late
last night. I brace myself and click to see more, knowing fine
well it's going to upset me.

I glance up at my maw, who's leaning forward. She looks
scared.

*I told them I've no seen that wee boy Jamie in ages. I thought
he'd moved away. He never looked well when I saw him walking
to school. So skinny.*

Aye, I said his maw's a weirdo.

*I think she's done something wi them. She knows where they
are.*

*The wee ginger wan's ma has been gone roon chapping doors.
No seen the other wan at aw. Thought it was strange she wisnae
oot looking fur him. If it wis ma boy I'd be oot 24/7 until I
found him.*

I think I recognise some of the names. I move my plate off my lap, put my phone down and hold my face with my hands.

'They're idiots, hen. Don't worry aboot it,' my ma says, but I can barely hear her. I feel like I have pins and needles inside my brain. I move my hands away and take a deep breath. When I open my eyes, my vision's all weird.

'I cannae handle this,' I say, and shut them again. 'I just want him hame.'

'He'll be hame soon. Don't worry. There's nothing we can dae the noo, but he'll be awrite.'

'Wit if he's no?' I say, but it comes out as a shout. 'Wit then? And everybody thinks I've done something tae him.'

'Well, ye've no, and he'll be fine.'

I normally like that my ma just tells me how she sees things and there's no bullshit or anything, but with something like this happening, I could do with a bit of tenderness.

'I need tae go an lie doon,' I say. I'm worried I'll start a fight with her.

'Away ye go up tae bed, then,' she says, gently. 'I'll stay here.'

I go up without my phone and crawl back under my covers.

I wake up with a fright. It's still light outside. Someone is rattling the letterbox and banging the door.

'Jesus Christ,' I hear my ma exclaim. 'I'm coming, bloody calm doon.'

I get up and put my shoes back on. 'Who is it?' I shout down. 'Is it the polis?'

'Where is he?' a man's voice booms. I recognise the voice. It's Danny.

'Go back up the stair, Fiona,' my ma says, as I stop dead halfway down.

He's right at the door, looking up at me. 'I said, where the fuck is he?' He sounds drunk. He's wearing a white T-shirt and a pair of shorts.

'Wit's it goat tae dae wi you, eh?' my ma fires back. 'Ye've never cared afore, so wit ye dain here noo?'

'She better no have fucking done anything ae him, I swear ae god,' he snarls.

'She's no done anything,' my ma says, shoving him back. 'Fuck off.'

'Am no leavin tae a find oot where he is. Where's ma fucking boay?!'

I stand frozen on the stair.

'Fiona, I said go back up the stair,' my ma shouts at me. She goes outside and slams the door shut behind her. I run up to my room and go to the window. Danny's motor is parked across the road with the driver door still open. I can hear them talking.

'She's a fucking psycho, an you know that,' Danny says.

'An wit dis that make you then, eh? Look at ye,' my ma says. 'You're a fucking tramp, and the wean's better aff withoot ye.'

'Is he aye?' Danny says, taking a step back.

'Aye, he is. Wit you gonnae dae? Hit me? You like hitting wummin, dint ye? Hit me, then.' My ma squares up to him. It's exactly what she said and did the night I left him. They both look so much older now than they did back then.

'Aw, fuck off,' he says, and takes another step back. 'When he's back, he's coming tae stay wi me, awrite? Clearly she cannae look efter a wean.'

'He's no a wean, he's nineteen,' my ma says. 'An when he's back, I'm gonnae make sure he knows everything that you fucking did tae her. Fuck off.'

Danny looks like he's going to fly for her. I wouldn't put it past him. 'I'll be back,' he shouts instead, and walks away towards his motor, spitting on the ground.

'You're a fucking coward,' my ma shouts, walking behind him. 'You'll no be getting anywhere near him again. No that it'd bother you though, wid it? No seen him in how many years? Wit did ye get him fur his birthday? Wit aboot Christmas? Aye, that's it, fucking walk away. Get in that motor and fuck off.'

Danny slams his door shut and speeds away. My ma watches his motor disappear down the street. I look up at the flats to see faces at every other window, while the curtains and blinds twitch in the other windows. Two lassies on their bikes are looking up at me. So is an old guy and even his fucking dug.

I kneel down under the window and start pulling at my hair again. Everybody in the whole fucking world is watching me, it feels like. I can't do this.

The front door opens and slams shut as my ma comes back in. 'Fiona, he's away. It's fine.'

Fine! As if any of this is fine!

I hear my ma coming up the stair. 'Fiona, ye awrite?'

'Aye,' I shout back, but she comes in anyway.

She stands looking at me with her hands on her hips, but it's as if she's looking right through me. She walks over to the window. 'He wis reeking a drink. Wi any luck, he'll wrap his motor roon a fucking pole.'

'I cannae dae this,' I say, pulling my knees up to my chest.

I let my kneecaps fill in the space between my jaw and my cheekbones. Maybe if I squeeze them together, I can make my head explode.

I start crying. My ma kneels down next to me. Her knees click as she does so, and she puts her hand on my back.

'C'mere,' she says and pulls me in close. 'It's awrite. It's gonnae be awrite.'

29

JAMIE

'There must be something we can eat,' I say quietly to Lee as he prowls through the drawers in the kitchen. I stand behind him, absolutely shitting myself in case Seb catches us. It's still early, judging by the light outside, but I don't know when Seb normally gets up. I check the fridge, and it's fucking stinking. There's no much in it, just eggs and weird glass jars. A block of mouldy cheese sits at the back. I think that's what's the smell is.

'Fuck,' says Lee, staring into the cupboard under the sink. He pulls out the bottle of acid Seb showed us yesterday. He turns it over in his hands a few times, then puts it back in and shuts the door. He turns and looks at me with eyes open wider than I've ever seen them.

'Pour it doon the sink,' I say reflexively. 'We'll refill it wi water. He won't know.'

'I'm no touching it, man, no chance,' Lee says, standing up. 'Wit if it melts the fucking sink? Wit if we get it oan us?'

'We could fling it oot the windae or something? He's no up, and then we can just bolt?'

'Awrite, big man?' Lee says, his eyes suddenly over my shoulder.

Seb stands in the doorway. 'Morning, boys,' he says, rubbing his eyes. 'Sorry there isn't much in for eating.'

'Aw, that's awrite. We're no really that hungry,' says Lee.

Seb looks at me and smiles. I gently close the fridge over. I don't know how long he was watching us for there, but I don't think he heard me, at least.

'I wanna go over the plan for today,' he says, yawning. 'Discuss your roles and that kind of thing, make sure you both know what you're doing. And then I'll see what I can rustle up for breakfast. That sound okay?'

'Spot on, mate,' Lee says.

'Come on,' says Seb and heads into the living room.

I glance at Lee, and he gives me a wink. 'It'll be awrite,' he says.

We walk through to the living room, and Seb is standing at the window with his back to us, wearing his housecoat. His pale legs stick out from underneath it. It's a washed-out grey colour. The couple of cans from last night are still lying on the floor. Lee kicks one gently. I stand with my hands in my pockets.

Seb turns round to face us, and I look at his feet. They look weird. The skin is grey, and the nails are a sickly yellow. He sits down in his chair and crosses his legs. I'm thankful that I can't see his cock and baws, but I think the brown soles of his feet might be a worse sight, actually. The crumbs and wee curly hairs stuck to them make me want to be sick. I hope none of the hairs are mine.

'Now, this *slut* we're going after,' he says. 'You wanna know why I hate her so much?'

'Aye, wit's she done?' Lee asks.

'Well, a couple years ago, I had this buddy. Richard, his name was. We met online and we met up when I moved here from the States. Anyway, one day we meet up for a beer, and he tells me he's fallen in love with this girl. She was his server in a coffee shop. He's telling me how she's the most beautiful girl he's ever seen. Now, Richard was like me and like you boys – he was an incel, but we didn't know about that word back then. We just said we were *undesirable*.'

I look at Lee, who's hanging on Seb's every word.

Seb reaches forward and starts picking at the skin on his feet. 'Richard didn't have a hope in hell of ever making this bitch his girlfriend, he knew that, but he wanted to try regardless. So we look online for advice on how to approach women, and we find this guy teaching a course, alright?'

'There's courses for talking tae burds?' Lee says. 'Did it work?'

'I'll get to that,' Seb says. 'So we watch all these videos about how to ask a girl for their phone number, how to get them to go on a date, how to fuck them within an hour of meeting them, all that kind of thing. It was all bullshit, but Richard lapped it *all* up and started to think he might have a chance.'

'So wit happened?' Lee asks.

'He knows this girl's every movement, right? He's obsessed with her. He finds her on Instagram, and she's always posting where she goes jogging. She posts this map and it says how fast she runs and how far and all that kind of thing, and it's around where he lives. So he thinks, "Okay, I'll just go for a walk in the same loop in the opposite direction from her, and we'll bump into each other." He thought she'd recognise him from the coffee shop and that he'd be able to strike up a conversation, and that'd be it – she'd fall in love with him.'

'Did it work?' I ask, feeling like I have to add something to the conversation.

'Of course it didn't. He was looking at his phone when she ran by him – he said he recognised her *smell*. He turned around and ran after her. He catches up and he's like, "Hey, excuse me," and she's like, "Yeah, what is it? Do I know you?" And he said that he just froze; he didn't know what to say. He had all this advice from these pick-up artists, he had a plan, but he froze. Instead, he tried to kiss her, and she screamed and ran. You know what happened to Richard?'

I shake my head.

'He jumped in front of a fucking train. My best friend died because this fucking slut wouldn't just give him a chance. Sure, he wasn't the best-looking guy in the world, but he'd have treated her like a fucking princess. He called me right after, told me what happened, said he was sorry, and then hung up. That was it. That was the last time I ever heard from him.'

'Fucking hell,' says Lee, looking at me. 'That's shocking, int it? Poor cunt, wit a fucking shame.'

A shame? I think to myself. *How's it a shame?* None of this is the lassie's fault, surely? I'd scream and run if someone chased me in the street and tried to kiss me. Just like that poor lassie last night. Fucking hell, I can't believe that actually happened. That I actually did that. Guilt brews hot and heavy in my belly.

'Aye,' I say, without conviction.

'Anyway, that's why I want you boys to do this for me. If I do it, if I see her, I'll go insane and end up doing something much worse. And, as much as I'd *like* to do that, this will teach her a lesson. Make her see what it's like to be an undesirable. To have people physically fucking recoil whenever they see you. To see what it's like to be us.'

'That's only fair if ye ask me,' says Lee, with a shrug of his shoulders. 'An eye fur an eye an aw that.'

I can't tell if Lee means it, or if he's just going along with what Seb's saying as part of a ploy to get us out of here. Keep on his good side and all that. Either way, I'm not doing this. I'll say all the right things, like I always do, I'll go with them to wherever it is we're going, then I'll just disappear. I'll hang back while they go on ahead, and then just run like fuck down an alley or something. It's a big city, like Seb says, and no cunt will ever find me, especially no them. Lee can handle himself. He knows what he's doing. He'll be fine; he'll know how to get back home and all that. Fuck knows what I'll do with no money and no phone. I'll just have to start a new life down here.

'You know that feeling you boys had when you were following those bitches?' Seb says, leaning forward in his chair. 'When they looked at you, you could see how much they hated you, right? I want you to remember that – that these sluts *hate* you. They fucking hate you, and they want you to die, and even if you were the last guy on the planet and the fate of humanity depended on it, they still wouldn't fuck you. They'd rather see you dead. They'd rather see your body and

252

blood smeared across a railway line than have you within ten feet of them. I mean every fucking woman out there. Fuck them. This is how we fight back.'

'I feel ready tae go ae war, man!' Lee laughs. 'Dae you no?' He turns and looks at me, widens his eyes again and gives me a subtle nod.

'Aye,' I say.

Seb reclines with a big smile on his face. Grinning like a villain. 'Just don't let me down, boys.'

'Don't worry, big man,' Lee says. 'We won't.'

'Good,' Seb says. When I look at him, sometimes he reminds me of, like, a pure bogging medieval king. King of some fucking shitehole in the middle of nowhere in a castle of mud. He has this aura about him, like he's used to getting other people to do things for him. I think if he was on his own, he'd be totally useless. Just another guy. But here, with me and Lee to do whatever he wants, he thinks he can do – and get away with – anything.

'There you go, buddy,' Seb says, holding out a plate of what I think is scrambled eggs, but they don't look very scrambled. He towers over me as I sit on the floor. As he hands me the plate, some kind of horrible, stringy liquid drips off it and on to the carpet.

'Thanks,' I say. This feels like what a prisoner in an old film would be given to eat, but he'd maybe get some stale bread as well. No such luck for me. I can see Seb's toes under my plate. Just inches away from my horrible breakfast. I can't decide which of them has made me not feel hungry. He sighs as he drops down into his chair, wee splashes of the eggmilk or whatever the fuck it is dripping off his plate too. Lee comes in with his own plate. He sits down next to me, and I notice he has less than me.

'Ye want some mair?' I ask him quietly, as Seb shovels his into his mouth, smacking his chops.

'Naw, I'm awrite,' Lee says. He pushes some egg around the plate with his fork.

'What was your black-pill moment?' Seb says out of nowhere.

'Wit d'ye mean?' Lee asks.

'You know, the moment you realised you'd lost the genetic lottery, and that you'd never find love? The moment you realised that all women are whores?'

'Ooft, eh, I'm no sure,' says Lee. 'Probably when I started talkin tae you an havin it aw explained tae me.'

'No, no, no,' Seb says, setting his empty plate on the floor. 'It must have been before that. Everyone like us has a story. I just helped you see the truth.'

'Fuck knows. Wit aboot you?' Lee asks me, just as I attempt to eat a forkful of eggs. I gratefully lower the fork from my mouth and let the eggs slide back on to the plate.

'Just at school, probably. When I started secondary,' I say.

'High school's tough,' says Seb. 'That's when I had mine.'

'Wit happened?' Lee asks. I go to answer, but I realise he was talking to Seb.

'My classmates all used to say I looked like a school shooter,' Seb says. That's what he said I looked like. Maybe he thinks I'm just like him. 'I had long hair and wore this long black leather jacket. I just wanted to look Like Neo in *The Matrix.*' He smiles and looks down at the ground. He reminds me of an old guy reminiscing, telling war stories or something. 'This girl sat next to me in math class. She'd never really speak to me, but she would smile at me sometimes. This was before I realised I'd never have a girlfriend. I thought, "Why would she be smiling at me if she's not in love with me? She *must* be in love with me!" None of the other bitches at school even looked at me, and here was this one smiling at me! Hell, that was it. I was in love. Same as Richard was. I asked her out, asked her if she'd go see a movie with me sometime, and she said no, of course. But she decided to tell everyone in the school that I'd asked her.'

'Fuck, man,' says Lee. 'I'm so sorry.' Lee says that as if he's saying it to someone who's just revealed they have cancer. If he's kidding on, if he's just trying to play along with this, he deserves an Oscar.

'They started filming me in school,' Seb goes on. 'This was when cell phones started having cameras in them, but before social media was really a thing. But the videos of me getting tripped up in the halls, spat on, punched, kicked, hair pulled and all that, they were still passed around everyone. Then people started saying I was a paedophile.' Seb looks up at the ceiling, and his eyes are glistening as if he's going to start crying. 'My mom and dad got divorced. He got a job offer here in England, and I came with him. I thought it'd be a chance to reinvent myself,' he says. 'But things are just as fucking bad here, if not worse. No matter where I go in the world, I've realised, I'll always be alone.'

'Och, mate,' says Lee, going over to Seb and putting an arm on his shoulder. 'You've goat us!'

Seb reaches up and touches Lee's hand. He smiles. 'Thank you,' Seb says. 'Thank you for coming here. For believing me. For trusting me.'

'It's nae bother,' Lee says.

'And thank you to you, too, Jamie.' Seb shoots me a look. 'I know you don't say much, but you do really listen. That's a nice thing you do.'

'Cheers,' I say, but my voice catches in my throat. Not because I'm emotional, but because I don't want to say it. I don't want to thank this cunt.

Lee removes his hand from Seb's shoulder and comes over to sit next to me on the floor.

'Fuck,' Seb says, wiping his nose with the sleeve of his housecoat. 'That's enough of that. I've just realised I haven't even showed you a picture of this bitch we're attacking later.'

He puffs out his cheeks and rubs his eyes. He looks scary again rather than upset. He pulls out his phone.

'Her name's Hannah. Works in a café during the day, goes for a run after work, then goes out and sucks the cocks of as many Chads as she can find. Here she is.' He offers his phone to Lee, who reaches out and takes it.

'Tidy,' says Lee, nodding. He turns and shows her to me. 'Int she?'

'Bit old for you though, Lee, right?' Seb says with a raised eyebrow. Lee hands him his phone back and gives me a sheepish look.

'But yeah, you know, before the stuff happened with

Richard,' Seb says, 'I'd have said, sure, she's a ten. Now, knowing what she did and the heartache she's caused and what she's like, how foul a person she is, I'd say she's a one. A good-for-nothing fucking cumslut. The worst of the worst, and the lowest of the fucking low.'

He spits the words out at us. Whether that story he told us about his pal Richard is true or not, he definitely hates this lassie.

'I don't want you boys to think that you want to fuck her. I don't want you to think that she's beautiful. I want you to hate her. I want you to ruin her life,' he says.

I turn to Lee, who's now going through the lassie's Instagram, one picture at a time.

'We are going to ruin this bitch's life, okay?' Seb says.

'I'm up fur it. She's fucking evil,' Lee says.

'Good,' Seb says. 'Time is marching on. I'm gonna get dressed, and then we'll go and do a practice run, okay?'

30

FIONA

I sit and stare at my phone, willing the police to phone me and say they're on their way with Jamie. I wonder what he'll be like when he gets back. He'll come back. I know him. He's not the type to go and get himself into any dangerous situations. If something freaks him out, he'll just run away and hide. Hide under the covers of whatever bed he's sleeping in. But what if he's sleeping on the streets or something? What if he thinks that's preferable to being here with me?

My phone buzzes. It's from a number I don't recognise and don't have saved.

What have you done with those two boys??

I stare as it buzzes again.

Everybody knows you've killed them

What the fuck? I throw my phone down and feel myself trying to edge away from it. It buzzes again and again, over and over, like it's filled with bees. I run to the toilet, lock the door and slump down to the floor, covering my head with my hands. I wish I could just wash myself away down the plughole. I imagine doing that, and the hand of a polis coming right down after me, grabbing me around the neck and hauling me in front of a judge, who immediately bangs her hammer and sends me to Cornton Vale for the rest of my life. I pull my hands away from my head, and when I look at them, they're covered in my hair again. Dozens of black strands, all knotted and curly. My scalp itches and burns. I shake my hands and watch the bundles of hair fall softly on to the white tiles. There's even more than I first thought. I run my fingers from my roots to the tips, and watch as more comes out and drifts down, piling up.

It sounds like the phone has stopped vibrating. I'd better go and check if I've missed a call from Graham or my ma or even Jamie. I stand up, but my body or brain or both just won't let me leave. I reach for the lock on the door, but my hands aren't working now. Pins and needles shoot up and down my arms, while the noise of the rain outside comes in and rattles around in my ears. If I go out there, I have to deal with something that could make me feel awful. If I stay in here, I don't. I can sit back down and shut my eyes and try and forget about everything. The problem's still going to be there, whether I leave the toilet now or in an hour's time.

I sit back down, my knees clicking as I return to the floor. I try and focus on my breathing, like a doctor once told me to do when I went to see if I could get some tablets that would help with the anxiety I had when I was with Danny. 'When you start to feel like this,' he'd told me, after I'd spent ten minutes explaining how I felt like I was going to die whenever I heard Danny's key in the front door, 'just breathe in and out, nice and slow, in through your nose and out through your mouth.' This is the first time I've tried to do it. It feels like it's working. I hate that it's working. I wanted to kill the guy for telling me to do that instead of giving me Diazepam.

The rain seems to have stopped. Maybe I just imagined those texts. I'm not in the best of states mentally, so I suppose, in a time of high stress like this, it's natural that my brain would be playing tricks on me. It wouldn't be the first time. The texts look like they've been pulled right from the part of my brain where my most horrible thoughts live. I stick to focusing on my breathing and try to empty all the nonsense out of my mind.

In and out. In and out.

I must have imagined those texts. They were worded to play into my biggest fears. My brain concocted them to scare me. In and out. In and out. There's nothing bad on the other side of the door. In and out. In and out. I use the palms of my hands to brush all my dead and broken hair together. In and out. In and out. I scoop it all up and roll it between my hands, into a wee ball. In and out. In and out. I lift up the lid of the toilet pan and throw the hairball into it. I'm fine.

I get up and unlock the door and open it. I feel dizzy and light-headed, but I don't have that sick-with-fear feeling I normally have. Maybe I've actually calmed down. Maybe I've gone beyond stress into a new state of being, and my brain doesn't know what to do so it's just short-circuited. I've somehow found my way into the living room without falling apart, so I pick up my phone.

1 missed call – Ma
23 new messages

I click on my messages without fear and without hesitation – I'm too far gone for any of that now.

Probably buried them out your back

Paedo cow

They were just wee boys

It's not your son's fault that you're evil

Scummy bitch

And on it goes. They're definitely real. The rest of the messages turn into a blur as I keep scrolling. I tap on the back button and then delete the lot of them in one go. I click on my ma's name in my phone and hold it to my ear before I realise what I'm doing. She normally answers after the first ring, but it keeps ringing. I'd be happy if I could go through life like this from now on – with my body making the decisions and just doing things without me thinking, while I watch on like a wee passenger.

'Fiona,' she says eventually. 'I was in the toilet, hen, I'm sorry.'

'That's awrite,' I say. 'I've got a missed call fae ye.'

'Aye, I wis just phoning ae say that I'm gonnae come doon and stay wi ye, if that's awrite.'

Instinctively, I look around to see if the place is tidy enough. Nothing is out of place, everything looks pristine and perfect. I haven't done anything but sleep and sit and have quiet melt-downs. 'Aye, that's fine,' I say.

'I'll be doon shortly.'

'Nae bother, see you soon.' I set my phone down and realise I'm no longer on autopilot. My body has relinquished its control and left me in charge again. I make the decision to run to the toilet and be sick.

My ma's sitting on the couch drinking a cup of tea. I had a panic attack on the floor of the toilet when I heard her coming in.

'Made ye a coffee, hen,' she says, nodding towards the wee table next to the couch.

'Ta,' I say. I sit down and rest the hot cup on my thigh. It burns a wee bit, but I don't move it.

'Ye awrite?' she says, not looking at me but towards the window.

'No really,' I say. This is the first time in my life, I think, that I've not replied, 'Aye, fine,' when someone's asked me that question.

'Murder, int it,' my ma says into her cup. 'Rotten situation. Sitting here wondering whether he's alive or deid.' She's still looking out the window. Her eyes look glazed over.

'I got a weird text,' I say. 'A few weird texts.'

'Fae who? Sayin wit?'

'I don't know who. It was somebody saying that I killed Jamie.'

My ma does a big sigh. 'People are horrible, int they?'

'I don't know wit tae dae,' I say.

'Wit *can* ye dae?' she says. 'I've never been in this situation. I didnae need tae worry aboot you dain anything like this. I wish I could gie ye some advice, hen, but I don't have any.'

My ma has always been keen to dish out advice. I think of all the times she's told me how I *should* have handled situations, how I *should* have behaved. The things I should say to solve problems. How if I was just more like her and less like myself then life would be all plain sailing and nothing bad would ever happen. God, she makes me feel so inferior to her and has done my whole life.

'That's no like ye,' I say, and it comes out a lot cheekier than I had intended.

'Wit?!' she snaps.

Fuck. I've done it now.

'Well, you've normally got plenty ae advice fur me. You're always the first tae tell me when I'm no dain something right.' I don't know why I've chosen this moment to finally challenge my ma. Adrenaline starts coursing through me. I feel angry.

'I dae that fur yer ain good. Maybe if ye'd listened tae me years ago when I was tellin ye how tae bring the wean up, tellin ye ae leave his da, then ye widnae be in this mess. Wid ye?'

I take a sip of my coffee and it scalds my throat on the way down. I turn to look out the window as I feel my ma's gaze boring into me. I hear her slurping as she drinks her tea.

'I think you should go hame,' I say. 'I need tae be oan my ain fur a bit.'

She sits for a second, staring at me, then sets her tea down on the floor. She groans as she gets to her feet, and I hear her zip up her jacket. 'Fine,' she says. 'That's wit I'll dae. Efter coming aw the way doon, I'll just go right back hame so you can be *oan yer ain.*'

'Ta,' I say quietly. I can't even look at her. If I do, I don't know whether I'll explode in anger at her or burst out greeting. Either way, I doubt she'll have much sympathy for me.

'Phone me if ye hear anything,' she says, and walks out. I feel my jaw unclench slightly as the front door slams shut behind her. I get a twang of pain from one of my back teeth. I've been grinding them a lot recently. I better try and stop, or Jamie will be coming home to a maw who's gumsy as well as baldy. I picture him coming home and seeing me and I look like an old hag. A wizened, decrepit witch with a hunchback, wearing old rags.

Jamie could be lying dead just now. That's just what happens. They don't ever seem to find missing people, they find their bodies. It's never the police who find them either, it's always someone out with their dog or something. I can't stop thinking about him lying on a pavement or down an alley. Or thrown into a skip somewhere. Jesus Christ, I hope he's okay. And if he is okay, then what happens when the police find him and he tells them how much he hates me, and how running away was better than being here with me?

I thought about killing myself a couple of times while I was with Danny, when it felt like there was no way out, but the thought of leaving Jamie behind to be raised by him stopped me. That, and the idea that Danny'd get any sort of sympathy from people because his mental partner had topped herself and left him as a single father. A few times I looked at boxes of ibuprofen on the shelves in Tesco, and wondered how many I'd need to do the job. A few times I thought about driving my motor off a bridge or swerving into the path of an oncoming lorry.

I've been lucky that those thoughts haven't been back since then, but here they are again now. What kind of life can you lead after your child has died, anyway? And when everyone seems to be pointing the finger at you for it? What's the point? I wish I could just crawl into a hole and fall asleep forever.

Jamie would be relieved to hear that I've died, I think. He hates me, and he can tell that I'm mental, that I'm not normal. I couldn't actually do it, I don't think. I couldn't kill myself.

My leg bounces up and down as I stare off into space, thinking about how I would like to go if I could. I find myself typing 'Quick painless suicide' into Google without even thinking about it. 'HELP IS AVAILABLE' it says in big letters, along with the number for the Samaritans. I immediately close the tab and throw my phone down, worried that it's going to automatically alert the police or something. I can imagine them outside the house with a megaphone, shouting that life is worth living. That's the last thing I need right now. Curiosity gets the better of me, though, and I pick up my phone again and scroll, clicking on the Wikipedia page for suicide methods.

A suicide method is any means by which a person chooses to end their life. Suicide attempts do not always result in death, and a non-fatal suicide attempt can leave the person with serious physical injuries, long-term health problems, and brain damage.

Maybe I'd end up in a coma if I didn't do it right, just lying there dreaming for years, existing in some perfect fantasy world in my mind until the life-support machine gets switched off. I scroll down the page, and it makes me wish I had a gun. I'm not hanging myself, because that looks horrible and sore. I wouldn't want anyone to find me like that. I'm not jumping, either – I'm scared of heights. That leaves me with asphyxiation or poisoning. It says something about using helium, but where am I supposed to get helium from? Go and buy a load of balloons? I imagine myself walking down the street in black and white while sad music plays, with my face tripping me, holding a big bunch of balloons like a sad clown in a weird film. I thought you could sit in your motor with the engine running in an enclosed space and that would be enough to kill you, but I don't have a garage. It says it's the carbon monoxide that would kill you if you did that. I type 'Carbon monoxide suicide' into Google for some inspiration. The Samaritans number comes up again, and I find myself saying, 'Gies peace,' and immediately scrolling past it. I click the first link that doesn't say anything like 'There is hope' and it takes me to an old, somewhat dodgy-looking website. It's a forum where people are discussing disposable barbecues. I remember seeing something in the paper once, about a young couple who'd went camping, lit a disposable barbecue in their tent to keep them warm, and were then found dead in the morning.

A couple of scientific papers about carbon monoxide poisoning appear further down in the search results, and I flick through them. In amongst a load of waffle about chemical analysis and other stuff that goes over my head, the word 'painless' keeps coming up again and again. It sounds just perfect – drifting away into a long sleep with nothing to worry about. I wish I'd thought of doing this years ago – I could have stopped all this from happening. I could've stopped myself from living this miserable, dull, monotonous life. I could've stopped Jamie from getting into the state he's in. The best time to do it would've been years ago. The second-best time would be now. I'm just doing everyone a favour. I need out of the house. I don't think I can be here tonight. It feels like the walls are closing in on me, like I'm going to be crushed. There's nowhere for me to go, though. No pals I could ask if I could sleep on their couch. And there's nowhere I'd rather go less than my ma's. Suppose I could just sleep in the motor. Take my duvet, get some sleeping tablets and maybe a bottle of vodka, park up somewhere nice and quiet. It'd be like camping. Maybe if I take all the tablets, they'll make the decision about whether or not to die for me – leaving it up to the gods and all that. At the very least, I'll be knocked out and won't care about anything for a while. Get a wee taste of oblivion.

I go up to my room and grab a pillow and my duvet so I can be comfy and cosy in the motor. I think as soon as you die, you shit and piss yourself, so this way it'll all be contained if I do, and I won't look too undignified when the police or whoever find me. I go out and stick them in the back seat of the motor, rolling them up and throwing a jacket over the top. I look up and see someone watching me from the flats across the road. I get a pang of anxiety and feel like I'm being judged, but it doesn't matter, does it? I might never see them again. Nothing that's happening now is my problem anymore. I hope whoever it is tells people they saw me getting into the motor with a duvet and driving away. I hope they add on extra lies to make me look even worse. I hope they tell people I looked up at them and gave them the middle finger, and that my hands were dripping with blood or something. I slide into the driver's seat, turn the key in the ignition and drive off towards Tesco for my camping gear.

31

JAMIE

Lee strips down to his boxers and rummages around in his bag. I feel slightly embarrassed that I've not changed my clothes since we got here, but no one's said anything. Maybe they just haven't noticed. When Lee turns his back on me, I pull my T-shirt up over my nose and inhale deeply to see if I smell. I just smell like how I normally smell, I think. I stick my hand down my joggies and rub it under my baws. It's roasting there, man. I bring it to my nose. It reeks of stale pish and cum, and I've not even had a wank since I got here. No one's going to be down there anyway, though, so it doesn't matter.

'Ye awrite?' Lee asks me as he pulls a clean T-shirt over his head.

'I don't know, man,' I say, hoping he didn't see me doing the scratch and sniff.

He stops dead and holds his finger to his lips while looking like he's trying to see through the closed bedroom door. Floorboards creak as Seb walks by the room. They get quieter as he walks down the hall, away from us. Lee comes round and kneels down next to me.

'We're getting oot ae here,' he says.

'I thought you were intae his mad plan tae attack this poor lassie? I was worried.'

'That's how ye deal wi guys like him. Just agree wi them and make them think yer oan their side. I've goat a plan.'

Lee looks wild-eyed. I can tell he's anxious. His eyes are bulging out their sockets.

'Listen, see when we leave, wance we get doon the stair, I'll say I've furgoat something and need tae run back up. You'll need tae wait wi him and act like ye don't know wit am uptae. I'll find oor phones, then we'll go wherever he takes us and we'll just bolt. Awrite?'

'Then wit? How dae we get hame?'

'We'll figure that oot later. We just need tae get away fae him first.' Lee stands up and puts a hand on my shoulder. 'We'll be awrite. Just follow ma lead.'

I nod. I hope these are the last few hours we spend here. I want to go back home. I miss my ma. I miss my horrible room. I miss my granny. I miss when Lee just lived in my headset and we spoke about stuff that wasn't incels and being virgins and running away.

I watch Lee slip on his trainers and tie his laces. Everything he does, every movement he makes, seems so fluid and confident. Whenever I do anything, anything at all, I'm all awkward and juddery, like I've only just been given this body and I'm still working out the controls.

'You're pure starey,' he says, and I realise I've been staring at him for the last minute or so without looking away, probably not even blinking.

'Sorry,' I say, moving my eyes around the room, looking for something else to direct them at.

'Coming here has made you weirder, mate,' he says with a smile.

'I know, man,' I reply. 'Think it's the lack ae food as well. I feel pure spaced oot aw the time.'

'Shhh, hang oan,' he says, standing totally still again. I can hear Seb's footsteps approaching once more.

'You boys almost ready?' Seb says from outside. I can't tell if he sounds fed up or no; I worry that we've taken too long to get ready or something.

'Aye, here we're coming,' Lee shouts. He comes over to me again and leans down so his lips are right at my ear. 'Just keep dain wit ye've been dain and follow ma lead, awrite.'

'Sound,' I whisper in reply, my voice catching in my throat.

He bounces back up and heads out the door. I get up and put my shoes on, and I hear Seb sounding as if he's lecturing Lee in the hall. I hope Lee knows what he's doing, because I certainly don't. I'm a motor that's been parked on a steep hill and its handbrake's stopped working, and now I'm just fucking rolling, hoping to god I don't kill someone. Or have to throw acid on them, in my case.

'Front door's this way,' Seb says sarcastically, as I emerge out into the hall and immediately head for the toilet with my head down. I stop and look back at him. He's wearing mad army-style trousers. Dark green with loads of pockets. His

271

long hair is tied back in a ponytail. He has a backpack on. He looks like he's going to war.

'I just, eh, need tae pish first,' I say.

He sighs and then says, 'Hurry up.'

I nod and run for the toilet, shutting the door behind me and leaning against it. I can hear Seb saying something to Lee under his breath. Slagging me, probably. I shut my eyes and imagine I'm just in the toilet in my own house, praying that when I open them, I'll be back up the road through some kind of magic. But no. I'm in the most evil-looking, filthy toilet in the world. Obviously I'm quite a bogging guy, and if even I think this place is too much, then it must be bad. The light from the exposed bulb over my head seems so aggressive. It's even got evil light. I look down at my arms and hands. Even though the light has that weird orange tinge, I look fucking *grey*. I go over to the sink and aim a pish right down the plug hole. Wee bits of black stuff end up flaking off from around about it. The plughole, not my dick.

'Come *on*, man!' Seb shouts, giving me a fright, and my stream of piss goes over the side of the sink as I swivel round instinctively. That's the closest the floor's probably came to getting cleaned in a long time. I put my cock away and run the tap, then splash some water on my face to try and make myself feel a bit more awake. I take a deep breath and head back out.

Seb opens the front door and gestures for me to walk through it. I look at Lee, who looks as if he's sweating. He seems nervous. I squeeze between them and out into the close. Lee follows behind, and then Seb comes out and locks up. He gives the handle a wiggle to make sure the door's locked.

'Okay, let's go,' he says, putting the keys into one of his many pockets. He brushes past me and Lee and goes down the stairs. We look at each other.

'It'll be awrite,' Lee says, and hurries to catch up with Seb. They both disappear round the corner as they descend, and I take a few seconds to try and compose myself.

'Wit's the plan, then?' Lee asks Seb.

'The plan is to go and fuck up this foid,' Seb replies. Normally when he says things like that, he's got, like, an excitement in his voice. Now it seems pure sinister and angry.

'I thought this was just a dry run?' Lee asks him.

'No time like the present, is there?' Seb says. He strides ahead and lets the main door swing back without holding it open for Lee. I run through the door as Lee holds it open for me. Seb walks straight across the road before Lee can execute his plan to get our phones back.

'Shit,' Lee says. 'Right, act natural.' He pushes me gently from behind; I take the hint and walk away from him.

'Here, big man,' Lee shouts.

Seb stops and looks back. 'What the fuck?! Keep your fucking voice down!' he snaps at Lee.

'Sorry. It's just I've furgoat something. Can I run back up and grab it?'

'What could you possibly have forgotten?' Seb says, getting close to Lee. He seems fucking raging. 'You don't need your phone. You don't have any money. What the fuck do you need?'

'Eh, never mind,' Lee says, looking deflated. 'It's sound.'

'Yeah, it is *sound*,' Seb says, and starts walking again. 'Come on.'

Lee looks at me and shrugs his shoulders. We are fucked. We're going to have to melt some lassie's face so this mad cunt doesn't kill us. I follow behind Seb and Lee follows behind me. I feel like a zombie. I'm under the control of the two of them. I will either do something horrible because Seb tells me to and I'm too much of a shitebag to not do it, or I'll do something that Lee tells me to do, which could be either something daft or something brave. Just depends on who tells me what to do first.

'I'll figure it oot, don't worry,' Lee says, as he hurries past me.

I watch him run to catch up with Seb. He walks alongside him, having to do a wee skip-jog type thing every couple of seconds to keep up. Seb reminds me of the Terminator. I speed up.

'Wit's the plan?' asks Lee.

'I already told you,' Seb replies, sounding annoyed. 'That we go and fuck up this foid.'

'Aye,' Lee says. 'But wit's the *plan?*'

'It's best if we don't overcomplicate it,' Seb says. 'The more instructions I give you, the more stuff you have to remember, the more chance of something going wrong. I'll tell you what to do when we get there.'

Lee looks back at me. For the first time, I see him as just a scared wee guy, like I am. I don't trust him to come up with an escape plan now, just from seeing the look on his face and his shoulders all tense and the way he's walking. I need to be ready to do whatever it takes.

As the three of us walk, people move out the way for Seb

and Lee, but not for me, so I have to sort of zigzag along, always having to twist my body so I don't brush against anybody. I worry that I might accidentally barge someone with my shoulder, but if that happens, it's me who will end up on my arse. I try and listen to what Seb and Lee are saying to each other but I only get wee snippets between motors going by.

'Ye don't need tae dae that, mate,' Lee says but I didn't hear what it's in response to. 'Come oan.'

'Well, do what you're told and I won't,' Seb replies.

After a few minutes, Lee slows down and walks beside me, with Seb staying a few paces ahead. Lee keeps his head down as we walk. I glance sideways at him, but he just stares at his own feet.

'Ye awrite?' I ask him.

'I don't know, man,' he replies. He glances at me, but quickly looks away again. 'I'm freaking oot a bit.'

'Same.'

'Wit if he makes us dae this, right?' he lowers his voice. 'Wit if we get caught? Wit if we get the jail?'

'We won't get caught, because we're no gonnae dae anything. We're no actually gonnae throw acid oan somebody, man,' I say. 'Surely no.'

'Wait out here a second,' Seb says. I look up and he's stopped outside a newsagent's. 'Don't move.'

Lee looks back along the road in the direction we've came. 'Should we dae a runner noo?'

'No yet. He'll chase us and fucking throw that shit oan us,' I reply.

'Fuck,' Lee says. 'Fuck me. How did we get intae this mess?'

I want to say, *It's cause ae you, mate. You found Seb oan a forum. You convinced me tae come doon here*, but I don't. Instead, I say, 'I need a fag.'

'I need two fags and a wank. I feel so fucking stressed. Is this how you feel aw the time?'

'Aye, basically.'

'Fuck me.'

I look in the shop and see Seb pointing behind the till. The guy hands him something blue and wrapped in plastic, and Seb hands him some cash.

'Is it cheeky fur me tae ask him fur a fag?' Lee asks.

'Nah, man. Ask him fur wan fur me anaw though.'

Seb comes out the shop and passes me and Lee a blue face mask each. I turn it over in my hands. I could probably have done with this back at the flat, especially for going into the toilet. Lee immediately puts his mask on, and Seb says, 'I'll tell you when to put it on. Put it in your pocket. It looks suspicious if you wear it now.'

'Sorry,' Lee says, scrunching it into a ball and sticking it in his pocket. I can see his hands are shaking.

'C'mon,' Seb says, and starts walking again. I pat Lee on the back and we start walking too.

'Gonnae you ask him for a fag,' Lee says to me. 'I cannae dae it.' I look at him, and he looks even paler than usual. He's in a bad way. His skin is practically translucent, almost blue. He brings a hand up and rubs his nose and then his eye. I think he might be crying.

'Aye, I'll ask him,' I say, and walk next to Seb.

'Cheers, mate,' Lee replies, but it's so quiet it's like he's just mouthing the words.

I keep looking at Seb's face as we walk, hoping he'll take the hint and realise I want to ask him something, but he just keeps looking dead ahead.

'Could I, eh, borrow a cigarette?' I say to him.

'What?' he snaps, screwing up his face.

'Could I have a have a cigarette, please?'

'Why are you talking like that?'

I clear my throat. 'Like wit?'

'Like you're talking to a teacher.' He laughs and reaches into his pocket, then passes me his packet of fags and his lighter. I turn and offer them to Lee, who reaches out and takes one. I take one as well and spark up. I try to give them back to Seb, but he ignores me, so I put them in my own pocket instead.

'We're almost there,' Seb says. I have never wanted to be further away from a place I've been going than at this very moment. I'd cut my cock and baws off to even just go back to Seb's flat right now.

I take a long draw from my fag and it makes me feel weightless. Like I'm just a floating brain gliding through London. I look at all the faces charging past me, all the bikes and buses and motors, and realise not a single soul knows what I'm up to, where I'm going or what I'm being told to do. No one's even looking at me. I feel invisible. I turn back to look at Lee, who looks like a lost wee boy. He looks at me with worry lines making ripples across his forehead. I smile at him, but he doesn't react.

After a few minutes, Seb stops and sort of shepherds us into the doorway of an empty shop. A few dead vapes litter the ground around us. There's a washed-out poster for a circus or something pasted on to the shutters.

'Okay, the coffee shop is just around the corner. You boys ready?' Seb says.

Lee doesn't reply. It seems like I am now the designated talker, not him. 'Aye,' I say.

Seb takes off his backpack, drops it to the ground and squats down next to it. He unzips and reaches in, bringing out the bottle of acid. I have a pure physical response to seeing that bottle. My stomach lurches and I feel cold. He takes off the lid and pretends to pour it over my feet. I jump back and he laughs. He goes back into the bag and screws a sports cap on to the bottle, secures it by winding black tape around the neck, and then wraps the whole thing up in a plastic bag. 'You take this,' he says, and hands it to Lee. Lee's hands visibly tremble as he takes it from him.

'I was gonna have you do it,' Seb says to me. 'But one of you needs to do the talking, and *he's* not gonna be much use since he seems to have lost his voice.'

I watch Lee's free hand curl into a fist. I feel a sense of mild relief that I won't have to touch the acid.

'We'll go around the corner and wait across the road from the café. She goes out for a vape every hour or so, and stands with her face glued to her phone. You go over first, Jamie, and try to talk to her. Ask her if she has a lighter, ask her for her phone number – anything, it doesn't matter. I just want you to get her to raise her face up, so we can get as much of it as possible. Then Lee, you walk by and point the bottle in her face and squeeze. Alright? Just try not to hit your buddy here.' He laughs and pats me on the back.

Lee doesn't react.

'Hey, it was just a joke,' Seb says. He leans in to Lee. 'You're not gonna pussy out, are you?'

Lee shakes his head. I have a feeling he's going to empty the bottle into Seb's face, but he doesn't. Instead, he looks at both of us in turn and says, 'I'm sorry.'

'Don't be sorry. Just don't be a pussy,' Seb says. 'You're about to do a good thing. Think of it as rebalancing the karma in the world. She caused Richard's death, and now you're getting some justice for him. Alright?'

Lee nods. 'Aye, you're right.'

'I'll make men out of you pussies yet,' Seb says, putting his backpack on again. 'Let's go.'

Seb leads the way again. We walk further along the road until we get to a set of traffic lights. Seb presses the button for us to cross, and the three of us wait for the green man without talking. I can't fucking believe that this is what my life's been leading up to. Every decision I've made, everything that's happened, has led me to this fucking horrible moment.

'That's the café,' Seb says, pointing across the road as motors zoom by. The café looks nice. It's got a pink sign and flowers in the window, and people sitting outside it. 'She comes out pretty much every hour for five minutes. As soon as she appears, I'll give you boys the signal.'

I look at Lee, confused as to what the fuck Seb means. Lee is still set to mute, so I ask, 'Wit's the signal?'

The green man flashes and we cross over. We walk past the café and Seb cranes his neck to look in. 'Yeah, she's there.'

I try and get a look, but Seb shoves me and tells me to keep moving so we don't draw any attention.

'The signal is I'll wave at you from here.' He stops a few doors down from the café outside a bookie's. 'You walk until you get to that sign up there.' He points at a lottery sign on the pavement. 'Don't draw attention to yourselves. Just have a smoke and a normal conversation. Okay?'

'Okay,' I say.

Lee nods. His head keeps swivelling to look over his shoulders.

'I'll wave once when she comes out, and Jamie, you put your mask on and go talk to her. Lee, you stay where you are until I wave again, then put your mask on and your hood up. You're just gonna walk by, aim and fire. Once you've done it, drop the bottle, throw it, whatever, just get rid of it. Then the two of you run towards me. This part of the city is like a maze. We only need to run for a couple minutes, make a few turns, and we're safe. Okay? Nothing bad's gonna happen as long as you follow those instructions.'

'Sound,' Lee says. I watch him wipe tears from his eyes, but Seb doesn't seem to notice.

'What are you waiting for?' Seb says. 'Go.'

We both start walking. As we pass the café, I can't bring myself to look in. Lee doesn't look either.

'Wit we gonnae dae?' I ask him.

'We'll dae exactly wit he says,' Lee replies. 'But I'll miss her.'

'I wish we could just run away noo,' I say.

'We cannae, man. He's still goat oor phones.'

'So fuck. Mine is just a cheap wan. Yours is auld anaw.'

'Aye, but . . .' Lee's face looks even more worried now, as he looks away from me and down at the ground. 'It's wit's oan it.'

'Wit d'ye mean?' We stop at the sign, just as Seb told us to. Lee is gripping on to the bag with the acid in it for dear life.

'I never told ye this afore, but I met Seb oan a forum where cunts wid send each other pictures ae lassies.'

'Wit, like, porn an that?'

'Naw, man. It wis . . .' Lee looks down the street towards Seb. 'He asked me fur pictures ae lassies I went tae school wi. An lassies a few years below me. Pictures aff their Facebook an Instagram an that.'

'Fucking hell, mate. Is he a paedo, then?'

'Fuck knows, probably. I just hink if we bolt, then he'll find us nae matter wit. He knows this place an we don't. An fuck knows wit he'll dae tae us. An if we try an get him the jail, then the polis will take oor phones as evidence or witever, and they'll see wit I've been sending him and saying ae him.' He covers his face with his hands. 'I told him I wanted tae rape wan ae them. I feel fucking sick. I'm a horrible cunt, man.'

All I can bring myself to say is, 'Fuck me, man.'

Seb is looking up at us, but there's still no signal. Lee rubs the back of his head and then shouts, 'Fuck!' He sounds like a wounded animal or something.

'It's awrite,' I say, knowing fine well none of this is alright at all. This is the singular most stressful moment of my life. Well, until Seb gives the signal, and I have to talk to a lassie and hope that my pal, who may or not be a beast, misses her with the acid he's going to throw at her on the orders of an American incel. Fuck me, indeed.

'I'm sorry,' Lee says. 'I'm sorry I roped you intae this. He made me say that shit tae him, called me names an aw that if I didnae dae it. Threatened tae tell people aboot me. Send the messages I'd sent him tae my maw.'

'It's fine, mate,' I reply. 'Just keep yer voice doon. Cunts are looking at us.'

A group of guys and lassies about my age are standing outside a pub a few doors up, smoking. The guys are sort of smirking while the lassies look a wee bit scared.

I look down to see Seb, and he's waving like the guy who directs the planes at an airport. Fuck. The lassie, Hannah, has appeared just outside the café. She smiles at a couple of customers sitting outside, and then takes her phone out of her wee apron and puffs on her vape. She's beautiful, just like in the pictures Seb showed us.

'Right, mate,' I say. 'It's gonnae be awrite. Just throw that shit behind her against the wall or something, anything, just make sure ye miss her, and we can get oot ae here.'

He nods in reply, and I start walking. Fuck knows what I'm going to talk to the lassie about. Should I tell her she should go back inside or something? Is that mental? I look at Seb, and he's moving towards me, gesturing towards his mouth. I reach into my pocket and quickly fire my mask on. Immediately, it feels like I've got a shield on. I feel a bit more protected knowing she'll only be able to see my eyes. My hot breath comes out my mouth and up my nose, and it reeks of shite. When I get home, I'm going to brush my teeth once a day from now on.

The blue light on the bottom of the lassie's vape lights up as she takes a draw. She turns her head to look at me as I approach and exhales. She looks back at her phone.

'Eh, sorry, excuse me?' I say.

Out the corner of my eye, I see Seb wave again.

The lassie looks at me and puts her phone in her pocket. 'Yeah?' she says.

'Eh, where can I get wan ae them?'

'I'm sorry?' she says, smiling and tucking her hair behind her ear as if she's trying to hear me better.

'Eh . . .' I start to panic. I glance back up towards Lee, who's just standing still, staring at me. He's barely walked two steps. I turn back to the lassie, who's looking at me as if I'm mental now. 'That,' I say, nodding at her vape. 'Where can I buy one?'

Seb is jumping up and down and mouthing something at Lee. I turn to look at him, and he's coming towards us now with his head down, walking fast.

'There's, like, five shops down there that sell them,' the lassie says, pointing down the road, and smiles again. She reaches into her pocket and takes out her phone once more.

'Awrite, eh, cheers,' I say.

She doesn't look up at me. I can tell I'm freaking her out, and I want to tell her she should go back inside, but my mouth's now as dry as the Sahara and I feel paralysed. I look down at my feet, and there's a wee white dug sniffing my trainers. It looks up at me like its staring right into my fucking soul, then it goes towards the lassie and sniffs around her feet. A woman sitting at a table outside the café is holding its lead. I look at her and she smiles and drinks her coffee.

I hear Lee's trainers slapping at the pavement as he comes up behind me. I feel myself tensing and freezing up, knowing what's coming next. The lassie screams and ducks down as Lee goes flying past me. The bottle skelps against the wall behind her and bursts open. I try to run after Lee, but my legs give way and I fall backwards on to the pavement. I can hear screaming again, but it doesn't sound human. It's the wee dug. It's wriggling about on its back, twisting and rolling, kicking its back legs in the air while its front paws scratch at its face. It must have went in its eyes.

Fuck.

People get up from their seats and run towards me and the lassie and the dug. The dug's owner is greeting and screaming as it screams right back at her.

'What was that?!' the lassie shouts. I think she's okay, at least.

'Oh, Lola, oh no,' the woman's saying to her dug between sobs. She picks it up and holds it like a baby. 'Oh no. Oh no.'

Its eyes are stuck shut and look like they're bubbling, all red and fucking painful-looking. I look in the direction where Lee ran, but him and Seb are nowhere to be seen.

'Are you okay?' the lassie asks me. I sit up and look up at her and want to say sorry, but all I can do is nod. She runs into the café, shouting that she needs someone to phone the police. An old guy in a suit with white hair and glasses comes over and offers me his hand. I take it and he pulls me up to my feet.

'Are you alright, son?' he asks me.

I nod.

'Did you get any on you?' He looks all over me, turning me round with his hands on my shoulders.

I shake my head.

'Good,' he says, and gives me a sympathetic look. 'I've read about this happening, but never seen it with my own eyes. Acid attacks, a vile and cowardly thing. That could've been you, me, or that young girl,' he adds, staring down at the dug. It's stopped screaming and is now whimpering softly and trembling. The owner pulls its paws away from its face and screams at the two holes where its eyes used to be.

He puts his hands on my shoulders and gives me a gentle shake. 'You're a lucky boy,' he says quietly into my ear, and goes to see the woman with the dug. I take a couple of steps back as people crowd around. I can't see Lee or Seb. Fuck, I can hear sirens.

I walk for fucking ages in the direction Lee ran, hoping he'll materialise in front of me, preferably without Seb, so we can figure out a way to get back home. I walk through the gates of a wee park and see an empty bench. There's perfect green grass behind it and flowers and nice big trees. Birds chirp from somewhere above my head, and a butterfly floats right by my face like I'm in a fucking Disney film or something. I take a seat and pull out the packet of Seb's fags. I spark one up and it's the best fag I've smoked so far. I exhale and watch the smoke make its way up towards the singing birds. I'm sure they'll appreciate it.

I shut my eyes and try to breathe, but the image of that wee dug writhing about on the pavement with acid burning through its eyes plays on a loop of infinite suffering. I've never heard anything make that kind of noise in my life, man. Suppose it would've been worse if it had hit that lassie, or the woman, or the old guy. Jesus Christ, the fucking carnage we've caused here is insane – and yet it could've been a lot worse. I wish it'd hit me instead. It wouldn't make a difference to me. If it got in my eyes and blinded me, I wouldn't need to work, surely. At least my maw would get off my back. Everybody would. Fuck, I miss my maw. I wonder if I'll ever see her again. I take another draw and think about Lee. My heart rate starts to rise. I keep moving between being angry with him and feeling sorry for him and worrying about him. I'm angry that he was sending pictures to Seb and saying that rape stuff. I'm sorry that he's found himself in this mess. And I'm worried that something's going to happen to him if he's alone with Seb.

I need to find him. I get up, flick my fag in amongst the flowers, and head roughly in the direction, I think, of Seb's flat.

32

FIONA

Tesco is dead as I walk up and down the aisles. The bright lights hurt my eyes. The staff make what I assume are snidey wee glances at me. They're probably thinking to themselves, *Why is this mental bitch out shopping at this time of night?*

I stand in the nappy aisle and check the supermarket website on my phone to make sure they do actually sell sleeping tablets. It says they do, and they're only four quid each. I'll get two boxes, just in case.

In the next aisle where all the medicine is, I grab some painkillers and the sleeping tablets. They're only herbal ones, but I'm sure they'll be fine. On the front of the box is a woman lying sleeping with a smile on her face.

The booze aisle is calling my name now. I'm not much of a drinker, I never have been, but I need a drink tonight. I head towards it just as a boy who looks younger than Jamie pulls a fabric barrier halfway across it. He looks me up and down and then says, 'We can't sell alcohol after ten. You've got five minutes.' I grab the cheapest big bottle of vodka and then turn on my heels and walk past a woman pushing a trolley with a wee lassie sitting in it. She's holding a magazine with unicorns on it. She waves it at me as I walk towards them. Her ma looks frazzled, leaning on the trolley as she pushes it.

I go into the next aisle, and they have boxes of flatpack garden furniture and water guns and all that. Sitting on a bottom shelf is a row of disposable barbecues. My stomach lurches as I see them, big orange flames shooting up around a burger and some sausages on the label. I pick one up.

I scan everything through and pile it up neatly on the scale. Vodka, sleeping pills, painkillers and a disposable barbecue. A red light above the screen starts flashing when I press the checkout button.

A young lassie and an older guy stand talking to each other, completely oblivious to me.

'Right,' I hear the guy say. 'Ye'll no know this wan,' and he starts humming a tune.

'"Hotel California",' the lassie says as the guy hits the chorus, adjusting her glasses.

'How'd ye know that? You're too young tae know the Eagles!'

'My da likes them,' she says, with a shrug.

'Oh shit,' the guy says, looking at me. 'Sorry, darling. I didnae see ye there.'

'That's awrite,' I say.

He comes over and presses buttons on the screen. He looks at my haul, then at me, and hits the 'Visibly over 25' button that's popped up.

'Trouble sleeping, aye?' he asks, revealing his yellow teeth.

'Aye,' I reply, and smile back. I think about saying, *No shit, Sherlock*, but I don't want to be cheeky.

'You'll be needing them fur the hangover anaw, eh? Efter yer barbecue,' he says, pointing at the painkillers.

'Aw aye,' I say with a fake laugh. I hit the button to pay, expecting the guy to go away, but he doesn't.

'It's tae be nice weather the morra,' he says. 'You've put me right in the mood fur wan noo. Enjoy.' He walks away and goes over to the lassie, who's on her phone. 'I might have a barbecue the morra. Dae you like barbecues?' he asks her. 'Cause I fucking love them.'

She mumbles something in reply. I grab my stuff and head out.

I drive around the industrial estate, making sure no one's about. There's a few factories that run night shifts; I saw some workers hanging about when I came here for my last meltdown a few nights ago, but it seems quieter tonight. There's a bit where they built a load of offices years ago, but they ran out of money and now the buildings just sit there, empty. I pull into the car park of the furthest away one and turn off the engine. It's on a hill, and during the day you can see for miles, all the way over to East Kilbride, I think it is. I can see lights away in the distance, twinkling like stars. I wonder if any of the lights are headlights from some other woman's motor as she prepares to do the same thing as me. I look down into the footwell at my vodka, barbecue and tablets. This is grim.

★   ★   ★

I pull out my phone to see if I can find instructions on how to do this right. I type 'Disposable barbecue suicide' into Google and scroll past the helplines again. I go through ten pages until I get to a forum that looks like it'll explain it.

'Just light them up and lie back lol,' someone says.

The packet says that the barbecue will burn for up to an hour. I hope that'll be enough time for me to die. I get out the motor and stand still in the cold night air. It's so quiet. All I can hear is the distant rumble of the motorway and the wind. I'm going to enjoy this silence for a wee while, and then I'll do it. I walk to the front of the motor and lean against the bonnet, looking out at all the lights in the distance. The vodka makes me wince as I hold it up to my nostrils. I take a big sip right out the bottle and force it down, covering my mouth in case I'm sick. I pop open the sleeping tablets and wash a handful down, then do the same with a strip of Ibuprofen. The vodka burns on its way down, but it feels nice until a shiver runs up the back of my neck.

I wonder what my funeral will be like, and who'll be at it. Probably just my ma and Jamie, if he comes back. Maybe Gillian from work. And that's it. Jesus Christ. My ma will be able to make the buffet after it herself with half a loaf. My da's funeral had a lot of people at it. People I'd never seen before were all greeting and telling me how nice he was and how funny he was. I turned to look at my ma as his coffin slid away, and she did a single sob and sniffle, took a deep breath, and went back to being stony-faced. I can't remember if I cried or not. Jamie didn't want to go – he was probably too young, anyway – but I let him have the day off school and stay in the house by himself.

I imagine meeting my da if there's an afterlife. He'd come towards me and smile and say, 'Hullo, hen. How ye getting oan?' like he always did. I'd reply, 'Aye, fine,' like I always did, and he'd say, 'That's good, hen,' like he always did.

I wonder if I should leave a note. What would I even write? It seems such a dramatic thing to do. I don't really have anything to say. I don't want to say, 'I'm sorry,' because I'm not. God, this is so depressing. What a miserable life, and what a miserable end to it as well. I go round to the passenger side and bring the barbecue outside to light it in case I set the motor on fire. That'd be the absolute worst way to go.

I strike a match and light the paper on the barbecue, watching it curl up as it burns. It smells lovely. I spread my duvet out across the back seat and place my pillow against the door. It looks so comfy.

I sit against the bonnet for a bit, waiting for the smoke and flames from the barbecue to die down. I hope Jamie's alright, wherever he is. He's a good boy, all things considered. Just, I don't know, *troubled* is probably the right word. Troubled because his ma didn't know what she was doing. Troubled because his da is fucking mental. Troubled because his ma is even more mental. He'll be fine, though. He's better off without me.

The last of the smoke from the barbecue floats away, and I move the white coals into the motor, placing them in the front footwell.

I take another couple of glugs from the bottle and stare up at the sky, but there's no stars, just clouds weakly reflecting back the light from down here. I feel a sense of calm that I haven't felt for a long time. My knees feel soft and doughy as I open the door to the back of the car; the vodka and tablets seem to have went right to my head. I fix my duvet and rest my pillow against the opposite door. I crawl in under the covers, curl up and shut my eyes.

33

JAMIE

It's dark now, and I still can't find Lee. I don't know where the fuck I am, and everywhere looks the same. It goes from houses and flats to endless roads with shops along either side. Vape shop, takeaway place, bookie's, pub and repeat forever. It's like I'm stuck in some mad anxiety nightmare. I'm starving, I'm thirsty, I need a pish, and I'm scared to fart in case I shite myself. I don't even know the name of the bit of London where Seb stays, so I can't even ask anybody, man. This bit looks familiar now as I turn a corner. I duck behind a skip and have a quick piss where no one can see me. I don't know if I was here yesterday, or if this is where we were earlier. It's getting scary because the cunts outside pubs are getting drunker as it gets later, and they're staggering about and shouting and all that. A group of guys up ahead seem to be looking at me. I put my head down and keep walking towards them. I pull out my fags and take out the last one. Maybe that'll make me look a bit more intimidating and they'll leave me alone. I spark it and look up as they part and let me through. The smell of their aftershave makes me feel a wee bit dizzy.

I pass a café with tables and chairs piled up outside it as if someone did it in a hurry. They're not all neatly stacked like other ones I've passed on my travels. I look up, and the café has a pink sign. Fuck me, I'm back exactly where I started. I've managed to walk in a big fucking circle. I take a draw of my fag and start coughing because I breathed it in too fast. I buckle over and cough like fuck. Eventually, the tickliness in my throat subsides, and I spit on the pavement. I instinctively go to take another puff, but I catch myself and throw the fag on to the road.

I stand up straight and look around. A group of older women look at me and laugh amongst themselves. They all look rich. Maybe one of them will take pity on me and be my new maw.

'Jamie!' I hear someone say. I spin round, looking for the source. 'Jamie!' It sounds like Lee, but I can't see him anywhere.

'Jamie! Here, mate.' I turn to my right and see Lee and Seb crossing the road. Lee runs over and grabs me in a tight embrace.

'I thought something had happened tae ye, man,' he says into my ear. 'Thank fuck yer awrite.'

Seb comes over with a face like a smacked arse. 'Fucking *finally*,' he says. 'Why didn't you just go back to mine and wait there? Where the fuck have you been?'

'I was looking fur you two. I got lost, I didnae know where I was gawn.'

'Fuck. We thought you'd spoken to the cops or something.'

'Sorry we ran an left ye,' Lee says. 'It aw happened so fast, man. Wan minute ye were right there, and then I looked back and I couldnae see ye.'

'It's fine, man. I'm here noo,' I say.

Seb eyeballs me. I can tell he thinks I've done something, even though I've not.

'You promise me right now you haven't spoken to anyone about what happened earlier, right?' he says.

'I've no spoke tae anybody,' I say. 'Aw I've done is look fur yous.'

He stares at me and squints his eyes slightly. It's like he's waiting for me to say something else. 'Okay,' he says. 'Good. Right, we need to get outta here. We'll take the train back: keeps us off the street and covers our tracks just in case. Come on.'

Seb starts walking in the direction he and Lee ran off in earlier. Lee gives me another cuddle when Seb turns his back.

'I'm so glad yer awrite, mate,' he says quietly. 'He's fucking raging, by the way, though.'

'Fuck sake, wit fur?'

'Cause I didnae get that lassie. He disnae know I missed deliberately, but he's still angry.'

I start walking and Lee does the same. He puts his arm around me and kisses my head.

'Fuck him, man,' I say. 'We'll get hame, get oor phones and get tae fuck, right?'

'I don't know if we can. He's been scary the day, mate. Like, actually mental. I'm worried aboot wit he'll dae if we try an leave.'

'Wit's he done? Has he hit ye or something?' I scan Lee's face, looking for any cuts or bruises, but I can't see anything.

He glances towards Seb, then lifts up his top slightly, revealing a purple bruise on his side. 'He took me doon an alley after we bolted, grabbed me by the neck, threw me doon and then booted me, man.'

'Fucking hell,' I reply. 'We'll find a way hame, mate.'

'Move!' Seb shouts at us, stopping and waiting for us to catch up. 'I'm not letting you two idiots out of my sight, all right?'

We walk along the road in silence. Lee walks with his head and neck slumped forward instead of up straight and tall like he normally does. Seb walks just ahead, but he keeps turning back to look at us, as if he's worried that we're hatching some plan or talking about him or something. I suppose he'd be right to think that. I'd love to kill this cunt.

'In here,' Seb says. A glowing sign hangs just above his head that says 'OVERGROUND'. We follow him up some stairs and emerge right beside the tracks. A few people who look like they've just finished work are dotted around on both the platforms. No one's talking to each other, they're all just looking at their phones, the blue light illuminating the bottom halves of their faces. We stand in a row, like birds on a wire, waiting for the train. A woman's voice booms from somewhere above me and says, 'Fast train approaching.' A few moments later, the fast train comes speeding through, screaming as it chews up the rails. It makes me want to cover my ears. I take a step back. It disappears down the line and through a tunnel, like it's puncturing a hole in fucking space and time.

'That's how fast the train was going when Richard jumped,' Seb says. 'All because of that fucking whore bitch. You had one chance to put it right. For me, for Richard and his family. And you couldn't do it. Neither of you could.'

I look at Seb just as he turns away from us. He looks across the tracks to the other side while he shakes his head.

'Should've done it my fucking self instead of putting my trust in two pussies like you,' he goes on. 'Waste of money as well.'

Lee tilts his head back, looking skywards, and lets out a sigh.

'If you've got something you wanna say, Lee,' Seb says, 'then just say it.'

I watch the two of them stare at each other for a second or two before Lee looks away, down at his feet.

'Thought so,' Seb says. 'You could maybe start with an apology. What a pair of fucking retards, honestly.'

'Aye, awrite,' says Lee. 'We get it.'

I turn to my right and look along the tracks. In the distance, I can hear a train coming towards us.

'This is our train. We get on it and it'll take us somewhere – isn't that magical?!' Seb says, talking to us as if we're children. 'Then we get off this train and get on another one, which takes us home. We could've been home by now and not have had to fuck around with trains, but neither of you can follow simple instructions, so here we are.'

The train slows down and comes to a halt in front of us. Seb motions for us to get on first as the doors slide open. Me and Lee exchange glances as we step on. Seb pushes me gently as we walk down the carriage.

'You sit there,' he says to me. He grabs Lee by the arm and sits him down in the window seat, and then sits so he's between us. I look over at them across the narrow aisle, and Seb's head wobbles slightly as the train moves off.

'Did you miss deliberately?' Seb says quietly.

I can't see Lee's face, but I can see his right hand is balled into a fist, veins bulging. 'Naw,' Lee says. 'I wanted tae hit her, I just missed by accident.'

'Interesting,' Seb replies. 'Because from where I was standing, you looked very apprehensive about doing it. Nervous.'

'Aye, obviously I wis nervous. Fuck sake.' Lee raises his voice slightly as he says this, and it makes me flinch. I'm fucking shitting myself for what could happen here. Seb's obviously got a temper on him, and he's clearly fucking unhinged too. If we had to fight, he'd win just because he's physically bigger. I can't fight, I've never thrown a punch in my life, so it'd be down to Lee. I don't think he's much of a fighter, even though he'd probably say he is.

'Did you two plan to fuck that up? Did you put both of your singular brain cells together, and that was the best you could come up with? After what that *bitch* did to me? You don't even fucking care?'

Did to *him*? Of course it was him she knocked back, and no some guy called Richard. Of course he's that much of a fucking freak that he'd spin a mad lie like that to try and get me and Lee to do that for him. Trying to make us feel sorry for him. He's fucking pathetic.

'Naw,' says Lee. 'If we'd planned it, we wid have done something tae *you*.' He's going to try and fight him; I can feel it in the air. Maybe he's giving off mad testosterone fumes or something.

'Is that so?' Seb says, leaning back in his seat. Lee cracks his knuckles one by one. 'Not a very nice thing to say to a friend, is it?'

'You're no ma pal,' Lee says.

'I brought you down here so you could start a new life. I'm letting you live in my home rent-free. I'm feeding you. I pay for everything. You should show me a little bit of gratitude.' Seb speaks slowly and deliberately. Even though Lee's being cheeky and argumentative, Seb's in control. I feel like he's playing Lee here. Like he's trying to goad him into doing something daft.

'I wish you hudnae bothered,' Lee says. 'I wish I'd never started talking tae you.'

'Well, you did start talking to me. And you certainly seemed to enjoy telling me what you'd do to those girls you sent me pictures of.'

'Fuck up,' Lee says. 'Shut the fuck up.'

'What was it you said about one of them?' Seb says. 'How you'd like to make her mom watch as you raped her?'

Lee bounces his foot up and down. 'You *made* me say those things.'

'Did I put a gun to your head?' Seb laughs. 'I don't know what this new holier-than-thou attitude is, or where it's come from. You're a scumbag, Lee. You're an incel. You're not *better* than me. You're the same as me, whether you like it or not.'

The train window is open just a crack, and I wonder if I could turn myself into a liquid and pour out of it.

34

FIONA

35

JAMIE

'This is our stop,' Seb says, as the train starts to slow down. 'Get up.'

Lee leans forward and looks at me, and I give him a sort of just-do-what-he-says nod. We follow Seb off the train and I whisper to Lee, 'We can still get away.' He just nods and wipes the snotters from his nose.

'We need to get on the next train heading back the way we came,' Seb says to us, without looking back. 'Makes it harder for anyone to track us on the security cameras if they're keeping an eye on us. We'll be home soon. There'll be a bit of a walk when we get off. Plenty of time for you to calm the fuck down, Lee.'

We follow Seb to the bridge that goes over the tracks to the other platform. Massive buildings rise up over our heads. We must be near the proper city centre. This station is even quieter than the last one, though. It's just us three as we step on to the platform. I head straight for a wee bench so I can sit down; I feel like I might pass out. The stairs and looking at the big buildings has made me feel weird and dizzy. Maybe it's the fact I've barely eaten anything since I got here. Seb walks to the end of the platform while Lee paces around in front of me. He keeps rubbing his eyes and wiping his nose on his sleeve.

'I want tae go hame,' he says, but as if he's just verbalising his thoughts rather than saying it to me. I can see silvery lines crisscrossing the cuffs of his black jumper.

'It'll be awrite,' I say, trying my best to sound reassuring. 'It's aw gonnae be fine.' I don't know that I believe any of it, but I'm just saying my hopes out loud.

Out the corner of my eye, I can see Seb sauntering towards us. 'You two better not be hatching another fucking hare-brained scheme,' he says.

'An wit if we are? Eh?' Lee says, squaring up to him. The two of them stand right in front of me. Lee pulls his shoulders back and sort of cranes his neck forward.

Seb doesn't look even the slightest bit intimidated. Instead, he smiles. 'Hit me if you wanna hit me, pussy,' he says.

My heart starts to pound. If they start fighting, Lee will need my help, and I don't know what I'll be able to do, if anything. Hopefully somebody else will turn up and step in, but there's nobody here.

Lee doesn't say anything. I can see his nostrils flaring as he breathes in and out, rapid style.

'You won't do it because you're a fucking coward,' Seb says. He grins and bares his teeth. 'Aren't you?'

'Fucking shut up,' Lee snarls at him.

'Why? Why should I? What the fuck are you gonna do? Have you ever been in a fight?'

'Just gie us oor phones back,' I snap. 'And we'll make oor ain way hame.'

Seb turns to face me. 'You wanna go home too?'

I nod.

'You're not going anywhere. You're both staying here with me until you've earned the right to leave.'

Lee launches himself at Seb, who staggers back but then gets Lee into a headlock. 'You little fucking shit,' he says. Lee pushes and claws and slaps with his hands, but Seb just laughs at him, tightening his arm around Lee's neck.

'Let him go!' I shout, getting to my feet.

'Shut up,' he fires back at me. Lee tries to pull Seb's arm away from his neck, but can't.

'He cannae breathe, man. Fucking hell.'

'Just you wait until we get home,' Seb snarls. I look around, but no one's about to help us. Lee's legs seem to go limp and he stops struggling. Seb lets him go and he folds like a clothes horse, hitting the ground. He gasps and holds his neck. I kneel down next to him.

'You awrite?' I ask, but he can't talk, he's making weird noises instead. Pure horrible hacking coughs and bubbling phlegm.

I look up at Seb. He's looming over us, still smiling. Lee manages to prop himself up with his arms behind him. His breathing starts to slow down, and he turns to the side and spits.

'Get up,' Seb says.

Lee's arms give way and he falls back, flat on the ground, looking up at the sky. I run my hand through his hair, as I think that's what my maw would do if I was lying like this.

'Maybe you two should become boyfriends,' Seb laughs. 'Look at the state of you both. Pathetic. You'd be great for each other.'

I try to stand up, but I feel off-balance, and Seb puts the sole of his shoe against my arm and shoves me. I fall over, wee stones digging into my palms and burning as I land. I turn to see Lee getting up. Seb goes to do the same to him, but Lee manages to dodge it.

'Fast train approaching,' a voice booms.

Lee flies for him again, but Seb gets him by the neck of his jumper and spins him, sending him sprawling to the ground once more. Seb stands in between us as we both lie on the deck. Lee bounces back up and goes for it one more time. Seb punches him in the gut, boots him in the baws and pushes him backwards.

Lee tumbles over the edge of the platform.

I hear the sound of his skull hitting the metal rail as he lands.

Seb stands motionless. 'Fuck,' he says, then turns and runs like a fucking sprinter up the stairs.

I scramble over to the edge of the platform and look down. It's more of a drop than I thought.

'Lee,' I shout. 'Lee, can ye hear me?'

No reply. No even the slightest bit of movement. He lies like a puppet that's had its strings cut.

I hear the train approaching. Footsteps come charging down the stairs to my right.

'What happened?' a guy in a blue uniform says. He looks like he works in the station. 'Did someone fall?' He comes running over and gets down next to me. He sees Lee and says,

'Oh fuck.' I want to climb down and help him, but I feel like I can't move.

'Help him,' I say. 'Please help him.'

The guy reaches for his radio and says into it, 'There's someone on the line. Ah, fuck.'

The train rumbles through the tunnel, getting louder and louder.

The guy grabs me and pulls me back, turning me away from the tracks as the noise of the train becomes deafening. I turn instinctively to see it come bursting out of the darkness. I shut my eyes and bury my face into the guy's chest.

36

FIONA

The world is upside down. I look up and see the ground, and look down and see the sky. My head is absolutely killing me. I blink a few times, and realise I'm lying on my back in the car park. My legs are in the motor while my body and head are on the ground. I roll on to my front and look down at the moss growing between the monoblocks. My pillow has flopped out and landed next to me. I slide my legs out from the car and try to get to my feet, but this pain in my entire skull is throbbing and making me feel sick and dizzy, so I lie back down.

It didn't work.

'Are ye okay there, hen?' I hear a woman shout. I lift my head and look around to see where she is. She's standing holding hands with a man in the entrance to the car park. She has a wee black dug on a lead. They look about seventy-odds.

'Let me help ye up, pal,' the man says, and comes towards me. He has a slight limp.

'I'm fine,' I say, and just lie there. If I move I'll be sick, and then they'll think I'm some kind of druggy.

'Wit happened?' the man asks. He puts his arms under my shoulders and manages to sit me up. He oohs and ahhs in pain as he tries to lift me; I swear I can hear his old bones creaking. 'Don't just stawn there, June,' he shouts to the woman. 'Come an gies a bloody hawn!'

I'm sitting with my back against the man's pristine black trousers. He smells like fabric softener. 'I'm fine,' I repeat, but I feel like I might pass out.

'Right, you get her by that erm,' June says, 'and I'll get her fae under here. Right, three, two, wan, up ye come.'

'Ta,' I say, feeling even more dizzy.

They both hold on to me for a few seconds as they get their breath back. Their wee dug sits in front of me, looking into my eyes and wagging its wee tail. 'I'm sorry,' I say.

'Naw, don't be daft, pal,' the man says and lets go of me. 'We saw ye as we were walking by, we couldnae just leave ye lying there.'

'We saw the motor and I said tae Ronnie, "Aw, that's strange, int it? Ye never see any motors in this bit." We never see anybody here, dae we?'

'Never. In aw the years we've been walking the dug here. Wit happened, hen?'

I don't know what to say. I can hardly tell this poor old couple that I was trying to fucking top myself and clearly it didn't work. My body must have went into survival mode and woke me up enough to open the door before I passed out again.

Ronnie looks over my shoulder and into the back of the motor, where my duvet is all crumpled up in the back seat. 'Ye should go somewhere nicer if ye want tae try camping!'

He laughs and picks up my pillow. 'Maybe get a tent next time anaw.'

I smile. I think June has maybe clocked that something's not quite right, as she gives me a look that seems laced with pity.

'Wit's its name?' I ask, as I bend down to clap their wee dug. It jumps up at me and tries to lick my face. 'I see ye, I see ye. Aw, you're lovely.'

'Henry,' June says. 'He's normally a grumpy wee thing. He must like you.'

Ronnie goes over and throws my pillow into the motor, taking a look inside.

'Aw, gie the lassie some privacy!' shouts June. 'For fuck sake. I'm sorry aboot him, hen. He's gawn doolally. He's furgoat wit bloody manners are. No that he had any tae start wi, mind you.'

'Ye burning that tae keep ye warm?' he says, nodding at the barbecue. He's right in the back of my motor, folding up my duvet for me.

'Eh, aye,' I say, thankful that he's drawn his own conclusion, so I don't have to explain what I was actually doing.

'Shouldnae be dain that. That can kill ye!'

'Aw, I didnae know that.'

'Yer a lucky wummin. I'll get rid ae it fur ye. Don't want ye driving aboot wi that in yer motor,' he says.

'Naw, honestly it's fine. I'll deal wi it.'

'Ronnie, stoap interfering. Leave her alane,' June says.

I get to my feet, and wee Henry jumps up and puts his paws on my leg.

'You've goat a new best pal there, hen,' she adds.

Ronnie takes the barbecue out of my car, ignoring his wife,

and tips the charcoals out on to the grass next to us. 'She could've died, June!'

June rubs my back. 'Are ye local? Will ye be awrite getting hame?'

'Aye, I'm just doon the road there,' I say, nodding vaguely in the direction of my house.

'That's good. We're just roon there,' she says, pointing the opposite way.

'Could use this fur cooking,' Ronnie says, holding out the empty metal tray. 'Could get a chicken in that. Yer veg roon aboot it anaw. Whack it in the oven. Can we keep this, pal?'

'Ronnie, Jesus Christ!' June shouts. I can't help but laugh. They remind me so much of my ma and da. 'Put it doon.'

'Fine,' he says, and tosses the tray on to the grass as well. He looks at me and smiles, then rolls his eyes.

'Honest tae god,' June says under her breath. 'Right, we better get gawn. He needs his breakfast.' She nods at the dug.

'Aye. Listen, you take care, pal,' Ronnie says, and starts walking away.

'Can I phone somebody fur ye, hen? Are ye sure yer gonnae be awrite?' June asks.

'Aye, I'll be fine.'

'Witever it is,' she says quietly, leaning towards me, 'it'll be awrite, hen.'

'I hope so,' I say.

She smiles at me again, and then walks away, arm in arm with Ronnie. I watch them go for a few seconds, and then get into the motor. I reach into the back seat for my phone so I can check the time. It's just after seven. I've no missed calls or texts. That feels like a bit of a relief. I couldn't deal with having to face my ma if she thought I'd went AWOL again. I gub two of the Ibuprofen I got last night, then turn the key in the ignition and head home.

BANG BANG BANG. I flush the toilet and run to the door, fastening my denims as I go. I open it expecting to see my ma but it's Graham standing there, looking sombre. I feel myself go cold as I dread what I assume he's about to say to me, what devastating news about my son he's about to impart.

'Hi, Fiona. I'll get right to it, Jamie's been found,' he says, but something in his voice, his eyes, says this isn't all good news.

'Oh my god,' I say. 'Is he alive? Is he okay? Where is he?'

'Is it okay if I come in?' he asks, looking over his shoulder.

I move aside and he walks in, down the hall and into the living room. My mind plays out a million grizzly deaths that could have happened to Jamie as I follow him and sit down on the couch.

'He and Lee were in London together. Now, Jamie's safe and well, but Lee has been found dead.'

I feel like I'm going to be sick all over his brogues as he stands in front of me. 'Jesus Christ,' is all I can say.

'Jamie was with him, but he's okay. A bit shaken up, under-standably, but we'll have him back home soon.'

I nod. 'Wit happened tae Lee?'

'I can't say too much right now, as there's an investigation underway, but Jamie's been helping the police in London with that, and we'll keep in touch with him when he gets back home. Jamie told the police down there that they went down to stay with someone they met online. They're now trying to trace whoever that was.'

'When can I see him?'

'He'll be brought home tonight; he'll be brought right to your door. Don't worry. He's okay, he's not hurt or anything. He doesn't have his phone, but I'll keep you updated whenever I hear from my colleagues down south.'

'Okay, that's good,' I say. *Good*. Poor Lee, that wee boy that was here the other night, laughing away in the kitchen, is dead and I'm feeling relieved, *good*, that it wasn't Jamie. My thoughts oscillate from happy to unbelievably sickened and guilty and back again with every passing millisecond.

'I need to get back round and organise some help for Lee's mum,' Graham says, moving towards the door.

'Please tell her I'm so sorry,' I say.

'I will. Look after yourself, Fiona,' he says, not smiling. 'I'll be in touch.'

I hear the door shutting and watch as he walks by the window, puffing out his cheeks.

'Wit's happened?!' my ma shouts down the phone as soon as she answers. I take a deep breath as she screams my name, but I'm in a daze; I can barely get the words out.

'They've found Jamie,' I croak. 'He's fine.'

'Aw, thank fuck fur that!' she shouts, sounding as excited as she would be if she'd just won the lottery or something. 'I thought ye were aboot tae say he wis fucking deid. Aw, thank Christ. I'm so glad, hen. Where is he?'

'He wis in London, he'll be hame later oan. Something's happened to the other wee boay though.'

'Aw naw, wit's happened?'

'The polis said he's deid,' I just about manage to spit out. Silence from my ma. 'Jamie was with him but he widnae tell me how he died.'

'That poor wee boay,' my ma says. Is she greeting? 'His ma must be in bits.'

I can't say anything. If it was Jamie who'd died I'd be out buying a gun and a rope, fuck barbecues and sleeping pills. My ma takes a deep breath and composes herself.

'Wit were they dain doon in fucking London?' she asks. 'Dae the polis know?'

'Meeting some guy they talk to oan the computer,' I say.

'That fucking *computer*. Never let him oan that again. Who wis it?'

'I don't know. It sounds tae me like he maybe had something tae dae wi Lee dying. This is horrible.'

'I hope they find the cunt,' my ma seethes. 'In fact I hope I find him first. I'm coming doon the noo, awrite. See ye soon.'

'Wait,' I say. 'I'm sorry aboot yesterday.'

'It disnae matter noo, hen,' she says, her voice softening. 'I'll be doon shortly.'

'He's fine,' my ma says down the phone to Danny. Delivering the news to him coldly. I can hear him saying something but can't make out what it is. My ma holds the phone away from her ear slightly and rolls her eyes. 'Naw, ye can fuck off,' she says. 'He's fine, an that's aw ye need tae know, awrite? If he wants tae see ye, he'll tell ye himself.'

'Is that right, aye?' I hear him shout.

'Aye, that *is* right, ya fucking arsehole,' and with that my ma hangs up with a flourish.

I smile. I wish I had even just a fraction of her ability to be so intimidating.

With my top up over my mouth and nose, I enter Jamie's room wielding a can of fly spray. I need to clean it; I need to make his room clean and perfect so this whole fucking episode can be behind me. A big reset. Make everything normal. Make us normal. Little fruit flies meander through the air as I step over piles of clothes and mountains of rubbish. I spray in every direction, holding the button down so the spray keeps coming out. The flies start dropping immediately. I keep going over every surface and into every corner for maximum coverage. I feel the chemicals settling on my clothes.

'Are they aw deid?' my ma shouts from behind the door.

'Aye,' I shout back, muffled by my top and trying not to breathe in too much in case I suffer the same fate as the insects twitching on the ground.

'Where's the mouse? Have ye seen it?' my ma says.

'Naw, I think it's away.'

The door creaks open and my ma comes in wearing marigolds, holding black bags and sprays and cloths. 'Worse than I remember,' she says, scanning the room.

'Right,' I say. 'We bag up aw the rubbish and then—'

'I know wit am dain, hen,' my ma says, cutting me off and immediately getting to work.

I let her take the lead and opt for clearing under his bed while she deals with the biggest pile of rubbish in the corner. I reach a hand through a gap in the detritus without looking

CHRIS McQUEER

first, and start to pull everything out from underneath. I can feel plastic bottles that seem full, and wince as I realise that they are full of piss. They come rolling out a couple at a time and nudge against my knees, which already have dead and dying flies stuck to them from kneeling down on the filthy carpet. Rock-solid crusts come next, along with equally hard chips and other bits of food I can't recognise. Balls of dust and hair come out like tumbleweeds. A big spider runs for its life. I scoop up as much as I can, trying not to think too much about what it is I'm touching, and drop an armful into a big bag. The smell is bad enough, but it's the textures that are really getting to me. Sometimes dry and brittle and sharp, sometimes cold and slimy and soft. All of it completely vile.

'This is never-ending,' my ma says. 'Two black bags full awready, no even made a dent in it.'

'I know,' I sigh. 'I didnae realise there was so much.'

We charge on without saying anything else. Just picking up and binning. Five black bags, bulging at the seams, sit outside his room door.

'Just aw his claes noo,' my ma says, out of breath but not stopping. We start trying to separate his clothes into clean and dirty piles, but they're all dirty.

'How does that even happen?' my ma says, holding a sock that she's found in his bed, so rigid it looks like it could be snapped in two.

'Ye don't want tae know,' I say.

She inspects it further with a bewildered expression on her face. She looks as if she's going to put it in the washing pile,

314

but instead drops it into a bin bag. Then his PlayStation catches her eye.

'I'm binning that anaw,' she says.

'That cost a fortune!' I say.

'Well, stick it up in the loft, then, and tell him ye binned it. I don't want him oan that ever again.'

'I will,' I say, but I won't. Imagine watching your pal die in front of you, and when you get home you've got nothing to distract you from thinking about that? That's a shame.

My ma gathers up his washing and takes it down the stair. I feel sad looking about his room. Taking away all the rubbish and his dirty clothes, he doesn't have anything apart from his bed and his telly and his computer. I haven't seen the mouse, though. It'll be all confused if it comes back. I run the hoover over the floor, all the dirt and detritus and mouse shit crackles as it's sucked up, swirling around inside with all the hair and other crumbs of unidentified matter.

I spray his bed with Febreze, then put on fresh covers and open the window. It's still not perfect, but at least it looks and smells like a semi-normal room now. It gives me a wee lift, seeing his room all nice and imagining him seeing it for the first time, but then I think about poor Lee again. If I had done things differently with Jamie, if I'd spent more time with him, maybe, and tried to engage with him more, he wouldn't have ended up in the state he was in before he left. He wouldn't have felt the need to run away, and poor Lee would still be alive. I've fucked everything up so badly. I feel myself about to start crying as I hear my ma coming back up the stair.

'Right, it's aw in the machine,' she says. 'Boil wash, since they were aw stinking. Wit's the matter, why ye greeting?'

'Nothing,' I say.

'C'mere,' she says, and gives me a cuddle.

'It's ma fault,' I say, and start to sob.

'Shhh.' My ma holds the back of my head and pulls me in closer. 'He's fine, he'll be hame soon.'

'It's ma fault that wee boay died.'

'Shhhhhh,' she says again. 'That's nothing tae dae wi you. You wurnae there.'

'Why am I bad at being a ma?'

'Ye did the best ye could, hen. Ye were oan yer ain an ye were dealin wi his arsehole faither anaw. Ye've been through a lot, but it's awrite noo. He's awrite and you're awrite.'

That's the first time my ma has ever said anything like that to me. I sob some more, and then the tears start to stop. 'I'm sorry.'

'Don't apologise tae me, hen,' she says, tears starting to pool in her eyes. 'Look at me – everything's gonnae be awrite noo.'

I nod and wipe my eyes.

'Look at wit the two ae yeez huv been through. An yer still here. There's nothing ye cannae handle noo. It can only get better fae noo oan.'

She's right, I realise. No matter what happens from now on, at least it can't be any worse than all of this has been.

'Come oan, I'll make ye a cup ae tae,' she says, and we both go down the stair.

*   *   *

My phone buzzes again. It's Graham.

'Right, Fiona. He's on his way; he should be home about nine o'clock tonight, I think.'

'Aw, brilliant,' I say. I look at my ma, who's gesticulating and mouthing something at me. 'He'll be hame aboot nine,' I tell her. She gives me two thumbs-up.

'I'll need to do what we call a Safe and Well check and talk to you both, but that can wait until tomorrow. In the meantime, just sit tight and give me a phone if you need anything. If not, I'll see you tomorrow.'

'I will. Thanks again, Graham,' I say, and hang up.

The clock on the fireplace finally hits nine o'clock, and I get up to look out the window for the millionth time.

'Gonnae sit at peace,' my ma says. 'Yer making me nervous.'

'He should be here by noo,' I say, craning my neck to see further down the road.

My ma sips from the sixth cup of tea she's made in the last two hours. God, I hope he's here soon. I can't take much more of this waiting.

'Will a phone something for his dinner?' my ma asks. 'Wit does he like? Pizza? Chippy?'

'Shhh,' I say as I hear the sound of a motor getting closer. Headlights shine on the wet tarmac as it approaches. It stops right outside the gate. 'I think that's him.'

I can see the heads of a woman and a man over the hedge as they get out the front seats. Then Jamie emerges.

'That's him!' I say, and run to the front door with my ma following me. I open the door and there he is, with the guy and woman either side of him. He doesn't look at me as he comes towards me.

'Please don't be angry,' he says. 'I'm really sorry.'

'C'mere,' I say, and grab him for a cuddle. 'Ye don't need tae be sorry. I'm just glad you're back.' I feel him, ever so slightly, cuddle me back.

'We'll leave you to it,' the woman says. 'But can I just give you these leaflets?'

'It's just to let you know the process of what comes next with everything that's happened,' the man says, 'and some helplines if you need them. Here's our cards as well.'

My ma reaches over my shoulder and takes them for me while I keep Jamie close. He feels even thinner than usual; I can feel every rib and every notch of his spine as I rub his back.

'You take care, Jamie,' the woman says. 'It was nice to meet you.'

He gently pulls away from my embrace and says to them, 'You tae, and, eh, thanks fur bringing me hame.'

'Right, come oan,' my ma says, and we go in and shut the door.

My ma goes into the living room while I have a look at Jamie. He's so, so skinny. His eyes look so dark and tired and heavy. His skin is dull and his face is all gaunt and drawn in. He looks like he's been away at war.

'I missed you,' I say, running a hand through his greasy hair, making a flurry of dandruff land on his black jumper.

'I missed you anaw,' he says, rubbing his eyes. 'I'm sorry.'

'I'm sorry,' I say, and grab him for another cuddle. 'I'm sorry for everything, but I'll make it aw better.'

'It's no your fault,' he says, holding me tight. 'I really, really missed ye.'

'I really, really missed you tae.' I let go and pull back so I can look at him better, and give him a smile so he knows that I mean it.

He yawns and rubs his eyes. 'Can I go tae bed?' he asks.

'The wanderer returns,' my ma shouts from the living room. 'Come in and let me see ye.'

'Just say hiya tae Granny first,' I say.

He nods and heads for the living room.

'Are ye awrite, son?' she asks him as I come in. He stands in front of her while she inspects him.

'I'm fine,' he says. He was never a good liar.

'Ye hungry? Ye must be starving.'

'Naw, they people goat me a McDonald's.'

'Awrite fur some!' She laughs and gives him a cuddle. 'We've been worried sick aboot ye. Too nervous tae eat, even though we knew ye were coming hame, and you're eating a bloody McDonald's!'

'I need tae go ae bed,' he says. 'I'm sorry. I'm so tired.'

'Away up tae bed then,' I say.

My ma says, 'Listen, don't ever dae anything like this again,' and lets him go.

'I won't. I'm sorry,' he says. He walks past me without looking up, and goes up the stair. I listen to his footsteps, so glad to hear them again.

I wake up during the night, after having a nightmare about poor Lee. Imagining what could have happened to him, what

Jamie could have seen, what could have happened to my own son. As I lie, drenched in sweat, I hear Jamie tiptoe down the stair and the sound of the shower turning on.

37

JAMIE

My room's spotless. It feels so much bigger than it did before. It's a pure sunny day, and it's nice waking up to the sun coming in instead of pure darkness. It smells so fruity and clean in here, like my maw's room does.

I can hear my maw moving about down the stair. She sounds like she's talking to somebody on the phone. It's so nice to wake up in my own bed, man. It's so good that it almost doesn't feel real. Some kind of muscle memory or something kicks in and I sit up, fully intending to put my headset on and hear Lee's voice, but then I remember. Fucking hell, I miss him. I miss waking up next to him – that was the single good thing about the last few days. I start feeling angry as I remember Seb sending him flying. I hear his head hitting the track, the smell of that guy's aftershave as he grabbed me so I didn't see the train hit him. The rush of air. Fuck.

I'm glad my maw cleaned my room for me, but I'm fucking mortified thinking about the things she'll have seen. I check down the side of the bed for my wank sock and see that it's missing, and feel my face instantly flush with the biggest, most intense riddy I've ever experienced. Hopefully my maw won't know what I used it for. I get up and search for clean clothes. Was much easier when everything was in an easy-to-access pile on the floor. I find a clean T-shirt hanging up in my wardrobe and denims lying neatly folded on the shelf above the rail.

'Morning,' she says, standing in the kitchen when I go down. She's smiling, but she seems tense, not like how she was last night. 'I made ye tea. Yer toast will be ready in a minute.'

'Cheers,' I say. I feel guilt, shame, sadness: every fucking horrible emotion possible.

'The polis phoned,' she says, folding her arms. 'The guy that was looking fur ye says there's gonnae be stuff in the papers and oan the news aboot you being found and aboot wit happened tae Lee.'

I nod my head. My maw hands me my tea. I've not had a cup of tea in what feels like ages. I take a sip, and it's the sweetest, most amazing thing I've ever tasted.

'He said we've just tae avoid it, no look at Facebook or anything like that.'

'Sound,' I say.

'I'm sorry aboot him,' my maw says. 'Aboot Lee. He wis a nice boay.'

'Aye, he wis.'

The toast jumps out the toaster, giving me a fright. My maw goes over and starts buttering it.

'I hope his ma is awrite,' she says.

'Me tae,' I reply. 'It wis horrible.'

'Wit happened?' she asks. 'You don't have tae tell me if ye don't want tae.'

'He goat hit by a train, but I think he wis deid before that. Seb pushed him oantae the tracks.'

'Jesus,' my maw says. 'Is Seb the guy you went tae meet?'

'Aye,' I reply. 'He wis horrible.'

'He wisnae half by the sound ae it.'

My maw puts my toast on a plate and hands it to me. Whenever she's made me toast before, she's gave it to me on a bit of kitchen roll. She must be trying to be nice to me.

'Will we sit oot the back? It's a nice day,' she says, grabbing her cup and the leaflets the woman that brought me home gave her. I've forgot her name already, the whole of yesterday – the whole of the last few days – just feels like a mad blur.

'Aye,' I reply and we head outside.

'Says here you'll be able tae get counselling,' she says, flicking through the leaflet.

'Wit's that?'

'I think it's the same as therapy.'

'Like, lying oan a couch and some guy asks ye aboot yer problems an aw that?'

'Aye. It says that I can get it as well.'

I never even thought about me going missing having an effect on my maw; I just assumed she either wouldn't notice or wouldn't care. And now she's going to need therapy. Fuck me, man. Running away caused my best pal, my only pal in the world, to die, and now my maw needs fucking therapy.

I wonder if anybody in the world has ever made a series of fuck-ups as bad as I have the last wee while.

She squints her eyes as the sun hits her face. She looks tired. I need to get a grip of myself; I feel like such a scumbag for putting her through all this. I need to become normal. I feel sick at the thought of all the times I was horrible to her. She's always just tried her best, in spite of everything. I missed her.

'I missed ye,' she says, as if she can read my mind. 'It wis weird no having ye here.'

'I missed you anaw,' I say, and have a bite of toast.

There's not a single cloud in the sky and it's already feeling warm. I wish Lee was here. I look over to where we stood and had our first fag together and think about how happy and normal I felt in that moment. How I told him I loved him and meant it and how I could tell that he was happy to hear me say that. I wish I could put my headset on and hear him slag me. I wish I could've woke up beside him this morning, but in my own bed. It was weird sleeping without him being there to steal all the covers. I miss him so much.

'It's the last day ae the summer holidays,' my ma says out of nowhere. 'This time a few year ago, you'd have been getting ready tae go back tae school.'

'I wish I could go back tae then,' I say. 'Dae everything different. Try and be mair normal.'

'Me tae,' she says. 'I'd dae a lot ae hings different.'

'Nothing's ever gonnae be the same, is it?' I say, but I'm no really asking her. I just mean it like a statement, because I know the answer.

'Naw, but that can be a good thing though,' she says. 'A fresh start fur the two ae us.'

'Aye,' I say. 'Never thought ae it like that.'

I take another bite and look at her. She smiles at me.

'Did my da know I was missing?' I ask her.

'Aye,' she says, and her smile fades away. 'He wis at the door, saying that I'd killed ye.'

'Fuck,' I say. 'I'm sorry. Fur swearing an fur my da dain that. An fur gawn missing anaw, I suppose.'

'Och, don't be sorry. Yer hame noo. An yer awrite. That's aw I care aboot.'

'Still, I'm really sorry. I'll no dae it again.'

She smiles again. 'I know ye won't. I'm gonnae make another coffee,' she adds. 'Ye want another tea?'

I nod and she gets up and reaches for my cup. With her free hand, she rubs her eye and then yawns.

'I love you,' I say, as she walks away, but I don't think she hears me. I look down at the grass and watch a bee rise up and float away up over the house.

ACKNOWLEDGEMENTS

Writing a novel is a lot more difficult than I thought it would be. I wouldn't have been able to finish this book without the help and support of so many of the brilliant people in my life. Thank you, Imogen, for your guidance, insight, patience and generally just being the soundest agent around. Thank you, Ella, for your edits, for taking a punt on this book and also for your patience as I went off the grid for months at a time. Thanks also to all the team at Wildfire.

Thanks to all the people I've worked with at Fife College and SPS over the last wee while, to the Scottish Book Trust (their Live Literature scheme helped me keep the wolves from the door and meet so many great writers), and to Laura and Heather at 404Ink for everything over the last few years.

My maw has probably been the biggest influence on me, both in terms of my writing and who I am as a person. So special thanks to you, Ma. No one knows how to give me a kick up the arse while also making me feel ten feet tall quite like my granny, so thanks for pulling me through the last few years. Thanks to my wee brother, Jay, for being such a class wee guy and to my granda for always kicking about with me. Thanks to Timmy as well, even though we had a falling out. Thanks to Anne and Frank for their generosity, hospitality and for being early readers of this book; and to Madeleine, for everything.

ABOUT THE AUTHOR

Euan Anderson Photography

Chris McQueer is the acclaimed author of the short story collections *Hings* and *HWFG*. Stories from *Hings* were adapted for TV by Chris and shown on BBC Scotland, and he's presented the documentaries *Noteworthy with Chris McQueer* and *Let's Talk About the English*. He has also appeared on *A View From the Terrace* and Damian Barr's *The Big Scottish Book Club*. He won the award for Outstanding Literature at the *Herald* Scottish Culture Awards 2019 and has had two plays staged. He has delivered workshops in youth clubs, for secondary school pupils, prison inmates, adult learners and HNC/HND level students. Chris lives just outside Glasgow. *Hermit* is his first novel.

If you or someone you know is struggling
with suicidal thoughts, confidential assistance
is available through the Samaritans
by calling 116 123.